Hawthorn Close

By Anna Jacobs

Hawthorn Close

ANNA JACOBS

Allison & Busby Limited
11 Wardour Mews
London W1F 8AN
allisonandbusby.com

First published in Great Britain by Allison & Busby in 2023.

A CIP catalogue record for this book is available from
the British Library.

First Edition

ISBN 978-0-7490-2881-7

Typeset in 11/16 pt Sabon LT Pro by
Allison & Busby Ltd.

By choosing this product, you help take care of the world's forests.
Learn more: www.fsc.org

Printed and bound by
CPI Group (UK) Ltd, Croydon, CR0 4YY

Author's Note

The hawthorn tree is associated with Beltane, the ancient festival celebrating spring, and it is one of the most sacred trees in Celtic mythology. It symbolises love and protection.

In March, the leaf buds start to open and pale green leaves appear, joined by masses of delicate white flower buds in May, whose blossoms have five white petals surrounding stamens with bright pink heads. They produce red berries in July.

Songbirds love hawthorns and they'll visit often in the autumn and winter to enjoy the bright coloured berries.

Hawthorn trees are most frequently used as hedges in the UK, and to have a whole street of very old trees would be extremely rare and precious.

Chapter One

Rob Carswell woke suddenly during the night. For a moment he lay there wondering what had disturbed him. Then he realised it was someone sobbing. It sounded like a woman's voice and was coming from the house next door, which looked to be in a very bad state of repair.

He'd never seen the person who lived there, but then he'd not spent a lot of time in Essington St Mary since he inherited this pair of semi-detached houses in Hawthorn Close from his great-aunt Flo three months ago in early January. That legacy had been a wonderful surprise, but it had hit him in the middle of a super-busy time at work in London, with a lucrative contract pending that would leave him able to semi-retire if he could pull it off.

To his delight it had all come together nicely and he had now stopped working full-time for others, but would take on occasional contract work as well as developing his own programs and apps. He'd moved here permanently a couple of days ago and put his London flat on the market. He was looking forward to starting work on the renovations this pair of older houses needed.

The woman next door was sobbing more quietly now but he could still hear her. She'd probably be horrified if she knew how the sound carried, but as long as it wasn't too cold, he preferred to keep his bedroom window open, and he lived next door to her in Number 4.

Heaven alone knew how noisy it'd be here when the damned builder who'd recently bought the first two houses on this one-sided street started knocking them down. Belkin was apparently youngish and a hustler. He'd no doubt be erecting several others in their place.

But at least the building noise would be a finite nuisance because he only had two plots of land to build on. Rob had been horrified, however, to overhear the builder arranging to have the two old hawthorn trees on the verges outside his houses knocked down.

How could he do that? They were heritage-listed. The trees lined the whole street and were over two hundred years old. They were glorious when they were all in bloom.

He'd played under them as a child when visiting his great-aunt, gathering their fallen blossoms in his toy bucket and making patterns with them on the paved area at the back of the house. Hawthorn Close wouldn't look right with the first two magnificent trees missing from the entrance.

Belkin had tried to buy this pair of semis from Rob the day after he'd found out that he'd inherited them, and you had to wonder how the man had got hold of the information so quickly. But Rob didn't intend to sell them, most definitely not.

Unfortunately, the fellow didn't seem to understand the word 'no' and had tried twice more since then, increasing his offer slightly each time and sending his agent to pester Rob about them.

No way was he selling! And if he blocked Belkin's progress up the street, maybe it would remain a quiet, happy place for the most part, not a noisy one crowded with tiny homes whose owners' cars were parked along the nearby part of the road.

Last month, Rob's long-term tenant in the other semi had given notice unexpectedly and moved out from next door almost immediately, saying he didn't want to live so close to a building site. But as no demolition work had started there yet, except for removing all the plants from the gardens, and there were two houses between his rental and the building sites, he had to wonder whether someone from Belkin's had bribed the tenant to leave.

Since Rob had been working long hours just then, sometimes well into the night, he'd simply left both houses empty. After a couple of windows had been smashed, he'd hired a local security firm to keep an eye on them.

He had sentimental reasons for living here as well as the financial ones. As a boy, he'd always loved coming to Essington St Mary to visit Auntie Flo. Such a charming little town. Those holidays were some of his happiest childhood memories and he'd put up a magazine picture of a blossoming hawthorn tree in his bedroom when he had to go home again. He still had it somewhere.

He'd never give away his inheritance to a 'property typhoon', as Flo had called builders like that one.

He turned over in bed, trying to ignore the sobbing

next door but couldn't, just could not. It wasn't loud but it sounded despairing. No one should cry alone like that. And she must be alone. In his four days of living here permanently, he'd been using the smaller front bedroom as an office and had seen no one enter or leave the old house next door, nor had the postman delivered any mail there.

In the end Rob gave up on sleep and went down to get a drink of water, not bothering to turn on the lights. He stood by the kitchen window, staring out at the stars sparkling in an almost cloudless sky. He noticed the vague outline of a figure on the back patio next door but she didn't have an outdoor light on, so he couldn't make out any details.

She'd stopped crying now, thank goodness, and he'd expected her to go back into the house, but she hadn't. Wasn't she afraid of being attacked, sitting out there alone? Most women would be, even in a peaceful little town like Essington. But perhaps she wasn't thinking clearly.

She got up and walked slowly across to sit on a two-person swing. As it moved to and fro, it let out a regular squeaking noise. It wasn't loud but it set his teeth on edge. That was more than enough to stop him getting back to sleep.

He didn't like to confront her about it just then. A strange man coming into her garden in the middle of the night would frighten any woman.

The squeaking went on and on, and when he went back to bed he could still hear it, even in the front of the house. He'd go across in the morning and offer to oil the damned thing. Like the house and garden, it was probably in sore need of maintenance.

Perhaps the owner was, too.

Even after the noise eventually stopped, it was a long time until he fell asleep.

The next morning, Rob woke late feeling heavy-headed. After breakfast, he sat scowling at his computer, too tired to feel inspired. The creaking of the swing could easily be stopped, but how to approach her tactfully to suggest he oil it for her?

He'd never even met her, hadn't particularly wanted to because since his divorce last year he preferred to keep himself to himself where women were concerned. He felt rather embarrassed at the thought of knocking on a stranger's door and betraying the fact that he'd been awake and heard the swing creaking.

If he did that, she was bound to realise that he'd have heard her weeping too. No, he'd leave it. She hadn't sat outside on that damned swing before and probably wouldn't again.

Chapter Two

Corin Drayton turned off the main road and drove through the village of Essington St Mary, glad to be nearly home after a long, hard day. As he started up the final hill, he suddenly caught sight of a new sign beside the road and slowed down, then drew up nearby to stare across at it, horrified.

DES BELKIN, BUILDER
COMING SOON

What had brought that scoundrel to this peaceful valley? He'd already crammed a lot of shoddy little houses on tiny building plots near Swindon. As an architect, Corin despised builders who short-changed the poor buyers who were probably making the most important purchase of their lives.

He had crossed swords with Belkin verbally a couple of

times over recent years at functions and meetings. Once, the fellow had even sued Corin for slander when he said publicly that one Belkin house design had a couple of potentially unsafe features. Corin had successfully defended that lawsuit and Belkin had been forced to pay his costs and make the necessary changes.

You couldn't do anything about the houses being built so close together since the council had approved that, just wince when you saw it.

Hawthorn Close was one of his favourite streets in the valley so he stopped the engine and got out to see exactly what was going on.

He stopped to smile at the lovely old trees, which were just coming into leaf. The left side of the street was occupied by a retirement complex with a small warden's house attached to the far end of the row of buildings. A high wrought-iron fence set on half a dozen rows of bricks separated their grounds from the street and there was a one-way drive behind it with an entrance at the near end and an exit at the far one.

The houses on the other side of the close consisted of a mixture of semis and detached houses from various eras, which somehow managed to form a harmonious whole. Sadly, Belkin's signs were in front of the two large old detached houses at the entrance to the short cul-de-sac and someone had already cleared their gardens of plants and trees.

Corin couldn't hold back a groan. What was going to happen to the hawthorn trees? When the beautiful old trees flowered in May, they formed a canopy of blossoms all along the street that brought in sightseers from all over the county. He'd only moved to the valley recently but had seen photos of it and had been looking forward to seeing the real thing this year.

He couldn't see a man like Belkin wasting parking spaces on the verge because of mere trees, heritage-listed or not.

The third house along on the lower side didn't have a sign in the garden but it looked very run-down so would probably be Belkin's next target to purchase. All three of those detached houses must have been beautiful in their day, early Edwardian probably. They could have been renovated and modernised tastefully to stand there proudly for several more decades.

Feeling depressed at what he'd seen, Corin went back to his car and continued up Larch Tree Lane, looking forward to getting home to his wife. Lucia was in the early days of pregnancy and they were both thrilled about that.

Near the top of the hill, he clicked his remote and turned in to an entrance on the right, waiting impatiently for the gates to the small estate to swing open.

Locals still called it the Marrakin. It had been appropriated during World War Two by the War Office, who had presumably used its collection of houses for housing staff working on special defence projects. They'd kept it for decades longer than usual, no one knew why, and had only released it for sale to the public last year.

Buying it had taken a big chunk of his savings but it had been an architect's dream come true. Renovations and extensions would be needed for the existing buildings and there was empty land at the rear where brand-new houses could be built. He was looking forward to designing that part of the development from scratch.

His purchase was already proving successful financially, and he had just signed a contract to renovate and extend another of the older houses for a couple about to retire.

This one was near the former underground site that the War Office had dug out on the lower part of the land. There was no sign left of what they'd used it for and he still wasn't sure what he was going to do with it.

Those tunnels and underground rooms certainly wouldn't make good dwellings, whatever you did to them, and their commercial use would be strictly limited, too. Well, he'd think of something eventually. It wasn't urgent. All you could see of them at the moment was a grassy mound.

As he stopped in their drive, he saw Lucia peer out of the front window and wave to him. His heart lifted as it always did at the sight of her.

He didn't remember to tell her about the new development until they were eating their evening meal.

She looked at him in surprise. 'Is Belkin that bad? I've seen his company's signs on the outskirts of Swindon. He looks to be doing well.'

'Only if you want to live in the slums of the future. He sells a lot of houses but skimps on both size of rooms and quality of the building products he uses. I hate the thought of him erecting his tacky little houses anywhere in Essington St Mary. We have a wonderful variety of periods of architecture here in the valley and some lovely old buildings. He'll simply knock them down.'

'It's really upset you, hasn't it?'

'Yes. Sorry to go on about it. How he got his plans for

the last lot in Swindon through the local council there, I do not know.'

'He must have useful friends on it.'

'I suppose so.' He picked up her plate and his own. 'Go and sit down, darling. I'll put these in the dishwasher and pour you a drink, and we won't talk about that man any more.'

'I'll have a Gaudy Lady tonight, please. Thank goodness for your brother's brilliant non-alcoholic drinks. I bet he makes the family firm a fortune with them.'

He handed her a glass and clinked his own against it. 'Here's to Pete and a more successful future for Drayton's drinks.' As they chatted happily, she snuggled against him on the sofa.

She was starting to look drowsy now. He couldn't resist dropping a stray kiss on her nearest cheek. Good thing they hadn't been late-nighters. Since she'd become pregnant, she seemed to need far more sleep and tonight he was exhausted too after driving back from London.

When her eyelids fluttered then closed, he stared fondly down at her. He might have married later than average but she had been well worth waiting for. She was, quite simply, his soulmate.

Chapter Three

The next day, after a good night's sleep, Rob woke in a better mood. He went downstairs to get a second cup of coffee and what he saw through the kitchen window took the smile from his face. Hang being tactful with the woman next door! A huge dog of nameless parentage was busily digging up the flower bed to one side of his patio, grunting happily as it tore into the soft new earth and scattered the delicate seedlings he'd planted yesterday.

He'd seen the trays of baby plants at the local supermarket and bought one as a token gesture to brighten up the place till he could get round to sorting out the garden properly. He'd already regretted the purchase by the time he got them home and planted because he had other jobs that were far more pressing.

He looked for his intruder's point of entry and quickly found the spot where it had pushed through a gap where the low fence between the houses had been broken. The dog looked vaguely familiar. It must live next door.

When it sent a particularly pretty purple petunia that had been the only seedling in bloom flying across the paved area in a shower of earth, he roared, 'That's it!' and rushed outside to do battle.

Only, he didn't have to worry about restraining the dog because it came when he called it, wagging its tail and giving him a broad doggy grin, then nudging him with its head to get him to stroke it.

He couldn't resist giving it a token rub, then grabbed its collar and walked it round to the front door of the next house. When he rapped on the door, he was surprised to see scratch marks on the frame, and new unpainted putty round the panel of frosted glass in the upper half, as if the window had been broken recently. Windows like that didn't usually break easily, so how had that happened?

The whole place was in a dreadful state, far worse when you saw it from close up. He was about to knock again when he heard footsteps come along the hall and a shadowy figure appeared behind the glass panel.

A breathy woman's voice asked, 'Who's there?' but the door stayed shut. He suddenly noticed that it had a shiny new peephole in it. A pang of guilt shot through him. Her voice had quavered. He didn't want to upset some poor old lady, so he would offer to help her sort something out to keep the dog in her garden.

'I have your dog here,' he began gently, then the rest of the speech he'd prepared died in his throat as the door opened.

She wasn't an old lady. Most definitely not. She was about his own age or perhaps a little younger, say thirty or so. And she was gorgeous in a pale, ethereal way. Her long, honey-brown hair had enough curl in it to make you want to wind it round your fingers. She had huge blue eyes and generous lips.

He blinked and the words he'd been going to say went right out of his head. All he could manage was, 'I'm Rob Carswell, your next-door neighbour. Is this your dog?'

'I'm Ilsa Norcott. I'm just looking after the dog for a few days.' As she stood on the doorstep, staring up at her tall visitor, Ilsa was torn between good manners and wanting to snatch Tiny's collar from him and slam the door in his face. She'd had enough of men towering over her.

She relaxed a little, however, as she realised he wasn't at all like the last man who'd hammered on her door. This one might be angry about something, but he didn't make her feel threatened personally or seem likely to break the window as that other one had.

In fact, he looked – well, rather kind, and 'wholesome' was a word that sprang into her mind to describe him, with his clear blue eyes, light brown hair and fresh complexion. She found that very attractive.

He was holding the dog tightly by the collar and although his voice had sounded a bit sharp, Tiny was wagging her tail. She only wagged like that when she was with people she liked but Ilsa's heart sank as she noticed the dog's muddy nose. Oh, no! Not again! Tiny had escaped custody and dug up part of her own front garden only yesterday.

The poor dog was bursting with energy, missing the hired dog walkers who'd been taking her for long walks three times a week previously because her late owner hadn't been well enough to exercise her. Perhaps that's why the poor creature had taken up archaeology as a hobby, hunting for buried treasure under every soft piece of earth she could find.

Ilsa should have asked the lawyers to continue paying for the dog-walking services, but she'd been too upset to think clearly. Well, everyone in the nearby houses and retirement flats had been upset when Judith died suddenly last week. Since she'd known her health was chancy, she'd told all the neighbours who her lawyers were 'just in case'.

When the visiting nurse found Judith lying peacefully in her chair, with Tiny at her feet, someone had phoned them with the sad news and a clerk had come at once to take charge.

Ilsa had promised Judith to look after Tiny if necessary, so when someone emailed her, she'd rushed back from Great Yarmouth. A friend had lent her a flat there for a couple of weeks to try the effect of bracing sea air on a lingering reaction to a virus. But keeping her promise to a dead woman was much more important than fresh air or even her first holiday in two years. And anyway, as the doctor kept saying, only time would sort out her body and see her fully recovered.

The lawyer's clerk had been intending to put Tiny in some kennels while they waited for Judith's heir to fly back to England from Spain, but Ilsa had taken her instead.

It had seemed a simple thing to volunteer to look after the poor creature. She was doing it partly because she liked the dog, and because Tiny looked a lot fiercer than she was and she was hoping that a big dog would provide some protection against Belkin's foreman, a bully who was trying various nasty incentives to persuade her to sell her home.

Only yesterday one of Belkin's men had parked his car next to her house and left it with its radio on loudly for three hours. She'd got dressed quickly and gone looking for someone to complain to, only she hadn't been able to find anyone.

To make her current situation worse, she was missing Judith greatly. The old lady had been more like a grandmother than a mere neighbour and had helped Ilsa through a few bad weeks.

She sighed. Her new neighbour was scowling down at the dog as if Tiny had committed a major crime. The tapping foot suggested he was waiting for an answer so Ilsa dug her fingernails into the palms of her hands, not wanting to cry in front of him.

'Well, is this your dog or isn't it?' he asked loudly, trying to glare down at Tiny. But when she wagged her tail vigorously and grinned up at him, the glare faded and he shook his head ruefully and spoke in a softer voice. 'Is it?'

'No. She's not mine. She's called Tiny, by the way.'

'I don't give a damn what she's called. Whose dog is she if she's not yours?'

Ilsa could feel tears overflowing, couldn't hold them back. 'She belonged to my neighbour and friend Judith, from Number 6. She died a few days ago so I'm just l-looking after Tiny till the heir gets here and takes over. Pam lives in Spain but she's been away in Morocco on some sort of holiday tour.'

'What? That nice old lady is dead? I'm sorry to hear that. I met her a couple of times, though I don't remember seeing the dog. But they were only flying visits and I spent most of the time sitting with my great-aunt.'

'Judith kept Tiny inside except when the walkers took her out.'

'Well, do you think you could keep the dog in your garden and stop her visiting mine?'

'I'll try.'

As he glanced at her, Rob saw more tears rolling down her cheeks. She looked unwell, as if a breath of wind would blow her away, yet she was doing a last favour to her late neighbour. And here he was shouting at her – he, who hated bullies.

She bent down as if to cuddle the animal, only she had suddenly lost every last vestige of colour in her cheeks and was looking dizzy. Was she about to keel over?

'Are you all right?'

She didn't reply and he saw her grab hold of the door frame and cling to it. 'I'm sorry. I'm – recovering from a bad virus and—'

He was barely in time to catch her as she started to crumple. He swept her up into his arms, surprised at how light she was and how protective he felt. He stood for a moment staring down at her unconscious face, wondering what the best thing to do would be, then moved into her house, muttering to himself, 'Lay her down somewhere, you fool!'

Fortunately, the dog followed him inside, whining anxiously now as if she sensed something was wrong, so he quickly nudged the door shut with his foot to keep Tiny inside.

It had been a couple of years since he'd split up with Siobhan, and this was the first time he'd been attracted to any woman in all that time. Well, Ilsa was lovely, no doubt about that, but her kind nature was just as attractive.

Not now, for heaven's sake! he told his body. *Hell, she isn't even conscious and you're lusting after her like a raw youth.*

He knew a little about first aid so laid her down on a shabby sofa in the room nearest the door with her head slightly raised. The first-aid rulebook said that if someone was unconscious for more than a minute or so you might need to call a doctor.

To his relief she was already starting to regain consciousness, stirring and moving her head from side to side. Thank goodness there would be no need to call for help. Well, not unless something serious seemed to be wrong.

She blinked at him, closed her eyes then opened them again, looking puzzled.

'You just fainted. How are you feeling?'

'Dizzy. Disoriented.'

'Do you often faint?'

'No. I – haven't eaten anything today. I'll be all right.'

'I'll get you a cup of tea and maybe a biscuit.'

She closed her eyes. 'Cup of tea would be lovely.'

He was still worried about her so went to find the kitchen and put the kettle on. After doing that, he opened the fridge to find her something to eat and stood staring at it in shock because it was almost empty. He looked round the kitchen for something else, but a container labelled *BISCUITS* contained only a few crumbs.

He went back to her and saw with relief that she had a slight trace of colour in her cheeks again. 'I've put the kettle on but you don't seem to have much food.'

'I was away for over a week and when I came back the virus flared up again, so I went straight to bed. I felt too ill to get to the shops, too dizzy to drive safely. I gave Tiny my last slice of bread this morning.'

'Couldn't you have got food delivered?'

'There's something wrong with my phone and internet connections. They're not working at all. I think the developer must have done something to them. He's trying to make things difficult for me to persuade me to sell to him.'

'He wants my houses too but he's not getting them. He's not even offering a decent price.'

'He's – very persistent. Or rather, the man he sends to pester me is.'

'Tell me about it. If someone ever looked shifty, it's him. Look, I'll nip home and fetch you something to eat. Won't be a minute.'

'No need to—'

But he was gone. Ilsa turned her head to watch through the window as he strode down the front path, pushing one of the bushes aside. Like every other shrub in her garden, it needed pruning. She'd spent the last of her money on buying this house but had fallen ill almost immediately and hadn't had the energy or money to do any outside work, or to find herself a new job.

The doctor had said it was a retrovirus, then when it came back again recently another doctor at the practice insisted it was only a minor relapse and assured her that she would gradually get better. This didn't help her earn a living. She usually had no difficulty finding jobs because she was good with IT.

Like the first doctor, the second one had advised rest

and eating a healthy diet to help her improve further. Only she'd been ill for long enough now to be running out of money and credit, because a payment for a big project that had been due hadn't arrived.

Tiny came up and licked the hand that was trailing over the edge of the sofa, so Ilsa patted the dog's head gently. 'I'm sorry, Tiny, but I'm going to have to keep you inside the house from now on. But I will find a way to get some food delivered.' Maybe Judith's lawyers would pay for the dog's food, at least? Only, she couldn't get a phone signal to ask them.

Rob came back as she spoke and stopped in the doorway of the living room. 'I can easily get you some stuff from the shops.'

'Would you really? I'd be very grateful. I do have a debit card you can use to pay for it.' But she was trying not to use that because it was all she had left. If she hadn't been able to buy this house with money left to her by her aunt, she'd have been homeless by now.

He frowned. 'Don't you have any friends or family to turn to for help?'

'My only close relatives live in Australia now. And I can't keep pestering my friends.' She scowled at him and added, 'I went through a bad divorce last year. It's needed a restraining order against him and the lawyers' fees weren't cheap, so I'm rather short of money. Luckily for me, he's found another woman now and stopped annoying me.'

'That must have been difficult. Look, I'll just get you a cuppa. Piece of toast with it be OK?'

'Yes. And – could you do one for Tiny? Since she's not my dog, I don't have any tins of dog food.'

'I've got a tin of corned beef. She can have that till I go to the shops. I'll go back for it once I've sorted something out for you to eat.'

She opened her mouth, looking as if she was about to protest but he forestalled her. 'At the moment, you're in a far worse state than she is. She doesn't look like she's about to faint on me so her food can definitely wait.'

He was right. Ilsa closed her eyes and when he brought her something to eat, she forced it down.

He then fetched the corned beef for the dog, after which he looked at his watch. 'Sorry, but I have an appointment in Essington shortly. It'll only take me about half an hour and after that I'll get you some food. Will you be all right for a while?'

'Yes, of course. Thank you so much for your help.'

'I've left some more slices of bread in the kitchen and a jar of jam. Tiny ate the tin of corned beef in a couple of gulps, so she'll be all right, and I filled her water bowl. I won't forget to buy some dog food.'

'Just a couple of tins. Judith's niece will be sending couriers to fetch the dog in a day or two. I don't want to be left with dog food sitting in my pantry.'

'Good thinking.' Another glance at his watch and he rushed away. She heard his car start up a few minutes afterwards.

She lay down again, feeling slightly better for her snack and sensing that she was about to take another nap. She still felt tired nearly all the time.

Chapter Four

Ilsa was woken abruptly by the sound of a large vehicle throbbing loudly just outside the front of her house. When she looked out, she saw that her drive was now blocked by a lorry, a vehicle she had seen a few times before. But it wasn't the foreman driving it this time.

Was this man going to leave it there as he'd threatened yesterday? Surely even he wouldn't dare do that?

The engine was switched off, and a beefy man she didn't recognise jumped down from the driving seat and started walking away from the house.

She got up and anger took her to the front door, which she flung open. 'Hey! You! You're blocking my drive. This is private land. Move your lorry!'

The man turned and came right up to her, grinning as he thrust his face so close to hers that she was pressed back against the door post by the rest of his body. She tried to move away from him, wrinkling her nose in disgust at the smell of stale sweat and beer that emanated from him.

He put one arm out to stop her edging away and spoke with a slight foreign accent. 'No, lady. I won't move it. My boss think this parking place is perfect for our lorries. Is convenient to the new development, right next door. We start work here soon. I come and see you every day.' He blew her a kiss.

It was like a poor TV show, she thought: stereotyped violence, sexual harassment and a huge nasty villain. Only it wasn't a show, it was really happening. She tried once again to shove him away but couldn't get him to move at all. She felt utterly helpless because even if she screamed for help, there was no one likely to be around at this time of day. Even her kind next-door neighbour was away in the village.

Her tormenter hooked one finger under her chin. 'Unless you change your mind about selling house.' He waved his hand scornfully. 'Is old ruin? Not good to live here.'

She batted his hand away and gave him another shove, but it was like pushing against a cliff face.

She yelled, 'Get off me!' right in his ear but he didn't move an inch. And everything was starting to waver around her again. She hadn't the strength to do more than hold herself upright. 'Go away. Tell your boss I haven't changed my mind and I won't do. I like living in Essington – it's where I grew up and I'm staying right here!'

She was unaware that her words were carrying clearly across the street as she added, 'Des Belkin can just find another plot of land to develop.'

'My boss want this one. Number 3 is right next to the other two houses he's bought, makes it perfect for further development. He'll get it, too, always does. You'll be sorry about saying no, lady, but you'll sell to him in the end. They always do.'

He ran one hand down her body in a parody of an intimate caress and she stiffened in shocked outrage. In desperation, she tried to scratch his face but he grabbed her shoulders and gave her a hard shake.

She could feel tears of helpless outrage rolling down her cheeks as dizziness swept through her again.

Despair filled her but also determination. *She would not sell!* She had been born stubborn and illness hadn't changed that. Besides, she had nowhere else to go. Closing her eyes for a moment against a surge of dizziness, she wondered if she was going to faint.

The heavy weight leaning against her jerked abruptly away and another man's deep voice said, 'Have you gone deaf? This lady has asked you several times to leave.'

Ilsa opened her eyes and blinked in astonishment at the sight of a complete stranger standing there. He was taller than her tormenter and looked strong and fit, also angry.

'Mind your own business.' But for all his bluster, when the stranger took a step towards him, the man moved backwards.

'Stop harassing her or I'll call the police.'

'I'm not harassing her. And it's only your word against mine.'

'And her word. I hear the police are cracking down on violence against women. And you can take that lorry away from here, for starters.'

'It's tired. Needs nice long rest.' Laughing loudly at his own feeble joke, the man turned and strode away.

The stranger watched till he'd gone round the corner and vanished down Larch Tree Lane, then he turned to Ilsa. 'Are you all right?'

'I am now.'

'I'm Corin Drayton. I live at the top of Larch Tree Lane.'

'Ilsa Norcott. I can't thank you enough for coming to my rescue.'

'Any decent person would have done that. You don't look at all well. Did he hurt you?'

'I've had a bad virus. I thought I was going to faint again.'

'Again?'

'Yes. I fainted earlier today.' She sagged against the door frame. 'Thank goodness for whatever brought you to Hawthorn Lane.'

'I wanted to see whether Belkin had started knocking these houses down yet. Then I saw that bully annoying you. I've heard he brings in men who cause trouble sometimes.'

She shuddered at the memory, staring in despair at the lorry. 'How am I going to get my car in and out? I need to go to the shops later today. I'm nearly out of food. And my internet and phone connections have stopped working properly so I can't order online. I think Belkin must have done something to them. I have no way of even complaining about the phone connection at the moment.'

'I think we'd better call the police about this because Belkin will no doubt find a reason to sue anyone moving his vehicle without permission. He can be tricky to deal with.' He gave her a conspiratorial smile. 'Fortunately, that fellow didn't see me approach and I was able to record him harassing you and refusing to move the lorry on my mobile phone.'

'Oh, well done!'

She watched him dial the police helpline and explain what was going on, then email them the film he'd taken. She winced when he said it was more urgent at the moment because the houseowner had been ill and hadn't fully recovered yet so needed her car to get around in.

That was bad enough but she felt even more embarrassed when he added that there might be a sudden need for ambulance access because she'd fainted earlier today and wasn't looking at all well after being hassled just now.

He listened intently and nodded, then put his phone away. 'They'll send someone round, hopefully within the next half hour. I'd better wait for them and keep an eye on your safety if you don't mind, and – are you sure you're all right? You're utterly white.'

'I'm just – a bit dizzy still.'

There was the sound of a car drawing up next door and she saw that Rob had just come home. As he looked towards her house, he frowned at the sight of the lorry.

When he came to join them, he glanced at the man who'd helped her but spoke to her first. 'Are you all right?'

'I am now.'

He turned to her companion. 'Aren't you Corin Drayton?'

'Yes. You look familiar, I must say.'

'Rob Carswell. We met at a seminar last year.'

Corin snapped his fingers. 'That's it. You're a specialist in putting together classy technical presentations.'

'Yes. Well, I was. I'm not doing so much of that now.' He

turned back to her. 'What exactly happened, Ilsa? You're looking as if you're going to faint again. And how dare Belkin park his lorry on your drive?'

'One of his employees left it there and harassed me but when Corin rescued me from his unwanted attentions, he still wouldn't move it. He said my problems would only get worse till I agreed to sell to them. But I won't. Can't. I don't have anywhere else to live and anyway, I like it here in the valley.' Her voice faded and she rubbed her forehead as if it was hurting.

'And all of a sudden her internet and phone access aren't working,' Corin said.

'They're still not working?' Rob asked.

'No.'

Both men shared angry glances.

Rob turned back to her. 'Did he hurt you?'

'He touched me.' She shuddered at the memory. 'I was afraid he might do worse, but Corin stopped him, thank goodness.'

'What's wrong with Belkin? Is he utterly crazy, thinking he can force people to sell to him?'

'Don't get me started on that man's faults,' Corin said. 'He's made his money quickly, mostly through luck and being in the right place at the right time. He isn't my favourite person, professionally or personally. How he manages to get away with things like this, I don't understand. Look, we should go inside and let Ilsa sit down while we wait for the police.' He grinned suddenly. 'I just happened to catch the incident on my mobile phone so the police have evidence and are taking it seriously.'

'Oh, brilliant.' Then Rob saw she was dizzy again and

put one arm round her shoulders, guiding her inside and hovering while she sat down. Tiny, who'd been shut in the house, came across, wagging her tail.

'I'll just bring in some shopping I bought for you, Ilsa, then you might like to eat something simple like a yoghurt. I got enough food to last you and your hairy friend for a day or two longer.'

'Let me pay you.' She fumbled for her handbag.

'I don't need paying. There are only a few things. We're neighbours. You can do me a favour sometime.'

She leant her head against the back of the sofa. 'Thanks. Please sit down, Corin. Rob, could you let Tiny out for a quick visit to the garden, please? She really needs to go, but I'm afraid I haven't had time or the materials to repair that gap in our mutual fence.'

'I've got some tough cardboard boxes left from my recent move. I'll use a couple of those to block the way through temporarily.'

A short time later, the dog bounded back in, sniffed Corin carefully, gave him a few wags of approval, then plonked herself down next to Ilsa again.

'Your dog's very friendly,' Corin said.

'She's not mine. My neighbour at Number 6 died a few days ago and I'm only looking after Tiny till her niece can sort things out.'

Corin looked thoughtful. 'Do you think the niece will sell the house or move in?'

'Probably sell it. Pam's been living in Spain for years and her aunt always said she loves it there. Trouble is, she's off on holiday in Morocco at the moment, so it's taking her a few days to get back.'

'Bad timing for you,' Rob said. 'You've enough on your plate without looking after this monster.' He reached down to ruffle Tiny's fur as he said that and she wagged double time at him.

'Yes. But she's good company.'

'Going back to your neighbour's house, unfortunately I should think Belkin will be first in line to make her heir an offer, may even have got to her already,' Corin said.

Rob nodded. 'He certainly got to me quickly when I inherited next door and he'll be even more anxious to get hold of our houses now, because Ilsa and I are in the next three houses, blocking his chances of doing a bigger development. He'll probably redouble his efforts to get rid of us.' Rob let out a little growl of annoyance at the prospect.

'Yes. Unless . . .' Corin's voice trailed away and he stared into the distance for a moment then said, 'Unless someone else comes up with a better offer for Number 6.'

'Are you volunteering?' Rob asked. 'I'm afraid I don't have that sort of spare money. I recently inherited 4 and 5 and they both need doing up, especially the one that's been used as a rental, if I'm to get another tenant.'

Corin shrugged. 'I'm not sure yet whether I want to buy it but I'll give it serious thought. I'll need to discuss it with my wife first and we'll have to crunch a few numbers to see whether we want to use some of our money that way. Do you have the contact details for your late neighbour's lawyer, Ms Norcott?'

Ilsa nodded. 'There's a business card on the mantelpiece. You can get the details from that. And do call me Ilsa.'

He did that, then pulled a couple of his own business

cards out of his pocket and gave one to each of them. 'In the meantime, this is how to contact me if you need any more help dealing with Belkin.' Corin frowned. 'Hmm. I really will have to think seriously about this. A Belkin housing development would spoil the whole tone of the valley and Hawthorn Close is such an iconic street, one of the earliest to be built. Not to mention the lovely avenue of trees. Oh, hell . . . Look, I'm going to contact that lawyer and tell him that I'm interested in buying the house, which I probably am. And it'll be a cash offer, so will probably be far more tempting than Belkin's.'

Rob and Ilsa said 'Good!' at the same time as they studied the business cards.

There was the sound of a car drawing up outside and footsteps approaching the house.

Corin stood up. 'I'll get it in case it's the police. I'm the one who called them in and I have the evidence about that guy on my phone.'

His voice floated back to them from the front door, explaining about the harassment and the lorry.

'You sure you're all right?' Rob whispered to Ilsa.

She nodded. But if truth be told, she was feeling distinctly shaky.

The conversation outside ended and Corin came back into the house. 'Will it be all right if these officers join us in here, Ilsa? They had just finished their shift and were on their way home when the call came into the station. That's why they're out of uniform and driving an unmarked car.'

'Yes, of course. Do bring them in.'

The female officer stopped in the doorway, studying Ilsa intently. 'You don't look at all well, Ms Norcott.'

'I'm getting over a bad virus.'

'She fainted earlier this morning,' Rob put in.

'No wonder the despatcher said it was urgent. Look, I'm Vicki and this is Murad.'

As the two of them questioned her about what had happened today, the male officer looked even more angry than his companion. 'This sort of behaviour utterly disgusts me. I'll phone my sergeant and see if we can get that lorry taken away for you.'

He went outside and, after a brief conversation, came back in smiling. 'They're sending someone immediately to tow it away, given that Ms Norcott can't get out if she has a medical emergency. There just happens to be a magistrate at head office at the moment and they're going to show her the phone images of you being harassed, then she'll no doubt approve the towing-away officially.'

Ilsa was glad of that, of course she was, but it also worried her. 'That's good in one sense but – well, what will Belkin do next? He'll be furious about his lorry being towed away. He broke the window of my front door a few days ago. He said it'd be a big rear window next. I can't prove any of it, though, since no one else was around. And the retirement housing on the other side of the street is behind a fence, so people there don't have a direct line of sight.'

'And she's suddenly lost her internet and phone access so she has no way of calling for help,' Rob put in. 'I wonder how they managed to do that?'

'I'll phone someone about looking into it,' Murad said.

'You don't have CCTV here, do you?' the female officer said thoughtfully. 'Might be worth installing it. That developer is going to be around for a while.'

Ilsa could feel herself flushing. 'I wish I could but I can't afford it.'

'Well, I can,' Rob said. 'I've been planning to install it on my own houses. I'll be doing most of the work myself, so it won't cost me much to extend it to your place as well, Ilsa, and no, you won't need to pay me. But I will ask you to let me have some extra cameras fixed on your house, both front and back, focusing on my two places.'

She looked at him, knowing he'd taken pity on her, but he nodded encouragingly and she couldn't resist accepting. 'Thank you. And of course you can put as many extra cameras in as you wish.'

'That'll be much more secure for me and my tenants, when I get some new ones.'

A couple of minutes later, a tow lorry arrived and backed up the drive to the illegally parked lorry, fixing an attachment to it so that its front wheels were off the ground. It left shortly afterwards with the large vehicle trundling along behind.

Ilsa was still looking worried and Vicki whispered something to her partner. At his nod, she then held out a different business card.

'Dial this number if you're ever afraid for your personal safety, Ms Norcott. Don't give the number to anyone else, though. It's only for vetted people with ongoing problems who are facing possible physical danger, most of them women.'

What did that say about Belkin? Ilsa wondered. The police must know something else about him. She saw Rob look at them thoughtfully too when he heard that.

'We'll connect an alarm button to both our security

systems as well,' Rob told them. 'It'll scream loudly and alert a security company if you have to call for help.'

'That'll make me feel a lot safer,' Ilsa said. 'I can't thank you enough, Rob.'

'Neighbours should help one another.'

Once the police officers had left, Corin looked at his watch. 'I'd better get off home now. My wife and I would like to invite you two round for drinks one evening soon. You might enjoy looking round the Marrakin while you're there as well.'

'What's the Marrakin?' Rob asked.

'It's the name for the gated estate where I live near the top of the hill, and was the previous local name for the whole of the nearby area. It was taken over during World War Two and wasn't released until fairly recently.'

Rob let out a soft whistle. 'There must have been something special going on to keep it for so long.'

'Who knows? The War Office doesn't announce its business to the world. There are some interesting old houses still there, some of them very well preserved. Others need quite a lot of work. And there's a former World War Two bunker. Well, we call it a bunker. No one's exactly certain what it was used for originally.'

'I will definitely look forward to seeing that estate. Who owns it now?'

'I do. I'm an architect and I suppose you'd call me a developer, but not one like Belkin. Anyway, I can show you around when you come for drinks.'

Ilsa looked at them doubtfully. Corin was clearly waiting for her answer to his invitation. These two already knew each other slightly but she wondered why she'd been included in the invitation. 'I'd love to visit you. It'll be nice to get to know some people round here socially now that I'm starting to feel better.'

Rob nodded agreement and they both started speaking at the same time, which made them all smile.

'Good,' Corin said. 'My wife will enjoy meeting some more people too, Ilsa. We're both fairly new to living in the area.'

When he'd gone, she turned to Rob. 'I can't tell you how grateful I am for your offer of a security system.'

'You already did. Belkin is trying hard to expand his business but he doesn't have a good reputation in the industry. I'd heard that bad things have been known to happen to those who refuse to sell to him, so I'm doubly happy to put in a joint security system.'

She shuddered and looked down again at the extra business card Vicki had given her.

He gestured towards it. 'You should memorise that special phone number they gave you as well as putting it in your phone. And you and I need to be ultra-careful what we do from now on.'

'I agree. I don't know what I'd have done without you today.'

'My pleasure.'

Rob was thoughtful as he went back into his home. She looked rather run-down, but she was still very attractive. He was looking forward to getting to know her better.

What did she think of him?

Chapter Five

The following morning, Corin's second cousin Deanna phoned him. 'I wonder if I could come and see you?'

'Of course.'

'Today?'

'OK. But it'll have to be this afternoon. I've things arranged for this morning. Do you know your way here?'

'Yes. Even if I didn't, I have a satnav; Mum knows Maggie Hatherall and we've been to visit her a couple of times. She pointed out your turn-off on Larch Tree Lane the other evening, Corin, and told us about the Marrakin for a development. It sounds a fascinating place. Anyway, see you later.'

Lucia came into the kitchen to join him. 'Who was that?'

'A younger cousin of mine. Deanna Drayton.' He frowned slightly. 'Wonder what she really wants. She doesn't usually have much to do with me.'

'Does she have to want something specific?'

'People from that branch of the family usually do. They can be a bit pushy.'

'Well, we'll find out this afternoon, won't we?'

'We? You're usually enjoying a nap in the afternoons these days,' he teased. 'I've even seen you fall asleep in the middle of a sentence.'

She stuck her tongue out at him. 'I shall make a huge effort and stay awake this time, Corin my love. I really am starting to feel better now that I'm past the first trimester. My goodness, it's hard work growing a baby.'

'Stick with it, my love. Any child of yours will be wonderful.'

'And of yours.' The glowing smile that accompanied these words said she didn't mind the hard work at all.

When Deanna arrived, she was wearing an outfit that looked more suited to the World War Two era than the present time and Corin hoped he'd managed to hide his surprise.

'Like it?' She twirled round and dropped him as flourishing a curtsey as you could manage in a knee-length skirt and tailored jacket with padded shoulders. 'I'm very much into this era. Did you recognise when it was from?'

'Of course we did. Those are very authentic World War Two fashions,' Lucia said.

'They ought to be authentic. These clothes are actually from that era and they didn't come cheaply. I know a second-hand boutique owner who looks out for vintage 1940s clothes for me. I've been fascinated by the World War Two years ever since I did a history unit about it at uni.'

She hesitated, then said, 'Um, I've been wondering about that air raid shelter I heard about. Have you really discovered an untouched one here? What are you thinking of doing with it?'

Lucia pointed towards Corin, who shrugged. 'We don't know yet. We're not even sure it was an air raid shelter. We call it the bunker. Less of a mouthful, anyway. All I am sure of is that I don't want to fill the hole in. Apart from the fact that it's so big it'd cost me a fortune to do that safely, it'd seem wrong. The bunker makes such a statement about the war. As I've said to Lucia, I think this generation and future ones should understand what lengths the war generation had to go to in order to defend our country.'

Corin stared blindly into the distance for a moment, then said slowly, thinking aloud, 'The trouble is, making it into a museum sounds a bit tame. And it'd need contents, curators and attendants finding. I definitely don't want to get involved in that sort of thing, either the initial setting up or the ongoing management.'

Deanna beamed at him. 'It sounds as if we're on the same page, though, about wanting to preserve it intact, and I wouldn't mind getting involved. I might even have an idea about doing something commercial with that bunker – if it's suitable, that is. I'd need to see the interior first.'

'Oh? Give me a hint.'

'How about turning it into a living museum and themed café, if there's enough space, that is. Café staff could wear World War Two styles of clothing, there might be murals of scenes from that era, and a relevant menu with food based on the rationing they had in those days – and also rooms where they can get a taste of sheltering from an air raid or something similar, with sound effects. We might also run special private parties there and hire out period outfits from the war years for those attending. As I said, it depends on the place being physically suitable.'

He didn't reply straight away, sat frowning slightly, thinking about her idea. 'Be a bit expensive to set up, wouldn't it?'

'Yes. But my partner Didier can provide the finance and he already owns some kitchen equipment from a café he used to run. He's sent me to do some preliminary scouting because he's a bit busy at the moment. He's a real live wire about making money.'

Corin exchanged surprised glances with his wife. 'Have we heard of this guy? Your use of the word "partner" sounds as if you're in a steady relationship. Your mother hasn't mentioned that.'

Deanna flushed slightly. 'Yes, we're getting very close. I may be a bit premature in calling him my partner, but I'm certainly hoping the relationship will last. Didier is rather special. Well, I think so. He's French, as you may have guessed from his name, but he's been living in England since he was a teenager, so he's also had a British input into his upbringing. It's really cute the way he switches languages sometimes. I've learnt more French since being with him than I ever learnt at school.'

She paused for a moment, then smiled and waved one hand dismissively. 'I'll tell you more about him later. At the moment I want to concentrate on this bunker of yours. He wants me to see if it'd be suitable for what we're thinking of.'

Lucia looked at him as if she wanted to say something.

'What do you think about this, darling?' he prompted.

'I'm not sure. It's mostly underground. It'd have to be

done carefully. You'll have a better idea what I mean once you've seen it all, Deanna, but Corin will have to do the showing round at the moment and I'll wait for you here. The going is rather rough for someone in my condition, even though I can still see my feet, which a pregnant friend of mine can't now she's in her eighth month.' She grinned across at Corin, blew him a kiss and made a shooing movement with one hand.

He quite liked Deanna's idea, well, he'd like any idea that dealt with the problem of what to do with the bunker, but he had a niggling worry that it might not be feasible financially. It'd need careful thinking about the details. If there was some way of making it work, it might be a good thing to do on principle, but parking might be a problem. He'd not even consider it if it was just Deanna, but she said she was working with an experienced businessman and he did want to find something to do with the bunker, which was the thorn in his flesh at the Marrakin.

Essington had a go-ahead local council that tried to encourage tourist activities and he didn't think they'd quibble at the idea of this one, as long as it wasn't going to make a lot of noise or cause disturbances. One of the important things to them would be that it could have spin-off financial benefits for the other local businesses in the valley because of people coming in from outside and spending money locally.

As he walked across to the shelter with Deanna, she said, 'There's another thing I need to mention, Corin. If it is suitable, we're hoping you won't charge too high a rent for the first year, and we'd need a long lease. We'd all need to think strategically and long-term.'

He tried to hide his amusement at the family chatterbox

telling him how to think but he needn't have bothered because she wasn't even looking at him. She'd stopped talking and was studying the approaches carefully, stopping every now and then to take photos.

He didn't spoil her concentration by asking any more questions at the moment. He still wasn't sure whether it'd work for her and her partner as a way of making a living and therefore for him as a way of using the bunker to generate income.

When they got to the underground shelter, he took the lead down the rather steep stone steps that had been uncovered when he explored it. These started at one side of the shallow sunken dome that covered the shelter, circling it and leading down to a small entrance area.

There, a metal grille barred the way and Deanna bumped into him, as if she'd expected to go straight inside. He edged her gently away from it and took out a large, old-fashioned key to unlock one of the entrance gates, then entered a code on an unobtrusive panel to one side. 'I made a modern addition or two to the original security system.'

'Do you really need such precautions?'

'Yes. And if you rent this place you will need to take care of that side of things as well. I don't want kids sneaking inside and getting locked in. It's bigger than you'd think and very dark once you're past the outer rooms.'

'Sounds promising.'

The entrance chamber had enough natural light for them to see clearly but beyond it he'd had some temporary strips of cheap LED lights fitted, which he switched on now. She paced this area out and scribbled down numbers of steps in a small notebook.

The door at the left side of the chamber also had a lock on it and he made no attempt to take her inside it before turning to her and asking, 'Want to go further inside? There are several smaller chambers. You're not claustrophobic, I take it?'

'No, I'm not. And yes, please. I'd also like to see it all, including whatever's behind that door.' She gestured towards the locked door.

'Sorry. That section is separate and won't be available to anyone hiring the rest of the bunker. I keep some of my own things there.'

What better place to store his business and personal records, not to mention some paraphernalia from his days as an architectural consultant to charities building homes in third world countries? He didn't miss those days though he was glad he'd made a positive contribution to the human race. As far as he was concerned, this was his personal time of life and at thirty-five he wanted to build a family and personal career now.

She consulted the notebook. 'Are there, you know, facilities installed?'

'What sort of facilities?'

'Running water, electricity, toilets and so on.'

'Well, of course there are. People of that era had the same basic needs as people of today. But the ablutions areas are extremely old-fashioned by modern standards.'

'That might be even better, as long as they work efficiently.' She gestured around them. 'This is a nice big entrance area. It could house the seating for a café and a place selling World War Two facsimile articles. Would that worry you?'

'Not if it were done properly. Do you know much about running such places?'

'I did work in shops and cafés several times when I was a student and even then I noticed that people spend more money when they're relaxed. But my Didier's run several small businesses and he's very knowledgeable about the management side of things because of his family background.'

'Good.' Corin grinned. 'Did you know that your voice goes soft when you speak about him?'

Even in the dim light down here he could see her blush. 'I've been seeing him for nearly three months now, my all-time record.'

That didn't seem a lot to him. 'Good luck to you. It isn't easy to find someone to live with permanently, though it's wonderful if you do. As for the idea of a development of that sort, I'll have to think about it and get more details from you if Didier is interested. I'm still concerned about the finance side of things and about the safety aspects for customers. We'll probably have to put in a fire escape of some sort, too.'

'You'll have to talk to Didier about that. He handles the financial side of things.' She gave him another of those quick sideways glances. 'But you are *considering* letting us rent it for that purpose?'

'The idea does sound to have some merit. Depends how well it's done, of course. Anyway, come back and have a cup of coffee with Lucia, then you can go away and tell your partner what it's like, then he can come and discuss it further with me.'

'Could we just go round it one more time? And I forgot to mention one other thing we thought of. I was a teacher for a couple of years and there's a lack of places round here for school day trips, especially ones for smaller groups of older students needing serious purposes for their outings.'

'You've certainly been doing your homework!'

'Yes. And just to set the record straight, I'm well aware that I've grown up a lot recently and found more of a purpose in life. I was a bit flaky before.' She spoilt the solemnity by grinning and adding, 'Though I had a lot of fun.'

'Glad to hear of both aspects.'

He led the way round again, not saying much but noting that she was still observing everything most carefully and scribbling occasionally in her notebook. This was a new side to Deanna and her lively interest in that era was very attractive, could be a good selling point as well if they were dealing with the public.

'The spaces are unusual, but I think it could work,' she said as they locked up again and left the area. 'But of course Didier will need to come and see it.'

'I'll look forward to meeting him.' He stopped at the top of the steps to look round, thinking about the other things that would be needed. Fortunately, the shelter was at the lower edge of the Marrakin, looking out over some as yet undeveloped and rather scruffy land at one side of the rear. They could put in a car park there, but they'd have to connect its entrance to a small country road on the other side of the hill, which wouldn't be cheap.

That way, the comings and goings wouldn't annoy the residents of this estate, or impinge on the additional properties he was planning to build one day on the unused land at the higher side of the rear. He would *not* create an estate like Belkin's crowded dormitory housing, though he would have to put in some lower-cost housing to meet council requirements, he was sure.

He'd give it all due consideration but wasn't rushing into anything.

Besides, he had another problem to deal with at the moment, one which might need some serious attention in the immediate future: Hawthorn Close. The more he thought of it, the more he loathed the idea of those beautiful old houses being knocked down and an ugly Belkin development being plonked in their place.

Not only didn't he want that man building his shacks there, he didn't want them anywhere else in this lovely little valley, either. He'd fought for sustainable, attractive housing developments in third world countries and he was prepared to do the same here in Britain too.

What's more, he truly believed that people benefitted from living with beauty around them as well as needing a roof over their heads. Those trees performed a valuable service for the whole community, they were so beautiful.

It was well known in the local building industry how Belkin had wangled his way into a couple of areas near Swindon, starting small and gradually driving local residents away by making them unhappy with their changed surroundings. They could be so desperate to move away in the end that he was able to buy their properties and extend his developments more cheaply than was fair. The man was a master of sneaky tricks.

Lucia shared his opinion of this potential invasion and his beloved was a savvy lady with her own contribution to make to the Marrakin and the world in general.

He was looking forward to finding out what sort of a child they'd create between them.

Chapter Six

Ilsa's phone and internet connections mysteriously began working again after the lorry had been taken away by the police, which was a big relief.

Her deceased neighbour's lawyer contacted her two days after that. 'Pam will be arriving from Spain tomorrow and has already begun making arrangements online for her aunt's funeral. She's asked me to tell you how grateful she is to you for looking after Tiny and will take her back to live with them in Spain afterwards.'

'Oh, good. Um, is it possible for me to be reimbursed for the expenses I've incurred with Tiny? I wouldn't ask but I'm still on sick leave, you see, and I'm a bit short of money and, well, Tiny does eat rather a lot.'

'My dear Ms Norcott, why didn't you let me know about that straight away? Send me a list of what you've spent and your bank details, and I'll see to the money being reimbursed at once.'

'Thank you.'

After a brief pause, he added, 'You need to get your phone and internet checked as soon as possible.'

'Yes. But that sort of thing can be rather expensive.'

'Your neighbour might be able to look into that for you, or at least give you the name of someone who won't charge like a wounded bull.'

'I don't like to bother him again.'

'I don't think you've got any choice. Your primary need is to protect yourself and your finances, and he'll understand that, I'm sure.'

'I suppose so.'

'And don't quote me on this but Belkin contacted me the day after Judith died about buying her house, asking me to urge the heir to sell to him quickly and telling me he was offering the best price the estate is likely to get. I thought it very unfeeling to contact her so soon, not even waiting till after the funeral. And he's lying about it being a good price. It's a pitiful offer. I would never advise her to accept it.'

'He offered a really low price for mine as well. And he won't take no for an answer but I will *not* sell to him. Um, did you know that a man called Corin Drayton wants to buy Judith's house? He lives further up Larch Tree Lane and he seems a decent guy. I'm sure he would offer a fair price. Shall I ask him to contact you?'

'Please do.'

'I'll phone him straight away.'

When the call was over, she found Corin's business card and was about to phone him to pass on the lawyer's message when he called at the house to see how she was.

She told him what the lawyer had said and he was

delighted to hear about him being interested in his offer. 'Thanks, Ilsa. I'm much obliged. I'll phone him as soon as I work out exactly how much to offer.'

'I'll be really happy if you buy Judith's house. Maybe if that horrible man can't get hold of any more houses in this street, he'll also stop harassing me.'

Corin looked surprised. 'He's still annoying you?'

'Yes. Or at least, not him but one of his men is. And things are still going wrong, or getting damaged during the night.'

'Unfortunately, unless we can prove it's this fellow who's causing these minor nuisances, there's not much we can do.'

'I know. He's got a new foreman for this development and he called in to introduce himself and make what he called an improved offer. Only it wasn't.'

'What's he called?'

'Harden.' At least this one hadn't tried to touch her or press against her. Ugh. She still had nightmares about the other man. She realised Corin had said something else. 'Sorry. I missed that.'

'I was saying that it was great having you and Rob round for drinks. Lucia and I both enjoyed your company.'

'I enjoyed yours too.' She'd also enjoyed walking up the hill to the Marrakin with Rob and walking back at dusk.

'You must both come round again.'

'I really ought to invite you and Lucia back here, only . . .' Ilsa hesitated, then told him the simple truth. 'Unfortunately I can't afford to entertain anyone at the moment. I'm rather short of money and will probably have to claim social security benefits when it runs out. I've never needed to do it before, so I'm not looking forward to that.'

'Any idea when you'll be well enough to return to work full-time?'

'Not really. I'm improving slowly but it takes a while to get better from some viruses.'

Her rate of improvement had been so slow she hadn't known how to cope sometimes. Life could be tedious when you couldn't do much. The doctor had warned her about taking it easy and not getting stressed during the next few weeks, and she'd do her best, but she'd never been one to sit around.

It was almost as if Corin was reading her mind because he suddenly said, 'You were working in IT, weren't you?'

'Yes. But it wasn't a permanent job. And I'm not fit enough yet to work full-time.'

'Which means this is the worst possible time for you to be dealing with someone like Belkin. Look, just a thought but I often have temporary or intermittent projects working on my various websites and I know my brother does too. Maybe that would be of interest to you?'

'Yes, it would. I could do an hour or two's work at any time of day then.'

'That'd be great, since our support needs change from time to time. I'll presume that you can spell accurately? You certainly use spoken English well. Don't get me started on the modern inability to spell I've encountered with some temporary help.'

She chuckled at that. She too had noticed the deterioration in spelling ability even in TV news headlines or newspaper articles, yes, and had shouted at her TV about it more than once. Which didn't do much good except for relieving her annoyance. 'I don't feel very intelligent at the moment but I definitely haven't forgotten how to spell.'

'And you come across as having a good brain even if you tire easily physically.'

His words cheered her up. He gave her one of his lovely warm smiles, then suddenly grew quietly serious again. 'In the meantime, if you're ever utterly desperate for money and most especially if Belkin is baying at your heels, come to me or Lucia. We'll lend you whatever you need and help in any way we can.'

She was nearly in tears at that kind offer because it removed the worst worry of all. She couldn't bear the thought of losing her home. She didn't have a mortgage, but even normal running costs and rates were a struggle at the moment. All she could manage was a choked, 'Thanks. I will remember. And I appreciate your kind offer.'

After he'd gone, she went to lie on her bed for a while, fretting at her need to do this. She hadn't realised that when you were ill for a long time, you grew bored with your own limitations – in between sleeping your life away.

There was a limit to how many books she could read because she found it hard to concentrate for long and she was fed up to the teeth of watching daytime TV or listening to the radio.

Rob kept an eye on the house next door, but didn't see any sign of Ilsa for several hours. Tiny was outside and had stayed in the patio area, sprawled in the shade, so the cardboard barrier must still be working. Ilsa had mentioned her need to take naps most days and there had been no sign of movement in the house, so that was probably what she was doing now.

He worked on the rental house next door, doing a series of small repairs, all the time wondering how to guard against

Belkin upsetting the next tenant or damaging his house.

When there was still no sign of Ilsa and a car drew up next door, he felt a bit worried. He recognised the police officers getting out of the car as the same ones who'd dealt with Ilsa before, even though they weren't in uniform, and went to join them.

'Is something wrong?' he asked, feeling anxious.

'We're just making a courtesy call, keeping an eye on your neighbour. It's taking Ms Norcott a long time to answer the door. Do you think she's all right? Is that normal for her?'

'She sometimes needs a nap in the daytime.'

'Ah. We'll give her a little longer, then.' Vicki looked round. 'This is a rather nice street. I love the hawthorn trees. I didn't realise they grew so big because I've only seen them as hedges in the country before. How nice that they've planted them all along the street.'

Murad had been staring up and down the street. 'Are there any rental houses around here, do you know? I'm sharing a really noisy flat at the moment and I'm looking to relocate. They're nice guys but they party a lot and it's especially hard going when I'm on night shifts.'

'And if he finds somewhere half decent, I'm going to share with him,' Vicki said.

Rob couldn't believe his luck and seized the opportunity. 'My other house is a rental.' He pointed next door.

They both stepped forward to study it.

'These two semis were left to me recently by an aunt and the tenant moved out rather suddenly.'

'What reason was given for that?'

'Building noise. Only, they haven't started any building work yet. I think Belkin got at him.'

'Ah.' The tone of Murad's voice said he understood the subtext to that statement.

'I'm just getting the house ready to advertise, only to be frank I've been worrying about the next tenant being driven away as well.'

They both grinned. 'How about renting to us? I doubt they'd manage to drive away my friend and myself and we'd pounce on any dirty tricks. Vicki's not only a police officer, she's also a black belt in martial arts.'

'Why don't you take a look round? If it suits you, I'd be very happy indeed to rent it to you. In fact, you sound like perfect tenants to me under the circumstances. Though I can't guarantee you won't have any trouble from Belkin.'

Vicki let out a sniff. 'Well, we can guarantee to deal with it. How much is the rent?'

He named a sum that was less than he'd initially hoped for but would cover running costs for the property and give him a modest profit.

If the way the two of them exchanged glances was anything to go by, they were indeed pleased at the amount he was asking in rent. And Rob was equally delighted. Having police officers as tenants was a particularly attractive proposition at the moment.

'Why don't you go and have a look round the house?'

Vicki nodded. 'We'll do that after we've seen Ms Norcott. If it's suitable, we'd like to move in without anyone knowing we're in the police as we'll be continuing to work in plain clothes for a while. It'll be convenient for some other work we're involved in.'

Rob stared at them thoughtfully, beginning to wonder whether this was a way of them keeping an eye on Belkin's doings or for some other reason.

Vicki winked at him and confirmed his suspicions by saying quietly, 'Don't ask us why we want to keep secret about who we are. Our moving in won't only be personal. Let's just say your needs and ours coincide with our boss's needs and then we'll not talk about it again. Murad and I are genuinely looking for a new place, and are likely to become long-term tenants at the house.' She paused for a moment, then added, 'Whatever else happens.'

At that moment they heard footsteps inside the house but though Ilsa's outline could be seen at the other side of the door, she didn't open it straight away.

'She's probably checking who's here through the spyhole,' Rob explained in a low voice.

Vicki looked suddenly angry. 'Very wise, given the circumstances, but no one should feel they have to do that, especially in their own home.'

Ilsa opened the door just then, stared at the police officers and asked immediately, 'Is something wrong?'

'No. We were nearby and thought we'd check that everything's all right. Just a courtesy call. Can we come in for a minute or two? Would you mind?'

'Not at all. This way.' She held the door open and began moving back down the hall.

'Thanks, Rob,' Murad said, clearly not wanting him to join their conversation.

So Rob went back into the rental house to finish fixing one of the kitchen shelves. When he heard someone at the back door, he went down the stairs quickly, so as not to keep the police officers waiting.

Only no one was there and he could feel himself falling.

Chapter Seven

When he regained full consciousness, Rob was shocked to find himself lying on the patio outside, feeling woozy, with two women who were strangers to him standing nearby. He began to struggle to his feet but was glad when one of them put her arm round his shoulder to help him.

What the hell had happened?

'You've been hurt,' the younger one said quietly as she helped him to sit down on the sofa. 'Just rest for a minute or two.'

He began to wonder whether she was a doctor, both from her tone and the way she was examining his forehead.

She frowned down at him. 'What happened? Did you have a fall?'

'Damned if I know. I opened the back door, that I do remember, and then next thing I knew I was trying to clear my head and you were helping me back into the house.'

'I think you were attacked and it's a good thing we

knocked on your front door just then. As my auntie was getting out of the car across the road at the retirement homes, she saw someone at the side of your house. She didn't recognise him and is paranoid about burglars. When this one saw her looking in his direction, he hid his face with one arm and ran away. We could see one of your feet on the ground and it wasn't moving so we came across to check what was going on.'

'I'm glad you did. Thank you so much.'

'There have been a few strangers I didn't like the looks of lingering in the street lately,' her aunt said, 'so I've been keeping my eyes open. I've taken a few photos of them too.'

He recognised her. 'I've seen you going in and out of the flats across the road.'

'Yes. I'm Marjorie Newall. And I've seen you occasionally too. You moved in recently.'

'Rob Carswell.'

'First things first. My niece Becky is a doctor. Let her look at your injury.'

'How are you feeling now?' the younger woman asked.

'I still feel a bit woozy,' he admitted.

When he was sitting near his kitchen table, Becky asked, 'Where is it hurting?'

'Side of forehead.'

'You've been hit by something and it's bleeding. Anywhere else hurting?'

'No. Just this.' He reached up to touch it and she moved his hand away.

'Don't mess about with it, Rob. Your hand is dirty. Do you have a first aid kit?'

He had trouble getting his words out coherently,

'Pantry, right side – um, middle shelf.'

'I'll get it, Becky.' Mrs Newall came back shortly afterwards, carrying the kit.

'Can you get me some boiled water to clean this with, Auntie? If there's any water left in the kettle, that'll do for starters and then you can boil me some more.'

'What's wrong?' he asked as she peered at his forehead.

'You've been whacked on the left side of the head. Luckily for you, it must have glanced off. Perhaps you were moving your head at the moment your assailant struck. It was still enough to knock you out, though. Sit still and let me clean it.'

When she'd done that, she dabbed something that stung on his forehead.

'Ouch.'

'Just lie down quietly on your sofa for a few minutes. I'll help you across to it.'

So he did as she told him. He was still feeling a bit spaced out.

The older woman took out her mobile phone and said, 'I think we should contact the police and report this.'

As Becky gathered the blood-stained mess of tissues together and threw them into the kitchen rubbish bin, he sighed and let his eyes close. He must have briefly dozed off because the next thing he knew, the two police officers he'd been talking to earlier were standing near him.

The doctor had a quiet word with them, then came to check how he was looking. 'Your colour's a bit better but you should take it easy for the rest of the day. If you start feeling worse, go to A&E.'

'Thanks for your help. It seems to be settling down.'

'Yes. You're lucky this time.'

As the two women left the house, Vicki, the female police officer, said, 'I'll just check the outside, see if the intruder left any traces.'

Murad came to stand by the sofa. 'Did you see anyone, Rob?'

'No, I didn't. I was lost in thought. I heard a sound and went to open the back door, thinking it was you. After that, the first thing I knew was that I was recovering consciousness only I was so dizzy I was afraid to move. My neighbour from across the street and her doctor niece had found me.'

Murad frowned. 'They told me they interrupted the attack.'

'Yes. I'm grateful for that. Do you think this is down to Belkin again?'

'No idea at this stage. I wouldn't be surprised.'

Vicki came back inside. 'No sign of anyone hanging around but there are some footprints behind the rubbish bins, as if someone had been hiding there. I doubt we'd get anything clear out of them as it's a trampled mess in a small space but there's one that shows the size of shoe, at least.'

Before she could say anything else, a young man hurried into the house through the back door without knocking. 'What happened? Is anyone dead?'

As he raised his phone to take a picture of Rob, Murad stepped between them. 'Who the hell are you? And why should anyone be dead?'

He flashed an ID card so quickly no one had time to read it. 'Press. My paper likes to keep an eye on public safety.'

Murad put a hand out to hold his camera to one side. 'Stop that! My friend here doesn't want his photo taken.

What brought you here today anyway?'

'We had a tip there had been an incident, a householder attacked.'

'Who told you that?'

'Anonymous source, someone who cared about public safety phoned the paper.'

'Well, if a guy falling down his own stairs and needing his injury checked by a doctor is a matter of public safety, that's news to me.'

'You're here, two of you. Are you the police? They said the police had been called. If so, why would they call the police in if it was something as simple as a fall?'

Vicki sighed loudly. 'No one called the police in. We're here to look at this rental property.'

Rob intervened. 'You have no business here, so please leave my property now.' He saw Murad get his phone out and take a photo of the so-called journo.

The man was now avoiding their eyes and had his arm up as if to prevent Murad taking any more photos as he edged back towards the door. 'I still don't understand why you were called in from next door if there was no trouble.'

'An elderly neighbour was worried that this gentleman might need to be taken to hospital,' Vicki said. 'If so, we'd have done that, since we're going to be renting from him and living next door.'

'Only I didn't need it,' Rob said firmly. 'I just fell down the stairs.'

The journalist frowned. 'Yes, but—'

Murad took over again. 'How did your anonymous source get to hear about the so-called accident so quickly?'

'How should I know? Ask the editor. He's the one

who gave the job to me.' The man had a shifty look as he said that and was still avoiding meeting their gaze while glancing round.

When he started to raise his phone to take another photo, Murad moved forward, getting between him and Rob. 'I hope your editor didn't pay this anonymous source a fee because if so, you lot have been cheated. *Man falls down his own stairs.* Big story, that. The public will be fascinated. Now, if you'll excuse us, we need to get on with our day and Mr Carswell needs to rest.'

When the journo didn't move to stand fully outside, Vicki walked towards him till he had to step back. 'Go away and stop harassing Mr Carswell. If you don't, I'll call the police myself.'

The man was right outside now and didn't reply, just muttered something under his breath and strode off round the house.

She came back in, shutting the door firmly behind her. 'At the moment I don't think he's quite certain who we are or what's going on.'

Murad turned back to Rob. 'All right if we have a quick look round your rental now?'

'Of course it's all right. The key is on the windowsill.' He leant back on the sofa because his head was aching. 'You can go round on your own. Come and tell me if you want to rent it or not afterwards.'

'Yes, of course.'

It wasn't long before they came back, smiling. 'It's a really nice house. We'll take it.'

Murad held out the key. 'We locked up. That journo is still lingering at the end of the street. Looks to me like the sharks are circling. I bet someone we won't name in public is trying to make properties on this street seem less appealing. How soon can we move in?'

'As soon as you like. I've got another key, so you can take that one and get a second cut. Let me know if you find anything else that needs fixing once you've moved in.'

'You don't want us to fill in any paperwork?'

'Another day. I can't think straight at the moment. Anyway, I trust you.'

'Thanks. We'll pay the deposit into your bank account later today if you'll give us the details, and we'll move in tomorrow morning as soon as it's light, if that's OK.'

'That'll be fine. The sooner the better.'

Rob had no hesitation giving these two his bank account details and he smiled as he watched them walk back to their car. Great that he'd found tenants he could trust.

It'd be even better if his guess was correct and someone in the police was taking an interest in what else Belkin was doing generally. The man didn't have a good reputation and he hoped the builder was heading for major trouble. If so, it couldn't happen soon enough or to a person who deserved it more.

He fingered the plaster on his forehead, furious at himself for being so careless. From now on all outer doors would be locked unless he was nearby, and that included locking up whenever he went next door to see Ilsa. He smiled. He hoped that would happen often.

On that thought, he locked his own back door then lay down for a while because his head was still throbbing.

Come to think of it, he ought to tell Ilsa to take the same precautions. He didn't want anything else happening to her. He'd go and warn her once he'd had a little rest. Thank goodness the aspirin was starting to take effect on the aches and pains. He sighed and felt himself begin to relax.

He woke an hour later feeling better for the nap and much more clear-headed.

After checking once again that all his doors and windows were locked, he left the back way and went to knock on his neighbour's rear patio door.

Ilsa was in the kitchen and the minute she saw who it was through the window, she went across to open the back door.

They smiled at one another as she locked it again and gestured to a chair, staring at Rob's forehead. 'That looks painful.'

'I've taken an aspirin so it's easing now. I'm just checking that you're all right.'

'That's kind of you. I'm fine, thanks.' He didn't move for a moment or two, suddenly wondering what she'd do if he kissed her, then telling himself not to be stupid. He hardly knew her. And yet somehow he felt as if he'd known her for years. Good heavens, what had got into him today? It had been a knock on the head, not an arrow to the heart!

He smiled at her again. The spear seemed to have lodged in his heart already. She had the loveliest smile.

Something touched his leg and he swung round, to find Tiny nudging him for a cuddle. So of course he obliged, which broke the spell. And thank goodness for that. He needed to slow down a bit.

'I was glad to see you had your door locked, Ilsa.'

'The police told me you'd been hurt by an intruder and

I should keep all my doors locked.'

'I was coming to tell you the same thing.'

'Thanks. You should be resting, surely, Rob?'

'I'm taking it easy.'

'Well, since you're here, why don't you continue to do that? Sit down and have a cup of coffee with me? It's only instant, I'm afraid.'

She was looking a bit flustered as she offered the invitation. Was she as affected by his presence as he was by hers? He wasn't usually a babe magnet. But he rather hoped she was attracted too. 'I'd love to stay for a chat and I'm not a coffee snob, so strong, black and wet will be fine.'

She stole another glance at his injury. 'Vicki said we should tell everyone you fell down the stairs.'

'Yes. It was what she told a journalist who suddenly appeared out of nowhere. They said afterwards they thought Belkin might be trying to generate some bad publicity for this area by publicising the attack, so that he could buy houses at a lower price. Ain't going to happen with my houses. I'm not selling.'

'I'm not either. Why were they suspicious of the journalist?'

'There hadn't been time for the news of it to get out, so the journo must have set out to come here before it happened.' He touched his forehead involuntarily as it twinged suddenly.

'Is it aching? Ought you to see a doctor?'

'I already have done. One was visiting her aunt who lives in the retirement housing across the road. The old lady had seen someone suspicious loitering so they came across and found me lying on the patio. She told me to take it easy for the rest of the day but no one said I couldn't chat to my next-door neighbour.'

'You're welcome to visit any time.'

'Thanks. Same applies to you coming to see me.'

Ilsa took a sip of her coffee and as she set it down, she asked, 'What lengths will that horrible builder go to next?'

'Who knows?'

'At least I've got Tiny acting as watchdog for another day or two. She makes me feel safer.' She gestured to the patio doors that led out from the dining end of the kitchen. 'Why don't we take our coffees outside?'

'I'd enjoy that.' Obviously she'd not be able to risk sitting outside when she was on her own, however fine the weather. And come to think of it, he shouldn't do that from now on, either.

He followed her outside and made sure to sit with his back to the house. No one was going to creep up on him again unless they had invented an invisibility cloak.

She stared at him across the outdoor table, an old-fashioned one of very solid wood, then pointed to the top of his head. 'What's the sawdust in your hair from?'

'What? Where?' He batted at his hair.

'You missed.' She got up and disentangled some splinters of wood, her touch light.

He was sorry when she sat down again. 'Thanks. I've been doing small repairs on my rental property. The sooner it's occupied, the happier my bank manager and I will both be.'

'How are you going to make sure the next tenant hasn't been planted by Belkin?'

He grinned. 'I've already got some new tenants and

they're absolutely trustworthy. In fact, you've met them.' He watched her face light up as he explained that the two police officers would be moving in.

'I wonder why they're keeping an eye on what Belkin's doing?'

'Who knows? Perhaps he's even more of a villain than we'd thought. It'll certainly suit me to have them living next door.'

She nodded agreement. 'I shall feel better too if they're within screaming distance, so to speak.'

'Exactly, but I hope you don't need to yell for help. And if you do, I'll be within screaming distance too and I'll come running, I promise.'

'Thanks, Rob.'

They continued chatting amicably and ended up agreeing to pool their resources and have a barbecue tea together. He provided the steaks and she contributed some salad and bread from the supplies he'd brought her. She had a tiny portable electric barbecue that she got out. He'd have to buy one of those. They weren't much use when you lived in a flat in London but it'd be a pleasant way of cooking tea sometimes.

He also brought his last bottle of cider for them to share. It turned out to be one of her favourite drinks as well.

He'd been pleased to see that she went into the kitchen while he fetched his contributions to the meal from his house and stayed there with the door locked till he got back. If this was overkill, he preferred it. 'Better safe than sorry' had to be their watchword for the present.

As the evening passed, they chatted or fell silent equally easily, talking about anything and everything. She was a sensible woman and well read, and they enjoyed the same sorts of music.

After a while she started to fade visibly, looking suddenly white and exhausted, so he helped her carry the dirty crockery inside, then left her to go to bed.

'I'll stay by the window and watch till you get back safely,' she said.

'There's probably no need for that extreme.'

'Humour me, Rob. I can't get past that bruise on your forehead tonight.'

He picked up his dishes and walked home with all his senses on the alert, ready to hurl his crockery at anyone who threatened him. He waved to her then put down the dishes on the outdoor table to unlock his door. After he was inside, he locked his door again immediately, annoyed all over again about the attack and having to be so careful now.

As he put his crockery in the dishwasher, he thought how much he'd enjoyed chatting to her. Or not chatting. She'd make a great neighbour and friend but would it be sensible to get romantically involved with her, tempting as that might be?

He smiled. In theory he needed to get his new life sorted out before he dated anyone, but it was probably too late for that now he'd met her. But he would keep an eye on the Belkin situation.

He was utterly determined not to let that villain steal his inheritance off him.

He'd rather let the properties rot away than hand them over to that crook. But it did make him feel better to know who his tenants were.

Chapter Eight

In Newcastle, after the funeral and a small lunchtime gathering of her mother's friends at a local café, Amy Hatherall changed out of her dark clothes and steeled herself to drive over to her mother's house. It would have to be cleared out and there was only her to do it, so she might as well start now. It was only two thirty and she had nothing else planned for the rest of the day.

Anyway, it'd fill the time. She felt rather lost and bewildered now the formalities were over.

Once she'd done this final task for her mother, she had to get on with her own life. She knew already that everything had been left to her because her mother had given her a copy of the will. There weren't any other close family members left, after all.

She parked in the drive and stared at the neat suburban street, then the house. No way was she going to move in here, even though the house was slightly bigger and a lot nicer than her own unit. It held too many memories and was buried in a part of outer suburbia full of older people, not convenient for her to get to work from. She planned to put it on the market as soon as it was cleared out.

And then what? Perhaps she'd buy herself a small place in the country. She was alone now and might as well be alone in a beautiful setting. And Northumberland was a lovely county.

She hadn't expected her mother to die unexpectedly of a heart attack at the age of fifty-seven, though she'd known there was some heart problem.

'Nothing for you to worry about,' her mother had said. 'Just a minor glitch that's manageable.'

Amy took a deep breath and told herself to get on with it. She'd changed into her oldest jeans and bought several rolls of bin liners to put things in. Her mother had been what people jokingly called a pack rat, never throwing away even worn-out old possessions in case they came in useful again one day.

Not being a hoarder and not sharing her mother's taste in fussy ornaments and patterned upholstery, Amy couldn't imagine wanting to keep much of the house's contents, apart from some of the books and a few pieces of tenderly polished antique furniture that had apparently been passed down from both sides of the family.

She'd taken a week's holiday leave from work and was debating giving in her notice now that she would have her mother's money behind her and be able to buy a house outright with it. Well, she would have once the house was sold. It wouldn't be a fortune but it'd be a comfortable sum and then maybe she could do temping and spend part of her life on painting, which was her passion, far more than just a hobby.

Once inside, she closed and locked the front door and stared at the hall and stairs. Would it be best to start at the top of the house and work her way down to the bottom? Then she shook her head. No, the kitchen should be first. She'd already removed the fresh stuff from the fridge and taken the usable food home with her, so it only took an hour to empty the cupboards of cans and unopened packets of food and pack them in boxes to take home with her.

After that, she went out into the small back garden for a breath of fresh air, found herself facing condolences from the neighbour and went back inside again, fighting tears.

She didn't want to talk about her loss, was still coming to terms with it, hated weeping in front of people.

After locking the back door again, she went upstairs, taking her backpack, which contained toiletries and a change of clothing. She intended to stay here and get this horrible job finished as quickly as possible. The spare bedroom where she'd slept occasionally during the past few years would be all right for as long as was needed.

She had to steel herself to go into her mother's bedroom at the front of the house. Where to start? 'The bed, of course, idiot,' she said aloud. 'Strip it and wash the bedding. Mum died in hospital, not here. This is all usable stuff.'

Once she'd done that and put on a load of washing, she turned away from the bare mattress and decided to tackle the big chest of drawers that had always stood near the window. She took a deep breath, expecting to face her mother's underclothing, but in the top drawer she found only a box file and nothing else.

Strange, that. She lifted it out and gasped. It was labelled in large letters: *AMY – OPEN ONLY AFTER I PASS AWAY*. That stopped her in her tracks. Something about the wording and the fact that it was the only thing in the drawer worried her.

After a moment's shocked hesitation, she set it down on the bed, sitting beside it, reluctant even to open it.

Was some ghastly family secret about to be revealed?

She'd seen TV programmes about reuniting lost members of families with relatives and there had been nasty shocks for some of the participants. Surely there wasn't anything like that in her own family history? They were from very ordinary stock if her mother was anything to judge by.

Whenever she'd asked about their ancestors, her mother had always said there was nothing much to tell on either side. Amy's grandparents were all dead and her cousins had emigrated to Australia. They'd kept in touch for a while, then the letters had been reduced to a card and short message at Christmas.

Her grandfather, John Hatherall, had always been a bit of a mystery but it had upset Amy's mother to talk about the father who had died young so she'd stopped asking about him. Now, she began to wonder if there was something to find out, after all.

In the end she took the box down to the kitchen, put it on the table and opened a bottle of white wine from her mother's store. She didn't know why but she felt sure she was going to unearth some problem or other.

After a couple of sips, she put the glass down, took a deep breath and opened the box. There was a sealed envelope on top with *AMY* written on it and three big kisses, *X X X*.

The latter was the way her mother had always ended letters during the years Amy had been away.

Tears came into her eyes and she blew kisses back at the written ones before slitting open the envelope and pulling out a neatly folded paper. It turned out to be a handwritten letter from her mother, who always said computers were for business stuff, not important personal communications.

My darling Amy,

What a lovely daughter you have been. I'm so glad I've had you in my life and so sorry to say my final goodbye like this.

The doctor has warned me that my heart problem is getting worse but I don't want to risk massive surgery with uncertain outcomes.

I need to tell you about your ancestry, though, because I'm the only one left now who can so here goes. I don't know whether I did the right thing in keeping this information to myself till now, or indeed whether I'm doing the right thing by 'revealing all', as the saying goes.

My mother did the same thing with me. She refused to talk about my father's background and left a letter for me about his family when she died. Her letter is included in the collection of family papers in this box.

When she wouldn't talk about my father except to say he'd left home at nineteen and never gone back, I always wondered why he did that. Was his family name really Hatherall or had he changed it so that his parents wouldn't be able to find him? I made up all sorts of stories about him as a teenager.

After I met your father, I lost interest in the past. I just wanted my own home and family, especially as I fell pregnant so quickly. He wasn't interested in getting married to make it official. He said we were together in every way that counted and somehow I knew he'd never leave me so I didn't let it worry me.

That means you and I are legally Hatheralls like your grandfather. Strange how that name has stayed in the family for over two centuries.

There is only one remaining Hatherall of the senior line left now, apparently, my father's sister, Maggie. I don't know anything about her because she was a lot younger than him, just her name and that she is still living in Larch House, the family home in Wiltshire.

He did say that she was a 'nice lass' in case you're interested in contacting her, but that'll be your choice and it won't worry me either way. Follow your own path, my darling.

Another thing that concerns me is that you'll let your horrible divorce from your dreadful ex stop you getting involved with a man again. Stay open-minded. The right man can make a wonderful life partner, as your father did for me.

There are no more secrets, not that I know of anyway, so I'll end with all my love and my very best wishes for a rich and productive life. Take some

time for your art now, dearest. You're good enough
to go professional. The money from selling my house
should last you a good while and give you time to get
established as a landscape painter.

Elaine

Amy wiped away a tear and pulled out the envelope
addressed to her mother. It was older and worn, looking as
if its contents had been pulled out and reread many times.

She took another mouthful of wine, set her glass down
and muttered, 'Here goes!'

The envelope contained another beautifully handwritten
letter, this one addressed to her mother from her
grandmother.

Dearest Elaine,

Your father asked me not to tell you about his family
background until you were twenty-one. He knew he
hadn't long to live and wouldn't see you grow up,
but he worried that his father might try to take you
away from me after he died if they found out that
you existed. I don't know why he felt so sure of that
but he did.

You know about my humble origins. Nothing else to
reveal there. Your father's family were anything but
humble, however, and there's quite a lot to tell.

I think 'landed gentry' would be a good word for
their status, though it sounds rather old-fashioned
nowadays. He kept his family name even though he
never wanted to go back to Wiltshire to see them.

The Hatherall family has lived in Larch House for a few hundred years, I don't know exactly how many. I remember it as 'the big house' of the district but I never went inside it. We ordinary folk didn't.

The estate and house still belong to the family but they've lost most of the other properties they used to own in the surrounding countryside, so are no longer wealthy. But they're still snobs, your father always used to say.

He never wanted to be rich, never looked down on anyone. He ran away because they didn't want him to marry me. He said I was his sort of person and the woman they were pushing him to marry was a boring fool. 'Thick as a brick' was the politest term he used.

His description of his family's lack of business acumen isn't flattering, either. He always earned enough to keep us in reasonable comfort and said that was all anyone needed.

Sorry if my mind seems to be wandering. This letter is harder to write than I'd expected.

Larch House is your father's ancestral home. It's situated at the upper end of a small valley that leads up only to a dead end from Essington St Mary, an insignificant little town that your father always called the 'last stop on the way to nowhere'.

He couldn't wait to get away from it. Well, there was no way a musician could make a living there. He always managed to do that but performed under an assumed name. It meant him travelling a lot but I had my home and friends, and later you to keep me company so I didn't mind too much. It would have been like trying to cage a rainbow to try to stop him.

Years after we left Essington, we heard that his younger sister, Maggie, had inherited everything. He said she was welcome to it. Presumably she has married and had children but I've no intention of trying to find out.

Now that you are over twenty-one, I feel you deserve the choice of whether to connect with the family whose name you bear or not. What you do is up to you. Go with your heart, dear girl.

With all my love,

Rose

Amy put down the letter and took a big gulp of wine. Why had her mother not said anything about this? And why hadn't she made any effort whatsoever to contact the Hatheralls when she was a direct descendant?

It only took a moment to work that out. Because Elaine had a cosy life, a job she'd enjoyed as a barmaid in the local pub, long-time friends nearby and no ambitions to do anything else with her life.

But her mother's home and life had felt rather claustrophobic to Amy and she'd gone travelling to a few other countries before she settled down nearby when she found out that her mother's health was rather fragile. She hadn't expected Elaine to die so young, though.

And yes, she did want to try being a full-time artist now.

She was twenty-eight and had a store of wonderful visual memories from her travels, not to mention photographs that she wanted to bring to life in oil paintings. She'd done several part-time painting courses to acquire the necessary skills to do it *properly*.

She stared down at the two letters, wondering what she should do about the Hatherall family. But she didn't have to make a decision straight away, did she? She put the box file with the few other things she wanted to keep, her family photographs, her grandmother's jewellery, her favourite childhood books and some vintage clothing.

She carried on clearing things out, relieved when she didn't encounter any more surprises.

She took an occasional sip of wine without really noticing how much and by the time she realised how late it was, she was exhausted and rather tiddly. Well, it had been a long, horrible day.

She'd finish her mother's bedroom first thing the following morning and hoped there wouldn't be any more confronting revelations there.

Of course, she couldn't resist rereading the two letters before she started work the following morning and then going online to make a quick search for Larch House. Only there was no sign of it. She did find Essington St Mary, though, and it looked like a pleasant little town. She'd look for the house another time.

As she worked, she kept wondering whether she wanted to stir up the past and wasn't at all sure about that. A workmate from Lancashire had had an old saying that amused Amy and she'd adopted it. It suited the current situation perfectly: *If in doubt, do nowt.*

There was no rush to do anything after all these years, so she'd concentrate on clearing out the house and then put it on the market.

But yes, she would give in her notice at work as soon as her mother's house sold. She felt burnt out from managing customer service for a chain of several small stores. No matter how well they paid her, she had other things she wanted to try doing with her life than calming down irate and sometimes highly unreasonable people.

There were no more surprises in her mother's house, thank goodness, and she was relieved to hand it over to an estate agent and move back into her own little home.

But she couldn't settle, still couldn't work out what to do about her grandfather's family.

She hoped her mother's house would sell quickly.

Chapter Nine

When Amy received a phone call from the estate agent two weeks later to say that he had received a good offer for her mother's house, she was so relieved she couldn't answer him for a moment or two.

'Are you still there?' he asked.

'Sorry. Just feeling happy. Yes, do go ahead and sell it to them at that price. And could you please come and look at my flat when you have time and tell me what you think it's worth? I'm thinking of selling it as well.'

To her surprise, he phoned an hour later to ask if he could come round that afternoon to get her signature on the contract. He'd be able to see her flat at the same time and give her an estimate of its value.

It didn't take long to show him round such a small flat, but she was pleased with the price he suggested putting on it. 'That's higher than I'd expected. Are you sure?'

'Yes. Prices have risen in this area because it's close

to town. And I doubt it'll take long to sell. These starter homes are going very quickly at the moment.'

So she signed up to use his company's services for a second time and when he'd left, she danced round her flat. It was all coming together.

A couple of days later, she received an unfair reprimand from the new manager about how she'd treated a customer whose language had been beyond rude. It was the second time this new man had accused her of something unfairly and refused to listen to her side of things.

And he might use politically correct non-sexist language and terms but the way he looked at her body made her feel distinctly uncomfortable. She didn't hesitate but marched round to the Human Resources department.

'I'm not enjoying working with the new manager, so I'm giving notice and I'd like to leave immediately.'

It took a few minutes' arguing and a threat to complain officially about the new manager before they told her it'd be all right for her to leave straight away.

There was no farewell party and she didn't care about that. The guy she'd worked most closely with whispered that they'd arrange something down at the pub one evening next week and he'd phone her. She didn't hear from him or anyone else, though, and she didn't care.

She sat alone in her flat on her second morning of not going to work and had a little cry, first for her mother, then for herself. Time had dragged yesterday because she wasn't used to spending whole days on her own. She stared at herself in the mirror and gave herself a talking-to. She had to focus on where to live, then what to do with her life.

Could she really earn her living as a painter? There was only one way to find out.

Perhaps a cottage in the country might be both inspiring and pleasant? They'd shown some lovely places on the TV programmes about moving out of towns. She drove out of Newcastle two days running to look at country properties that she'd seen advertised but she didn't feel drawn to them or, indeed, to anywhere in the area. Not for a permanent home, anyway.

Northumberland could get very cold in winter. She'd done a lot of shivering last year, her first winter after working in Australia for a few months.

Only, she hadn't wanted to settle down in the Antipodes either, or anywhere else that she'd visited on her travels.

She'd stayed in Northumberland to be with her mother, who was so eager for her to hang around that she'd given her the deposit money for the flat. Amy would always be glad that she'd had that year of living nearby, even though she'd had to take a job she didn't enjoy to manage financially.

Maybe she should look round some of the prettier parts of the south now, not the big towns and certainly not London, just somewhere where there was a pleasant little house with room for a big studio and where the winters weren't so harsh.

She'd never been able to settle properly to her painting in this flat. Perhaps if she had somewhere pretty to live, it'd inspire her. Or perhaps she was fooling herself about her artistic skills. What if she'd never be more than a talented amateur? She needed to find out and face that honestly.

But she'd be on her own in the world wherever she

lived. And she still hadn't decided about contacting her grandfather's family. Oh dear, she wasn't usually so indecisive.

After showing a couple of people round her flat, the agent lingered to speak to her.

'They both said the same thing: it's too small. I think you'd have a better chance of a good sale if you could clear a few things out. Your painting gear looks very unsightly when I'm showing the place, for a start. And you should get rid of some of your furniture too, if you can. There's rather a lot. Could you maybe park a few pieces with friends?'

She told him the simple truth. 'I don't have any friends close enough to do that with at the moment. I just quit my job and I had a bad divorce a few months ago, which ruined some of my so-called friendships.'

She'd been surprised at which of her so-called friends had stayed with her ex and his new partner socially. She could only guess that couples preferred to associate with other couples. And to cap it all, her best friend had moved down to London a few months ago to take up a big promotion.

The agent gave her a sympathetic look. 'Been there myself. It can be difficult moving on. Give it time.'

She nodded and managed to scrape up a half-smile.

'The thing is, if you can get rid of nearly half the furniture, the flat will sell more easily, I promise you. You'll be surprised at how much bigger it'll seem. Do you need all this stuff?'

'No. I brought a few special pieces here when I cleared out my mother's place.'

He seemed so certain and he was the expert, had sold her mother's house quickly, so she took his advice on board. 'I guess I can hire a storage unit for a month or two and dump stuff there.'

'I'm sure you won't regret it. Actually, I can recommend some storage units nearby. Other clients have used them and been very satisfied. I have some of their cards in my briefcase and it's not because I get paid to recommend them, because I don't; it's because I like to help smooth the way for my customers and make sales more likely.' He got out his wallet and handed her a card.

As she watched him leave, she thought what a pleasant man he was to deal with. Then it occurred to her that hiring a storage unit would have the added benefit of giving her a place to leave her things when she went to search for another part of the country to settle in.

Just like that, things began to fall into place in her head. As soon as this flat sold, she'd dispose of the stuff she no longer wanted and then go down to Wiltshire. She really ought to make the effort to see where her grandfather's family came from, even though she was a bit hesitant about approaching her remaining and apparently elderly relative.

The following afternoon when she got back from taking the last load to the storage unit, the agent rang to say he had a client who wanted to look round. If she could stay away for a while, he'd phone when he'd finished.

So she went to a local café and bought a coffee and piece of apple pie, then got out her phone and ate slowly as she began reading a book that had just been released by her favourite author.

It was a full hour before the agent phoned from his office to say the client was interested in buying her flat under certain conditions and had just left after signing a provisional offer. Could he meet her at the flat to explain what the client wanted?

That took her breath away. She'd only just cleared the extra furniture out, hadn't expected anything to happen so quickly. 'Yes. Yes, of course.'

'Great. See you there in half an hour.'

When she let him in, he beamed at her and declined a coffee. 'Never mind refreshments, let's get on with talking about the offer.'

'Fine by me. Please sit down.' She took the other armchair opposite him. There were only two left in the flat now and to her it felt uncomfortably bare, as if she were living in a furniture showroom.

'This is a cash buyer who has just come back from living in Spain. She wants to get her own place and move in as soon as possible, so her offer is conditional on an expedited sale. If that can't be done with yours, she'll look for something else to buy.'

'What exactly does that mean?'

'Things could be finalised in about a couple of weeks if we push the paperwork through. Would you consider leaving so quickly?'

'I thought the paperwork took several weeks.'

'It's possible to do it more quickly. I think you've nothing to hold you here now. Am I right?'

'Yes. Oh, wow!' Amy took a deep breath and said it. 'And yes, please. Just go ahead and do it. I'd prefer to move as soon as possible.'

'That's great to hear.'

When they'd done the initial paperwork and he'd left, she stood motionless for a few moments staring round.

Would she miss this place? Not at all. She'd bought it to be near her mother and because it had good public transport into town to get to and from work.

She hadn't really settled anywhere since she left school. Her mother's house had been too small for her to share it as an adult. She'd worked in a couple of boring jobs, taken some important painting classes, then felt she ought to see something of the world. She'd thought she was ready to settle when she got married but it had taken only a few months of living with her ex to realise how nasty he was under that charm that was brought out when he wanted something.

He'd thumped her once but she hadn't given him the chance to do it a second time. Because the lease to the flat was in her name, she'd simply packed all his possessions and dumped them in the front garden.

Was there something wrong with her that she hadn't been able to attract a decent man? Oh, who knew anything? She didn't, that was certain. But it was good that the unit had sold so quickly.

She dived into clearing out her possessions, putting those she wanted to keep into storage with the other items.

She woke in the middle of the following night and lay awake for a while before taking another firm decision. She'd contact her sole Hatherall relative to see if Maggie wanted to meet. If she did, Amy would be happy to give a new and friendly relationship a go in her life. And she'd absolutely love to see the old family house.

If this great-aunt didn't reply to her, she'd simply move on and try to find somewhere pleasant to live, then hopefully make a few friends. She could look at her ancestral home from the outside at least, whether she got on with the present owner or not. What you'd never had, you didn't miss.

Or did you? She was surprised to realise how much she wished she had had a bigger family now she'd lost her mother. It was rather frightening to be completely alone in the world.

She couldn't find an email address or phone number for any Hatheralls in that part of the country, just the postal address of Larch House in an old newspaper article, which had a small photo of the house at one corner. She didn't have a house number but she was sure the post office would know where exactly Larch House was on the street, so she sent off a letter to explain to the great-aunt who she was.

She said she'd be coming down to Wiltshire in a couple of weeks and would like to call in and meet her grandfather's family, if that was all right. Sadly he'd died nearly two decades ago.

She received an email two days later from Maggie, who sounded genuinely delighted to hear of her existence and who invited her to stay at Larch House for a few days and get to know her family's long-time home properly. There were plenty of spare bedrooms and it was a lovely, welcoming old house.

In for a penny, in for a pound, why not? Amy thought and replied at once to say she had just sold her flat and would be free to visit as soon as the sale went through. She'd send Maggie a date as soon as she had one herself, but it would be about another ten days or so. She'd be happy to accept the invitation to stay the night.

She didn't sleep well, wasn't sure she was doing the right thing, wasn't sure about anything. When she caught herself wishing she had someone to discuss the situation with, she knew it was right to go there.

The poet John Donne had been so right:

No man is an Ilsand, entire of itself; every man is a piece of the continent, a part of the main.

How had she ever come to think of herself as an Ilsand? No home, no real friends, no relatives except one stranger in Wiltshire and some distant cousins in Australia. Her mother had always had a lot of people to talk to, but they had been her friends, not Amy's. After her death they'd have no reason to contact her daughter, who had been overseas for most of the past few years and was a stranger to them.

Were the Hatheralls loners? Did she take after that side of the family? After all, there was only one Hatherall left apart from her.

Oh dear, she had to stop overthinking this till she knew more. She should just . . . well, stay open to getting to know her great-aunt. That would be a start, wouldn't it?

She wasn't going to chicken out now, so she researched Wiltshire online and camped out in her flat with increasingly few furnishings, getting rid of her life piece by piece through adverts in the local shop windows and community newspaper, as she waited for the purchase money to be paid.

Chapter Ten

Deanna phoned again two days later. 'Hi, Corin. Would it be possible for me and Didier to come and look round your underground bunker?'

'Certainly. When?'

'You couldn't let us do it today, could you? He's just had a private lunchtime function cancelled, so he's free this afternoon.'

'As it happens, yes, I am available then. I was only going to work on my accounts and I can do that any time. But I'm not tying myself to setting anything up with you yet. I'll need to look into the whole situation more carefully before I make such sweeping changes to the bunker site. Is that clear?'

'Yes, yes.'

He'd just sent off a draft design for modifying and extending one of the old houses and now had to wait for the potential client to think about it and get back to him. He'd enjoyed working on it and was finding it hard to settle down to another creative task until he got some sort of reaction to his efforts, so this meeting would fill in a couple of hours nicely.

It took only quarter of an hour for his two visitors to arrive. Didier was a very ordinary-looking guy, not very tall and with mid-brown hair going rather thin on top. Corin was surprised at how adoringly Deanna was gazing at him. But unless he was much mistaken, Didier wasn't looking at her in the same doting way.

As they walked round the bunker, the visitor's comments showed him to be a shrewd businessman. Corin remained puzzled that he and Deanna had got together, though, and didn't feel sure that he genuinely cared for her. This might affect the long-term viability of the project.

Indeed, Corin couldn't help thinking that Didier's attitude towards Deanna was more suited to someone dealing with a rather stupid pet dog.

After a while he left them to go round again on their own, so that they could continue their discussions without an audience. When he next looked, they had come out but gone beyond the bunker and were studying the nearby terrain. Now why would they be interested in that?

It was a full hour since he'd left them before they came back to the house. Didier was doing the talking and she was listening and nodding.

Corin took them to sit with Lucia while he went to lock the bunker up again.

'You're very careful about access,' Didier commented when he returned. 'Isn't that a bit of a nuisance? And is it necessary? I mean, who is going to come poking around that old place?'

'I'd rather be careful than sorry, and I'd require you to be just as watchful if you did open up a business here. I don't want people getting trapped underground when the place is locked up at night.'

'I would be careful anyway. I always hire a waiter or kitchen hand who is prepared to help with security if necessary.' He smiled reminiscently. 'I had a kitchen hand once who was into martial arts. You should have seen the surprise on one drunken guy's face when a woman literally threw him out.'

'You can't be too vigilant these days,' Lucia said. 'I've done a self-defence course myself.'

'Have you?' Didier sounded surprised and was looking at her as if she'd grown a second head.

Corin glanced at his watch and returned to their business discussion. 'I can give you another quarter of an hour if you'd like to ask about anything else, after which I need to leave as I have another meeting arranged.'

He saw Lucia smile briefly at that because she knew he had no other appointments that day and was simply avoiding spending unlimited hours with these two oh-so-verbose people. Neither of them ever used one word when four could be crammed into a remark instead. And they liked to gild the verbal lily in two languages whenever they could, too. Good thing he spoke French reasonably well after working in one former French colony in Africa for a couple of years. He didn't let on that he understood what they were saying.

After they'd gone Lucia heaved a sigh of relief. 'I can see why you set a time limit to this meeting, darling. I thought they'd never stop talking.'

'Imagine how I felt going round the bunker with them. I don't enjoy going over the same ground several times, whatever I'm talking about.'

'Rather you than me if you allow them to put the café idea into operation, Corin.'

'Yes. But underneath all the chat, they may have some quite good ideas. I'm not sure yet whether there would be enough financial reward to their labours, though.'

'She's so young and enthusiastic, isn't she?'

'Delightful to see. He's more guarded. Only, something about the project has me rather concerned and I can't quite put my finger on it. I'll have to think about it most carefully.' He shrugged. 'Anyway, that's enough about my cousin. What do you want to do with the rest of the afternoon, Lucia my love? I'm at your service now for the rest of the day.'

'I've already accepted an invitation on your behalf. Maggie rang while you were showing them round the bunker. She's invited us to Larch House for afternoon tea and I said we'd love to go. She apparently has something exciting to celebrate.'

'It's always good to catch up with her, whether her news is exciting or not. I haven't seen her for a week or two. Or my friend James, for that matter. He seems to have settled in permanently in his bedsitter there.'

She smiled and he studied her, eyes narrowed. 'You've guessed what their surprise is, haven't you? Out with it.'

'It's only a guess, so I think I'll keep it to myself until I'm more certain I'm on the right track.'

He stared at her. She usually smiled like that at what she called 'courting couples'. And it suddenly fell into place. 'Are you thinking they may be an item?'

She nodded and her smile deepened. 'I've been wondering since I last saw them in town. And hoping so too. She's a lovely person and she was so kind to me when I was running away from my horrible ex. I thought then that she seemed lonely. At her age you start losing your friends permanently to the grim reaper, you know.'

'Well, I'm sure you'll never have to run away from your ex again. I doubt he'll come anywhere near Wiltshire after getting mistaken for a criminal here and arrested.'

'Justice couldn't have been done to a nastier fellow. It took him weeks to get released, too,' she said with a smile.

'Didn't it!' He winked at her.

She gaped at him. 'You didn't have a hand in that?'

'I might have mentioned his behaviour towards you to a certain friend of mine who was in charge of mopping up after the raid, and whose daughter had had a similar experience of being stalked.'

'Why didn't you tell me that before?'

'I hadn't intended to tell you now. Not a word to anyone, mind, or my friend will be in trouble.'

'I won't say a single word. But I'll relish the thought of it. It was dreadful to have Rattus turn up wherever I went and play nasty tricks on me, even after our divorce. Men like you make good role models. In fact, you're almost the perfect man.'

He swept her a mock bow. '*Merci du compliment.*'

'You've earned it. And I know it's childish to call my ex by nasty names, but it helps me feel better about the past and that's how I think of him now: Rattus. As he got worse, his viciousness seemed to show in his face and make him look uglier each time I saw him. Now, your face' – she grabbed his ears and pulled his face closer – 'just gets more kissable all the time.'

And she spent the next few minutes proving it.

He didn't mind that at all.

Corin would normally have walked across to Larch House, taking the back route through their adjoining estates and then climbing over the wall into Maggie's territory. When the time to leave drew near, he looked at Lucia thoughtfully. 'I think we'd better go by car, don't you?'

'I'm afraid so.' Lucia patted her stomach. 'The ground is fairly rough if we cut across on foot and this temporary inhabitant of my body is already slowing me down, even before he grows really big.'

'Can't be too careful in your condition.' He laid one hand over hers and it felt as if they were cuddling their unborn child together, which always brought a lump to his throat.

Going by car meant driving to the main road, going uphill on Larch Tree Lane for a hundred metres or so then turning off on the lower of Maggie's two drives and going back parallel to the way they'd just come out from their land, only a little higher up the hill. Their neighbour's other drive also ran parallel to these two, but was further up again. The two drives had apparently formed a one-way system in the old days when Larch House had been a much busier place, because horses and carriages moved more slowly than motor vehicles.

But the number of visitors and employees had declined steadily as the twentieth century moved towards and into the twenty-first. Motor vehicles had speeded up the way the world moved around, too, so Maggie's upper drive was rarely used nowadays and was rather overgrown.

Corin slowed down as Larch House came in sight. 'Is it my imagination or is the garden around the main entrance looking tidier?'

'It's looking a lot tidier. I gather James enjoys gardening so Maggie's turned him loose on her grounds.'

'He was like that when we were working together in Africa, always starting garden projects or getting the people we were helping to try to find better ways to cultivate their food crops as well as build their houses. And sometimes he learnt better ways to grow things himself from how they did things. It wasn't all a one-way information flow, by any means.'

As usual, they continued round the classic Georgian building to the rear entrance of Larch House. No one who lived locally even tried to use the front door these days.

The Hatheralls had once owned a good part of the valley, but sadly, Maggie was the last of the main line and now owned only the estate on which the house stood and a few small rental properties in Essington St Mary itself.

James came to the door to greet them. 'We're taking tea in the main sitting room to mark the occasion.'

They exchanged quick glances, wondering again what special occasion this was, but he'd already said, 'This way,' and walked ahead of them so they didn't try to find out. He and Maggie would tell them when they were ready.

They found nibblies set out and a bottle of champagne chilling in an ice bucket, plus some of Corin's family brewery's non-alcoholic drinks for Lucia, so they kissed Maggie's cheek in greeting then sat down to enjoy the sort of relaxed chat that close friends can start without any trouble whenever they meet.

After a preliminary catch-up, Maggie looked at James and he nodded, then turned to their visitors. 'We have some major news for you, my friends, then we'll open the champagne and drink a toast.'

'There are two sets of major news, actually,' Maggie said.

He turned to smile at her, such a loving smile that Lucia gave Corin a quick triumphant glance.

'First, and by far the more important of the two, Maggie and I have decided to get married.'

There was a moment's silence at this because Maggie had recently celebrated her seventieth birthday without ever having married and no one quite knew how old James was or when his first wife had died. He was at least a couple of decades older than Corin, with whom he'd worked with for several years, but was still fitter and stronger than many men younger than him.

'Congratulations! I'm so pleased for you. When did this happen?' Lucia asked.

Their two hosts exchanged more of those happy, loving glances and Maggie said softly, 'It happened gradually over the past few weeks, sneaked up on us, you might say. I'm still a bit surprised, actually. In the nicest possible way, of course.'

'When's the happy day?' Lucia asked.

'We haven't fixed a date yet, only decided that we aren't having a fancy wedding at our age,' Maggie said firmly.

James rolled his eyes and added, 'I had one of those the first time round and boy, what a palaver it was. So much fuss for a few hours and my bride hardly looked at me, she was so worried about something going wrong. In fact, she didn't seem to enjoy it at all and I certainly didn't. I merely endured it because I wanted to marry her and everyone in those days assumed that was the proper way to do it.'

He looked into the distance for a moment or two and Corin didn't interrupt because he knew James's first wife had died at a fairly young age and that he'd loved her.

Maggie kept an eye on James, not looking upset at this reminiscence, but as if she understood what he was feeling. It wasn't until he smiled at her again that she continued the conversation. 'It'll just be a simple civil ceremony and we'd like you two to be our witnesses. Will you?'

'Delighted,' they said at the same time and both kissed Maggie again, then Lucia kissed James and the two men hugged and shook hands.

'I don't intend to invite any of my family to the wedding,' James said. 'They'll only make a fuss about me getting married at my advanced age and at least one of them will be worrying secretly that Maggie will inherit all my money. She probably thinks I have more than I do.'

'I wouldn't have expected that from a child of yours,' Corin said.

'It's my daughter-in-law. She's been trying to find out how much I'm worth for years and planning how to spend it after I die, though to give her her due, she plans to spend it on their farm, not on living the high life. She'll be disappointed, though. I'm going to enjoy spending what's left on Larch House and leave them only a token amount of money, since I've already signed the family farm over to them.' He stared round happily. 'Maggie and I are going to enjoy modernising this lovely stately home and restoring some of its original beauty. A worthwhile final project for my life, I think.'

He turned back to the visitors. 'Will next month be all right with you two for being witnesses? There will still be plenty of time before your sprog is born, won't there?'

'That will be perfect,' Lucia said. 'I've still got months to go. Now, what's the other good news?'

'Maggie's been contacted by a family member she didn't even know existed,' James said. 'She thought she was the last Hatherall left from the senior branch.'

'Talk about a bolt from the blue. It's a young woman called Amy, who is my brother's granddaughter, which makes me her great-aunt. I never found out what had happened to him after he left home until now. He died a long time ago, poor chap.' She let out a deep happy sigh and added, 'That gives me an heir for this place.'

'She's only a potential heir at this stage,' James corrected gently. 'We haven't met her yet. What if she's like your cousin Sheila?'

'Ugh, yes. That'd be dreadful. And you said you'd check that she really is a Hatherall for me.'

'Easy enough. I did it this afternoon while you were fiddling with the food. She is definitely a Hatherall born and bred, because her mother never bothered to get married, so never changed her surname. But you have to bear in mind that being a Hatherall doesn't mean this Amy will automatically be a suitable heir. We shan't know that till we've met her and got to know her.'

Maggie looked at the others ruefully. 'I know it's sensible to think of her only as a *potential* heir at this stage but I hope she'll prove worth leaving it to so that it can stay in the family for at least one more generation. You all know that I don't want to leave Larch House to Sheila. She's only a second cousin and isn't at all attached to the place. She'd sell it before my coffin was nailed down. I'd just about decided to leave it to the National Trust.'

'I thought Sheila was your closest relative.'

'So did I. I'm so glad there is someone else. I was amazed as well as delighted when this Amy contacted us and introduced herself, saying she'd like to meet us.'

'Didn't your father know about this at all?'

Maggie shrugged. 'He probably did. He was very good at finding things out and keeping them to himself. He certainly never told me anything about her. To say that he didn't approve of the woman my brother married was putting it mildly. Father was born in a different era and was an utter snob about social class.'

Lucia couldn't resist asking, 'What was so bad about the woman he married?'

'She was a gardener's daughter apparently, or something similar. He even chucked her family out of their house and livelihood because of her marrying his son.'

'Wow. You'd think your brother would have told him that he'd had a child, though.'

'Kyle had never got on with Father and didn't care about the house, only about his music. As he grew older and insisted he wanted to become a musician, they had huge quarrels that used to echo round the place at regular intervals. That was probably why my brother stayed away after he got married. My father wasn't the easiest man to live with, but he and I got on quite well. Strange, that, isn't it? He always said I was like my mother and he'd loved her dearly.'

'Have you never lived anywhere else?'

'No. I never had a job, either. I wanted to paint but of

course, a Hatherall couldn't make a living as a painter. That was the only thing my father and I disagreed about. And actually, he was right about one thing: this house always did feel like my main job in life. My father neglected it, just wanted to be with his books. Fortunately, the house is big enough that I was able to get away from him when I wanted time to paint and he just about lived in the library, but we usually shared our evening meals fairly amicably.' It was her turn to stare into space for a few moments, then she shrugged and changed the subject. 'I'm really looking forward to meeting my brother's granddaughter, though. It sounds as if she's alone in the world, as I have been until recently.'

The way she smiled at James made Lucia sigh happily for her.

'Good heavens. What a fascinating situation,' Corin said.

'Isn't it? Amy is coming to visit because she wants to meet her sole surviving relative and see the family home. I didn't say anything to her about being the heir to Larch House.'

James cleared his throat to get her attention and she stuck out her tongue at him but corrected herself. '*Potential* heir.'

'That's better.'

She assumed a meek voice and said, 'Yes, dear!', which made them all laugh.

James looked at his watch. 'We need to get the other thing sorted out now as well.'

'Oh yes. There's something else I'd be grateful to you two for. Seeing that James and I are going to get married, I've written a simple will leaving the estate and everything I own to him in case anything goes wrong and I drop off my perch unexpectedly. I'm determined now that Sheila isn't having it, whatever happens to me and whatever this Amy is like.'

James took her hand. 'We'll sort something suitable out, my love.'

Maggie nodded but it was a few moments before her smile returned fully. 'So, first things first. Will you two witness my signature on the will?'

They both nodded.

'Good. We need to get it done quite quickly. It's a very simple will so we did it ourselves. James gets everything if I die before him.'

'And I've written a similar will leaving everything to Maggie,' he said. 'I've already given the farm and some other substantial bequests to my children so they're not missing out.'

'Yes, of course we'll witness the wills, but you two are not allowed to die,' Lucia said firmly. 'I don't know why you even feel you have to cover that possibility. You're only seventy, Maggie, and you don't look your age at all.'

She gave them a wry smile. 'This is partly because it makes me feel old to realise I'm a great-aunt, which is silly, but that *does* sound old.'

'And although you'll never tell us your exact age, James, it has to be similar to Maggie's.'

'Yes. Similar.'

They both smiled at that.

Maggie said thoughtfully, 'You never know what's going to happen as you go through life, do you? Best to be prepared. So, let's all sign the wills, then we can relax and celebrate our engagement. Oh, and we've made extra copies, which we'll also sign. Will you take them away and put them somewhere safe?'

'Is this all because of Sheila?'

'Not only Sheila. It's because of life and fate and how events can take you by surprise. We've both learnt that. Believe me, I intend to keep taking my vitamins and exercising regularly to ward off old age – especially now.' She gave James's hand a quick squeeze and he raised it to his lips and kissed it.

Lucia exchanged sentimental glances with Corin, who blew her a kiss.

'Champagne now!' James said. 'This one is rather special, to mark the occasion.' He picked up the bottle and showed it to Corin, who whistled softly, then James opened it and poured three glasses. He hesitated before holding a fourth glass up and looking at Lucia. 'I know you're not supposed to drink when you're expecting, but how about a mere inch of bubbly just to give you a taste?'

'I'd love that.'

They settled down to continue chatting and it was eight o'clock before the two visitors left.

'I think they're a good match,' Lucia said softly as she drove them back. 'I'm so glad they found one another.'

'Just like you and me,' he said.

She patted his hand. 'Yes. I love you and I love living here, and James feels the same about Larch House, which is so beautiful. I love our home already. It isn't a minor stately home like theirs, but you've made it so beautiful, it's a pleasure to live in.'

That compliment pleased him greatly. He loved designing homes for people.

They put the car in the garage and walked up to their front door hand in hand.

Chapter Eleven

Ilsa woke up and lay listening to the night noises, still feeling drowsy. What had disturbed her? Then something warm touched her hand and she realised that Tiny was standing beside her instead of lying on the rug at the side of the bed.

The dog nudged her hand again and whined as if to say, *Something's wrong.*

Why had Tiny woken her? She jerked fully awake as she smelt smoke and rolled quickly out of bed, heart hammering. Had Belkin's henchman set her house on fire now? Surely even he wouldn't go that far?

She grabbed her dressing gown from the chair by the side of the bed. Its pocket contained the alarm device that Rob had given her only that afternoon. As she rushed downstairs to investigate, she held it at the ready.

Tiny followed closely behind and pushed past her into the kitchen, pattering across to stand looking out of the French windows then turning her head and barking, as if to tell Ilsa to come that way.

The smell of smoke was getting stronger all the time but it didn't seem to be coming from anywhere inside the house. When Ilsa saw flames outside at the rear of the patio, she pressed her hand-held alarm instinctively. It shrilled loudly in her hand, echoed a few seconds later by the main alarm, which was situated high up on the side of Rob's house.

Had she caught the fire in time to stop it spreading into her home?

Tiny nudged her as if to ask to be let out, but she didn't do that. She wasn't having someone injure the dog she'd been looking after and grown fond of. She was quite sure that if this was a Belkin trick, neither he nor his henchman would worry about the safety of a mere animal or hesitate for a second to kill the dog if it attacked them.

A door banged somewhere outside and footsteps thudded towards the house but she didn't open her rear door till she saw Rob clamber over the low wooden fence and run onto her patio. As she let herself out, she pushed Tiny back into the house, shutting the dog inside.

To her surprise, after Rob had run across to the low fire at the rear of the patio, he simply stood staring down at it and didn't make any attempt to extinguish the flames.

'There was nothing lying around there that could have caused a fire, nothing at all,' she called.

'There is now.'

'Shall I put the house lights on?'

'No, not yet.' To her surprise, Rob circled slowly round the fire, then left it burning as he joined her at the back door.

'Don't we need to put the fire out? It might spread towards the house.'

'I don't think it's intended to do that, Ilsa. I'd guess this is another way of upsetting you and pushing you into selling to Belkin.'

There was loud whining and scrabbling at the glass from inside the house.

She turned to look at the dog. 'I'm afraid if I let Tiny out she'll chase after whoever did this and they might injure her.'

'Sadly, I think you're right. Look, I need a rake of some sort to break apart the firelighters that have been piled there and lit. It won't spread to the house, though, even if we don't extinguish it.'

'Firelighters?'

'Or something similar, I'm not sure what so I'm not going to use the hose on the fire. Who knows what they used to start it?'

'I don't have a rake.'

'I can't kick them apart. I've only got my slippers on. Ah!' He ran across the back gardens up to Judith's fence and picked up a piece of wood from a pile leaning against one corner.

These had been left by some builders who had been working on the house when the old lady died and had simply stopped work. They'd left a few oddments like that here and there. Folding her arms across her chest in a protective gesture, she watched him use one of the longer pieces of wood to nudge apart the pile of burning firelighters.

To her amazement, they still continued to burn slowly and steadily. What were they made of? And what would that horrible man and his thugs do to her and her home next?

She shivered as she glanced round. This felt like a scene from a horror movie, not real life. Everything was illuminated by bright moonlight, which threw Rob's shadow across the patio, making him seem much larger than life and rather threatening.

He finished what he was doing and came back, took one look at her and dropped the piece of wood, pulling her into his arms. 'You're shaking. It's all right, Ilsa. You're not in danger, nor is your house.'

She huddled against him, not wanting to let go.

His voice was low and soothing. 'I doubt this was intended to hurt anyone because that would cause too much bad publicity for the development.'

Before he could deal with the fire properly, more footsteps sounded and they both tensed and stared in that direction, but to her relief it was the two police officers who were now neighbours coming to join them.

'We've only just come off duty and we saw the fire. Why haven't you put it out?' Vicki asked.

'Because there's something strange about it.'

Vicki went straight across to study whatever it was that was still burning sluggishly at one side of the patio. Picking up the piece of wood he'd dropped, she moved one edge of the burning pile slightly. Almost immediately she muttered something that sounded angry.

'It's a strange sort of fire,' she called to Murad. 'If it's what I guess, I don't think we should touch it.'

Murad came across to stare at it, then moved away to make a couple of phone calls before rejoining them.

'This won't have been intended to burn the house down because it's too far away, but it's close to the fence and could have spread along that. And you're right about there being something strange about the way it's burning. I've called it in as a dangerous incident as well as a fire. Come daylight, we'll go over the surrounding ground and see if whoever did it has left any traces.' He scowled at the burnt area where several small fires were still burning sluggishly, muttering, 'Why haven't those smaller fires died down?' Then he turned to stare at the two nearest houses. 'Is the CCTV switched on yet, Rob?'

'Mine is but yours and Ilsa's aren't. I was going to finish setting them up today.'

'How about checking yours and seeing if it's recorded anything? Just whizz through the last hour or so and stop if you see any figures moving about. I doubt that fire has been burning for longer than that.'

'Will one of you stay with Ilsa while I do that?'

'Of course.'

'Back shortly.' Rob gave her hand a quick squeeze and hurried away.

Vicki went to stand at the edge of the patio and watched him until he was safely inside his own home and had locked the door again.

Murad turned to Ilsa. 'Any chance of a cup of cocoa or something? I doubt the fire service will be here all that quickly as it's not a dangerously large conflagration.'

'Yes, of course.'

He watched her pull herself together visibly.

Vicki stood where she could still keep an eye on Rob's house. 'I bet those sods are planning to do something each night.'

Ilsa drew herself up. 'Well, they won't drive me away from my home, whatever they do. My parents taught me not to give in to bullies, and besides I don't have anywhere else to go or the money to start again, especially if I accept their offensively low offer.'

Vicki spun round at the sound of a door opening and closing.

Rob came hurrying back from his house. 'My CCTV caught someone but not clearly enough to recognise them. It's someone of the same build as that new foreman, though.'

'Can you email it to us?' Murad asked.

'Tell me which number to use. I've already sent it to my own phone.' He waved it at them.

After he'd passed on the recording, the two officers studied the images.

'You're right. The man's face doesn't show clearly enough to identify him.' Murad sounded regretful. 'But we'll pass it to the IT experts in the morning to see if they can make it any clearer.'

Ilsa edged the sliding door open with her hip, shut it again with one fingertip to keep Tiny in, and carried a tray of mugs out to the outdoor table. 'Help yourselves.'

They stood sipping their cocoa and watching the remains of the fire. Even now a couple of the smaller patches of fire were still glowing and shooting out occasional flames.

It was over half an hour before one of the smaller fire-service vehicles turned up. The man and woman inside it introduced themselves, then checked Vicki and Murad's IDs and listened to a rapid explanation of what had happened as they studied the fire.

The central part of where the fire had been was mainly dark now, but an occasional flame was still shooting up an inch or two from one edge.

'I've never seen anything take that long for all the pieces of firelighter to burn out,' Vicki commented, frowning.

'From the smell of it, these aren't normal firelighters but a similar-looking product that's banned from being sold in this country,' the female firefighter said grimly. 'It's a good thing you didn't spray water on it or it might have spread further. If it's what I think it is, it's been used as a terrorist weapon, because it's impervious to water. It usually breaks up into smaller lumps and continues burning for far longer than you'd expect. Tiny pieces can even float away through the air if there's a strong wind and they'll stay alight long enough to set other fires. People who use this should be roasted on a big fire themselves.'

Her male companion shook his head in disgust and looked at the group of people. 'Has someone got a grudge against the householder, do you know?'

'It's Ilsa's house and there's a builder who is trying to force her to sell it,' Murad said.

'Ah. I can probably guess who that is.'

'Better not name him openly. He's sued people for slander and won before now.'

'My mother lives across the road at the retirement complex. Only yesterday she was worrying about what they're going to build here. She said it would ruin the whole heritage area to have small houses crammed together on those two end plots.'

The other firefighter chimed in. 'Someone did the same thing in Swindon about three years ago when a builder wanted to buy some houses and used this pernicious stuff, as well as playing other nasty tricks. My mother's friend was ill and couldn't cope with the stress so gave in to the threats and sold. She got a very low price and had to go and live with her daughter, couldn't afford to buy anywhere close enough to her again.'

'We were shown a video and given a talk about that stuff in a training session,' his partner said. 'It's really dangerous. If you ever get any proof of who did this, we'll help you nail him to the nearest wall.'

'The builder in question is too cunning to do anything himself,' Murad said bitterly.

'We'll come back when it's daylight and see if they've left any clues. Probably not, but we may as well check.'

'And we'll ask our colleagues who patrol the valley at night to swing past here more often from now on.' Vicki still looked angry.

'I think we need to do more than that,' Murad said. 'For the next few days we should take it in turns to keep watch on your house and patio at night, Ilsa. We'll do that officially from tomorrow night onwards but it'll be from our new home. But I worry about Ilsa, and Rob's two houses are also going to be prime targets, I should think.'

'I've been having regular offers to buy ever since I inherited,' Rob said. 'Extremely low offers. I'm not selling even if they make higher offers. I really want to live here.'

Vicki gave Ilsa a concerned look. 'I doubt the guy who set the fire will be coming back tonight, so you may as well go back to bed.'

'I doubt I'll be able to sleep.'

'You should lie down and rest, then. I gather you've been ill. Don't worry. We'll be taking it in turns to keep watch.'

She hesitated, then added thoughtfully, 'Belkin's getting a reputation for dirty tricks and wearing people down, but I don't think he'll have found out about the CCTV cameras that are being set up yet. If you can position them out of sight, Rob, we might stand a chance of catching a shot of this guy

Harden trespassing one of these nights. He's a bit of a dark horse, but I doubt Belkin will ever get involved physically himself, though. From what I've heard, he doesn't usually, just orders other people around.'

Rob looked up, head on one side. 'Luckily these three houses all have decent eaves, so I'll probably be able to hide all the cameras completely. I'll finish fitting the other two as soon as it's light and try to get the job done before most people are out and about. I might set the odd booby trap near the house, too.'

'Don't do anything that will harm an intruder. That sod would pounce on that with glee and sue you for all you've got.'

'I would never hurt anyone. I just want to discourage intruders. And don't worry, I'll include your rental house as well as Ilsa's home in the CCTV coverage.'

'Good. If you need any help tomorrow morning, just sing out,' Vicki said. 'We like to help the public to help themselves. I'll go and grab some sleep now. I'll spell you in a couple of hours, Murad. Where will you be hiding?'

'In the garden, in your wood store if that's OK, Rob? The front is open-ended but it's dark at the back. I'll make myself a little wall from your chunks of firewood to give me some extra cover if you don't mind me rearranging it a little.'

'Be my guest.'

Ilsa yawned and walked slowly back into the house.

Rob watched her go, hoping this incident wouldn't have slowed her recovery. He might be mistaken but he rather thought anger was making her more alert, not less.

He went inside his own house, checked online exactly when it'd be daylight, then set his alarm for just before then.

* * *

Ilsa slept only fitfully and woke up completely when it began to get light. She immediately remembered the events of the previous evening and hurried into the back bedroom to stare out of the window.

It wasn't fully daylight yet but the greyish light was enough for her to see that everything looked peaceful except for a blackened strip at the rear edge of her patio. There didn't seem to be any flames burning now, thank goodness, and someone had scattered soil over the area of the main fire.

When she looked to the left, she saw Rob coming out of his house with a small pack hanging at the front of his body. He didn't see her as he climbed up a ladder to the eaves and began fiddling with something.

She watched him for a while, smiling slightly, feeling better just to have him nearby.

When Vicki came round the corner of the house a short time later, she positioned herself out of sight at the back of the wood store and Murad returned to their house.

Ilsa relaxed a little, realising that with these three people around she felt safer than she had for a while. Rob had promised he would have her part of the security system working by tonight, including a better panic button that only the recipients could hear. It would make such a difference to know that she could call for help.

She got up and put the kettle on, took Tiny out on a lead to attend to her needs, then went to ask if anyone fancied a cup of tea or coffee.

Vicki bobbed up to shake her head and put one finger to her lips, but Rob gave a small nod of the head, then turned back to what he was doing. Ilsa went back into the kitchen, annoyed with herself for calling out so loudly.

She put the kettle on, ran up to get dressed then came back to make the coffee. By the time Rob had finished, she'd also prepared a plate of toast as well. He seemed to have a very healthy appetite.

He put away his tools and stepladder and joined her, then the two police officers slipped one at a time into the kitchen.

'The outer connections are in place. I just have to finish the overall control system in my house,' he told her.

'That's great. Thanks.' Ilsa indicated the plate of toast. 'I'm sorry I can't offer you a more substantial breakfast, but please help yourselves.'

Rob beamed at her. 'How did you know I was hungry? Thanks.'

'Me too. Toast is always welcome,' Murad said. 'Besides, I don't eat pork, so bacon would be no good to me.'

The toast vanished like snow on water and Rob said cheerfully, 'I think we've cleared you out of bread and jam. I'll just fetch another loaf from my freezer.'

He was gone before she could say anything.

Murad smiled at her. 'The hospitality is as welcome and warming as the food. You'll remember not to tell anyone we're police, won't you?'

'Don't worry. I haven't forgotten that.'

Rob rejoined them with a tub of butter and a jar of jam as well as the loaf, and she made another pot of tea and another round of toast.

It felt good to have a civilised break with friendly people and, best of all, when the two police officers left, Rob stayed on chatting for ages.

Chapter Twelve

Jane Keevil parked her car at the end of Hawthorn Close and got out of it armed with a clipboard and camera. As she began examining and photographing the street trees, a burly man came out of the end house and marched across to her, scowling. He jabbed his forefinger at her to emphasise what he was saying and she had to step back to avoid it digging into her upper body.

'What the hell do you think you're doing?'

'Checking the trees in case they need attention.'

'Are you from the council?'

'No. From the heritage society.'

'Then these two trees are no damned business of yours, so you can just push off.'

She didn't move but stared back at him and said quietly, 'It is my business, actually. We work with the council because this row of street trees is heritage-listed. They're over two hundred years old and have been considered one of the treasures of the valley for decades. Our volunteers check them regularly and report back to the council.'

He let out a harsh snort of laughter. 'Well, get a good photo of them this time, lady, because those two are coming down soon. I'm the foreman here and I'm about to arrange for a guy to come and do the felling.'

She gaped at him in horrified shock. '*What?* You can't do that. You'll be prosecuted.'

He gave another of his mirthless laughs. 'Then my boss will pay a fine and it'll all be forgotten. End of trees getting in people's way.'

'But why would you want to knock them down when they're so beautiful?'

'We're going to need that space on the verge for parking. Belkin's are about to start building a development here, so our workmen will need access to the plots and somewhere to park and later the owners will need somewhere for their visitors to park.'

She stood perfectly still, then took a photo of the nearest tree and turned the camera on him immediately afterwards.

'Hey! You can just stop that!' He reached out, trying to grab the camera and she darted back to her car, glad she'd not locked it and was able to jump in quickly. She slammed the door in his face and clicked the lock hastily.

He glared at her then took out his keys, pointed them at her and ran them along the side of her car, laughing at the shock on her face as he scratched a long groove into the paintwork of her neat little car.

He thumped the driver's window next to her face when he'd finished and yelled loudly and slowly, 'If I see this

car here again, *ever*, I'll really damage it, you stupid cow!
These plots of land and their contents belong to Mr Belkin
now and he is *not* a sodding greenie.'

Corin had watched the incident from a little further up the
street, standing outside Judith's house. He'd just had his
offer to buy this house accepted by the niece even before
she arrived in person to clear her aunt's house. He'd taken
several photos of what had just happened in the street,
including one of a guy he'd not seen before deliberately
damaging the car's paintwork.

He was not only shocked by this behaviour, but by what
the man had said. Surely even Belkin wouldn't be so stupid
as to cut down these very special and much-loved trees?
Every spring, people from Essington and also elsewhere in
Wiltshire and the neighbouring counties walked along the
street to enjoy the beauty of the canopy of bridal-white
blossoms.

Threatening to chop them down showed how little
Belkin understood about the valley. People here lived
quietly and peaceably, but from what he'd heard they came
together when necessary to defend their town and land.

The ones whose families had lived in the older parts
of the town and valley for generations were apparently
particularly vigilant about anyone damaging their local
beauty spots and environment.

He was quite sure Belkin wasn't going to find it as easy
as he thought to flout the law here, whatever he'd got away
with elsewhere. Apart from anything else, it was far harder
to hide what you were doing in smaller communities than
in big cities.

He watched Jane Keevil drive her car away, her expression furiously angry. Even a newcomer like him had quickly become aware that the local heritage society was a force to be reckoned with and she was its chairperson this year.

It did a lot of voluntary work in and around Essington and its members were fiercely protective about their valley's history and beauty. And most of it was truly beautiful. He had quickly grown to love the place.

He'd soon realised that the locals had been watching to see what sort of houses he would design and develop once the government had released the Marrakin for public use and he'd managed to buy it.

His wife had overheard favourable comments on his first efforts to renovate a few of the older properties that were still soundly built, and that had pleased them both. He'd never design something that stuck out like a sore thumb.

If Belkin attempted to chop down those trees, he was going to have a major fight on his hands, not just formally with the council and heritage society, but in the many small ways local people could use to seriously impede his building efforts.

Corin would join in this sort of environment protection if necessary. For a start, he'd rarely seen anything as beautiful as this particular row of street trees in full blossom last year when he was first looking round the area. It was far more impressive than hedgerows of hawthorn. Indeed, it had made him stop in his tracks to stare the first time he'd seen it the previous May. He'd stood there for ages, lost in admiration and pleasure.

He wondered if Belkin, who was a relative newcomer

to property development, had ever come up before against fierce oldies who were at the core of informal local affairs, as they were here.

He'd already learnt which of them filled a leadership role here, people utterly devoted to the district where they'd lived all their lives and taking care to pass that love down to their descendants in practical ways. He'd heard tales of how they could act like gentle steamrollers. Jane's elderly father, Arthur, was their informal leader. Protests were not only the province of the young, not by any means.

What's more, he was now one of the owners Belkin would be trying to force into selling a house in this street. The man didn't seem to have found out yet that Corin's offer for Judith's house had been accepted and his own offer turned down. Well, it hadn't been anywhere near the true value of the beautiful old house, which might be run-down and in need of modernising internally, but had what he thought of as 'good bones' to work on.

Jane marched into the council offices and strode round to the parks and gardens section to report the incident.

The supervisor, whose desk was at the back, took one look at her angry expression and got up from his desk at the rear to join the clerk at the counter. As they listened to her tale, both of them gaped at her.

'That builder is intending to knock down our heritage trees? Over my dead body.'

She banged on the counter for emphasis. 'He will have to climb over a pile of dead bodies, George. Now, if you'll report it to the council, I'll let the heritage society committee know about it. I've just called an emergency meeting.'

'It's going to take time after I report the incident to get official action taken. You know what bureaucracies can be like.'

'Especially since Peter Singleton got on the council.'

George sighed and nodded to the clerk to go back to work, then lowered his voice and continued chatting to Jane, whom he knew quite well. 'Real nuisance, that fellow, as people are finding out. I don't like having the older Singleton for MP and the younger one on our council. The councillor wouldn't stand a chance of winning a second term of office if it weren't for certain newcomers who have no feeling for our valley. Though that fight won't be till next year via the local elections due then.'

'Yes. We'll work on that when the time comes but the immediate problem needs dealing with and I'm hoping you can nudge things unofficially in the meantime. I'm worried that Belkin might get that horrible foreman of his to chop the trees down during the night. It has been known for ruthless developers to break the law openly and simply pay the fines.'

'Can you get your lot to do something about this?'

'We can try but it's not going to be easy. They'll presumably bring in a JCB to push them down. And even if we block that, it'll take less than an hour to bring those trees down by hand with chainsaws.' She stared into the distance for a moment or two. 'We'll have to make sure they don't get near them, not even tonight.'

'If anyone can do that, it's your lot.' He spun round suddenly and tiptoed across to fling open a door at the back and glare at the man standing there. 'What are you doing in this part of the building?'

'Er – I was just coming to see you.'

'What about?' George asked.

'Er – doesn't matter now. I can see you're busy.'

'Get back to work and give your friend Singleton my regards. I've caught you eavesdropping in this area before and if I do so again, I'll report you to HR. Today's verbal warning will go down on your record.'

The man scowled and edged away.

As he moved off down the corridor, Jane called, 'And give Terence Singleton a message from me next time he visits his brother on council meeting days. He and his pals won't succeed in getting rid of those trees, whatever it takes to stop them.'

George closed the door on the clerk and turned back to her. 'I don't like what's happening here, Jane.'

'I don't like what's happened today. I'm going to report Belkin's foreman for threatening behaviour towards me to the police, as well as showing them the damage he did to my car. I was frightened for my personal safety, George, and I don't frighten easily, as you know.'

He nodded. She was well known and admired in the district for her feisty attitude to life. Arthur Keevil's daughter wasn't a coward about taking action any more than he had been in his prime. 'Who was this fellow who threatened you?'

'Someone pointed him out to me in town as the new foreman. I don't know his name but I got a photo of him. Big as a gorilla, he was, crew cut and his nose must have been broken at some stage.' She took out her phone and showed the photo to him.

'I saw one of my staff dealing with that man only yesterday about a minor building regulation. She thinks he was just testing them out to see how closely they stuck to the by-laws. She isn't in the office this morning but she'll know his name. She has a memory like a steel trap. Send me a copy of that photo and I'll show it to her.'

'Corin Drayton was further up the street and saw the whole incident as well. He fits well in the valley and is the sort of builder we *do* want here. I'm going to ask him if he'll act as a witness to the damaging of my car.'

'Drayton seems a decent guy. The couple of houses he's upgraded look really good.'

'I went to sneak a look at them last week and they certainly do. But fancy that foreman of Belkin's telling me not to go back there. Well, I'm not letting him frighten me away, as he'll find out.'

He looked at her in concern. 'You'd better not go back to Hawthorn Close alone, Jane lass. It'd be asking for trouble.'

'I won't. We're already making plans.'

'Who's "we"?'

'I'm going to take my dad with me.'

He smiled. 'Good man to have on your side in a fight, Arthur, even now.'

'He's been working on a special wheelchair. He'll no doubt be bringing that to the close.'

'Special wheelchair? What's special about it?'

She gave a wry smile. 'A lot. He's been working on it for a while "in case of an emergency". It kept him happily busy, so I left him to it. I never thought we'd actually need to use it. Plus he's got a defensive walking stick.'

'He's good at making gadgets. I still use a couple of his modified tools in my own garden. I hadn't heard about a special wheelchair, though.'

'Come along to the close and see it.'

'I will.' George couldn't hide his grin. He'd had dealings with Arthur Keevil years ago and had come off badly until he'd learnt not to cross the old man. Arthur didn't care what he had to do to protect 'his' town and valley but he never broke the law without it being a necessary act to indicate a genuine problem, as George had found out.

The local magistrates had always let Arthur off with a warning or a tiny fine in the past for that very reason.

George wished he could be a fly on the wall and see what happened if Belkin's new foreman ran up against Arthur about the trees, by hell he did.

Jane's next stop was to visit the home of the president elect of the Essington St Mary Heritage Protection Society.

Nellie was at home and listened to her tale with the same shock and horror as George had. 'This is a really major emergency, then.'

'Absolutely. You should have seen how that baboon treated me as well as damaging my car. Arrogant devil. I don't know why he was so confident about chopping down our trees but he won't succeed.'

'Unfortunately we can't be sure of that, Jane. Tread carefully, please. We can only do our best to keep an eye on things.'

'I'll do more than that. I'm going to take my dad round to hold the fort so that they can't sneak in and chop those trees down before the council takes action. And I know a good few others who'll join him.'

'Is he still capable of it?'

'Oh, yes. He's only in his mid-eighties. My family usually

get well past ninety. And he's certainly not giving in to old age. He just uses a few more gadgets to get around and help him do things, that's all. But there are two trees so we need someone else to guard the second one.' She looked questioningly at Nellie.

'Ah. I see. I'd better send my auntie Mavis to join him, then, if you don't mind keeping an eye on her as well. No, my husband can leave his staff to cope at the shop. He'll take her and set her up, then hang about nearby and make sure she's all right. I shall take great satisfaction in chairing this emergency meeting and setting up a full roster to keep an eye on things.'

They smiled at one another.

'If it weren't so important, it'd be quite exciting,' Jane admitted. 'Early retirement gets a bit boring after a while, I've found.'

'I'm thankful we've got our own shop and don't have to retire till we're sure we want to. You're right. It will be like old times. We haven't had any excitement for years.'

'No. That's because we don't start fights, but we don't let people trample on us or damage our valley, do we, Nellie?'

'Definitely not. If someone starts a fight with us, you can be sure we'll finish it. Our heritage group hasn't failed in any important venture yet.'

They shook hands, then Jane went to visit her dad while Nellie phoned her aunt Mavis, who jumped at the chance to get involved, and her husband, who sighed but agreed.

Arthur Keevil listened to his daughter without interrupting her, so she knew she'd caught his full attention.

'You were right to come to me. We'd better get down

there straight away, lass. No telling how quickly they'll try to attack our trees. You get out my special wheelchair while I get a couple of things out of my workshop. Good thing I haven't been wasting my time.'

She went into his front room, which he had used only for storage since his second wife's death. The special wheelchair was in a corner, covered by a dust cloth, and she knew it'd be ready to go because he was meticulous about maintenance.

He walked slowly into the room and put a few other small items into pouches on the sides of the chair. He stared down at them, counting under his breath. 'Right. All there still. You OK to put everything in the car for me?'

'Oh, yes.' She pushed the chair out and he followed her, with the slow arthritic gait that annoyed him, though at eighty-four even he should have expected his body to show a little wear and tear. It was amazing that it wasn't worse after what he'd done to it over the years. Talk about an active life.

'Who else is coming to keep watch?' he asked as they set off.

'Nellie's husband is bringing her auntie Mavis over to join you because there are two trees to guard.'

'Oh good! Mavis is a good person to have on your side in a fight. And Nellie?'

'She's running an emergency committee meeting of the heritage group. We thought I'd better come back and keep watch.'

'She's a good lass, Nellie is. She'll have a roster of guards sorted out by teatime.'

He patted his daughter's arm. 'And you're a good lass too.'

Chapter Thirteen

Someone in a neat little van labelled *Pedro's Pet Transfers* came to pick up Tiny mid-morning. It had been sent by Judith's niece to deliver the dog to her home in Spain.

The house felt strange without the sound of the dog's pattering feet and the sheer companionship Tiny had offered. Ilsa hadn't expected to miss her canine friend so quickly or so much.

When she heard a loud voice shouting from somewhere close, she didn't go outside to look, but ran upstairs to look out of her front bedroom window, then opened it to eavesdrop.

It was that new foreman, of course it was, shouting at a woman Ilsa didn't recognise. Well, she was too new here to recognise many people yet. The stranger suddenly flung herself into her car and slammed its door shut.

Ilsa was shocked to see him scrape his key along the side of the stranger's vehicle, leaving a long pale line in the dark paintwork. The woman drove off straight away, not attempting to take issue about this.

He laughed as he watched her go and the only way to describe how he moved back towards the house was 'strutted', acting as if it had all been a bit of fun. Only, damaging someone's car could cost that person a lot to put right.

That left Ilsa with nothing but questions. Who was the woman? What had she done to upset him? Did he go through life bullying everyone who didn't do as he wished or was this on the orders of his employer? And how on earth did Belkin get away with it?

As Ilsa started to go downstairs, someone rang her doorbell so she stopped to peep out of the landing window to check who it was, then ran happily down the rest of the stairs to let Rob in.

'Did you see how that fellow behaved?' he asked.

'Yes. Do you know what the shouting was about?'

'From what I heard, she was telling him that he can't knock these trees down because they're heritage-listed and he was saying that Belkin would do whatever he wanted now he'd bought the first two houses. Then he yelled at her to go away and when she didn't, he damaged her car.'

'I saw that last part. He was *laughing* as he did it.' Ilsa shuddered.

'Yes. I couldn't see him clearly but I could hear him.'

'I was in the kitchen and missed the first part of their quarrel but I ran upstairs to see what was going on.'

Rob shook his head in disbelief. 'I'm going to report the vandalism to that woman's car to the police and since you also saw it happen, would you mind if I give them your name as well?'

'I'm happy for you to do that. Vandals are cowards, if you ask me.'

She looked down and saw a piece of dry dog food on the floor, so bent to pick it up, smiling at it sadly before tossing it in the bin.

'Missing Tiny?' Rob asked in a different tone of voice.

'Yes. I've never had a dog of my own and it surprised me what good company she was. I felt safer at night with her here, too.'

'I bet she'd have tried to protect you if someone had attacked you. My family had a dog when I was a lad. I still remember him fondly. He was a golden Labrador. Big fellow so we called him Maxie.'

He stared blankly into his memories for a moment or two, then focused on her again. 'We're a pair of softies, aren't we?'

'I'd rather be soft than be a nasty bully. And I prefer to have softie friends, too. Would you like a cup of coffee?'

'Yes, please. I always seem to be imposing on you for coffee. I'll bring you a fresh jar of instant next time I visit.'

'You don't need to do that.'

'I think I do.'

'Well, I'll give you some cake once I've done my baking. It's much cheaper to make your own, and healthier too. Not stuffed full of chemicals to make it look pretty.' She stopped, head on one side. 'I just realised it's ages since I had the energy to do that.'

'I thought yesterday you were looking better, more alert in spite of the trouble.'

'Oh well, I'm glad you think so.'

'And I'd love a piece of the cake. Homemade cakes are

so much nicer. And actually, it can feel a bit quiet sometimes with just me in the house so it's nice to have someone to chat to occasionally.'

She was starting to wonder if he was as attracted to her as she was to him. She certainly hoped so. 'How about an orange drizzle cake?'

'Sounds delicious.'

'It shall be yours.' She felt a bit shy, didn't know what to say next, so turned to busy herself putting the kettle on and making their coffee.

By the time Rob and Ilsa had finished their coffee, cars had begun to turn in to Hawthorn Close and park along the street, and a few pedestrians had arrived too. So they moved into the front room and watched for a while.

'I like the people here,' she said softly.

'So do I. And I like you, Ilsa.' He stared at her with a question in his eyes, not rushing her to reply.

That made her feel good, so she gave in to temptation and smiled back at him. Then, because she'd had one very bad experience with a man and wanted to go slowly, she quoted the last line of Yeats's poem: *Tread softly because you tread upon my dreams.*

She felt it was worth tiptoeing forward a few more paces with him, that was sure. It had been quite a while since she'd dared do that.

When Jane and her father arrived in Hawthorn Close, a good part of the street was already full of cars and people were coming on foot. Small groups were forming here and there, but no one was parked near the entrances to the two empty houses.

'Park next to the first tree,' Arthur told her firmly.

When she did that, he sat staring for a few moments, then sighed. 'I shall be sad to see those two houses go. I remember a lad from school lived in the first one and I spent many a happy evening there playing with him.'

She studied them. 'The builder doesn't seem to have done any work on them yet.'

'No, but he's had the gardens flatted for easy access and we shan't be able to stop him demolishing the houses, unfortunately. But they're damned well *not* chopping down our special trees.'

He stared down the street and pointed. 'We'll have to station someone near that snicket. We don't want any of Belkin's workers sneaking into the street from the park.'

She couldn't help chuckling, for all the seriousness of the situation. 'I swear you and your friends have kept that old-fashioned word alive way beyond its use-by date in the rest of the world.'

'And why not? "Snicket" is a friendly little word and that narrow path between the end houses had been there for as long as the hawthorn trees, which is why we also got it and the park heritage-listed as well.'

'It's the heritage group that's kept Magnolia Gardens in existence. At one stage the council wanted to build on that land.'

He let out a scornful huff. 'If you want folk to exercise and keep fit, you have to give them somewhere attractive to move about. We all get lectured on the importance of exercise these days but who wants to walk along a main road and breathe in fumes from cars and lorries? That can't be good for you.'

Jane didn't answer or he'd have gone on and on. It was one

of his pet theories about what was wrong with the modern world, the lack of local amenities and shops. She focused her thoughts on today. This was the lull before the storm, she decided as she looked at the cars already parked in Hawthorn Close. But the storm would break soon, one way or the other.

She doubted a builder with Belkin's reputation and hunger to make money would give up easily and who knew what other dirty tricks he had up his sleeve?

But he was an outsider, didn't know the valley folk, did he? They always looked after their own.

An hour later, Rob and Ilsa were still sitting chatting when once again they heard voices outside.

'Let's go and keep an eye on what's happening,' he said. 'It's not Harden yelling this time, at least.'

'We can stand in my hall.' Ilsa opened the front door so that they could look out but not be noticed by most of the people out in the street.

'What is someone in a wheelchair doing here if there's going to be trouble?' she wondered aloud.

'Do you mind if I stay here and find out? Your house is closer to the action and the company's great.' He gave her a cheeky wink. 'You don't have anything else you need to do urgently?'

'No. And I'm as nosy about what's going on as you are.'

He put an arm round her and they stood away from the front door in the narrow hall. It made it easier to stand there though she had to resist the temptation to cuddle up to him more closely. But oh, she wanted to.

* * *

Jane parked in front of the first house in the close. She rolled her father's wheelchair down the ramp that opened easily from the back of her car, thanks to his modifications, and set it into place on the verge next to the first tree.

After that she took out the specially made piece of steel, threading it through the metal loops he'd had made and welded to the rear of his chair and then hammered it into the soft ground. If someone tried to drag the chair along the ground, they'd find it difficult to move it.

She gave him a fond glance. He was clever at thinking of these little gadgets and amendments to equipment. Nothing wrong with his brain, however much his body was slowing down and getting twisted by arthritis.

He insisted on taking over when it came to chaining what he called his 'trusty steed' to the tree trunk. After that he sat down in it and wriggled into a comfortable position, before attaching another chain from the back of the seat round his own waist.

He was taking no chances and there was even a little chain to attach his walking stick to the chair. She wasn't at all sure this was necessary but he'd enjoyed devising the whole system so she'd not tried to stop him. After all, he'd been right when he told her that they'd have to put on their activist hats again soon, though how he'd found that out, she couldn't work out. It came from his network of old friends, she supposed.

After locking all the chains into place, he reached out to pat the rough bark of the tree trunk beside him. 'My word on it: they'll not knock you down without getting rid of me first, my old friend.'

A gust of wind ruffled the branches above him just then,

making it look as if the tree was nodding agreement, and he let out a loud cackle of laughter and patted the trunk again. 'See that, Jane love. Even the trees approve of what we're doing. Eh, I'm looking forward to these beauties coming into blossom all along the street. Mother Nature does some things far better than us mere humans can ever manage.'

As they were finishing their preparations, another car drew up and parked outside the second house right next to them.

The driver waved a greeting as he got out. He too rolled a wheelchair from the rear of his vehicle, then helped his wife's aunt out of the passenger seat. 'Will you be all right standing there for a minute or two while I set it up, Auntie Mavis?'

'I'll be fine, Les. I keep telling you that I can move about as long as I do it slowly. I'll enjoy a chat with Arthur while you're putting my chair in place.'

Les got out the oddments needed to install her chair on the verge of the second house as close as possible to the second tree and Jane helped him position it and dig it in.

Mavis stood beside Arthur and they had a quick chat about possible tactics and he reminded her of the signals they'd agreed on. Both of them chuckled once or twice as they watched the preparations for putting this second 'trusty steed' into place.

'Auntie Mavis is in fine form,' Les whispered to Jane.

'So is Dad. I think they've been finding life a trifle dull lately.'

When Mavis saw that they'd finished, she went across to sit in her chair and she too chained herself in place. Like Arthur, she was facing the street so that she could see as much as possible of what was happening at either side of her and people were already greeting her or stopping to chat.

The two helpers were just finishing their tasks when a small lorry swung into the street, its driver so sure there would be nothing parked near the end of it that he had to stamp hard on the brakes to avoid crashing into the other vehicles standing there.

Then he caught sight of the two wheelchairs and gaped in shock. He didn't so much get out as throw open the door of his lorry and erupt onto the street, striding across to glare at Jane, who was standing next to her father.

'I told you not to come back here, you stupid—' He saw someone recording what he was doing on a phone and finished the sentence in a quieter voice. 'Are you deaf or what?'

Jane gave him a cheerful smile. 'Not deaf, stubborn. I never did like obeying orders, especially when someone has no right to give them, only you weren't in a mood to listen to reason. I thought I didn't have any witnesses then and I didn't feel safe, so I got out temporarily. This time I've got plenty of witnesses in case you lay one finger on me or do any more damage to my car.'

'What damage?'

She pointed to the long deep scratch. 'And by the way, your vandalism has been reported to the police by two different witnesses who photographed you doing it.'

'Who cares about your old rattletrap of a car?'

'I do. You might like to bear in mind that there are people inside some of the nearby houses. Useful things, windows. You'll never know who's watching you or recording your attempts to damage our town's heritage, will you?'

He stared round and suddenly realised that the occupants of the two wheelchairs parked on the verges were chained to the trees and pointed. 'What are they doing there?'

'We're keeping watch on our trees and you won't chase us away,' Arthur called across to him and rattled his chain for emphasis.

'You'll need to remember from now on that people are legally entitled to walk wherever they choose on the streets of our town,' she said loudly and slowly, then she turned her back on Harden. 'Are you comfortable now, Dad?'

'Aye. For the moment.' Arthur lowered his voice to add, 'You'd better stay here till more of the cavalry arrive, though. He's a nasty-looking chap, that one.'

Harden came a couple of steps closer. 'I told you not to come back and I meant it. This is a building site now, not an old folks' home, and it might not be safe. And why has that old fool chained himself to our tree?'

'That isn't your tree nor is the land it's on. It's a public thoroughfare and will remain so whatever your company does on its own land. What's more, if you do anything to make the public area unsafe, your company will be sued.'

He grabbed her arm and when she tried to pull away, he shook her, upon which her father leant forward and poked him with his walking stick.

'Stop that, you.'

When Harden yelped in sudden shock, Arthur grinned at the success of one of his own grandfather's inventions, which was still working as well as ever over fifty years later. If you pressed the button just below the elaborately carved handle, the retractable spike in the bottom end of the walking stick popped out.

The spike jabbed once more into the soft flesh of Harden's buttocks, then, as Arthur pulled the stick away, the spike slid swiftly back into its hiding place again.

With a yell of pain, Harden let go of Jane, rubbed his backside and turned round to see what had hurt him. But all he saw was Arthur sitting smiling at him and a group of nearby people laughing uproariously. He tried to pull the old fool and wheelchair away. Only he couldn't get the thing to budge.

It was only then that it registered with Harden how firmly the chains were holding the wheelchair to the tree and that it was also anchored to the ground. He shook the wheelchair furiously and in vain just as a police officer turned the corner into the street. But he had his back to her and didn't notice her.

Arthur immediately slumped down and called in a faint voice, 'Help! Someone help me! I'm being attacked.'

The officer strode forward, yelling, 'Hey, you! Let go of him at once!'

Harden let go and swung round, breathing deeply but doing as she ordered.

'Thank goodness you're here, Officer,' Arthur exclaimed, still in a feeble and shaky voice. He'd had to practise this several times to get just the right quavering tone and was rather pleased with it now. 'This man has just attacked me, Officer.'

'I saw him doing it, Mr Keevil. Do you want to prosecute?'

'Not this time but if he does it again, I shall definitely lay a complaint.'

She turned to Harden. 'Think yourself lucky that poor old man is not pressing charges. If I see you laying hands on him again, I'll arrest you for assault and you'll be brought before a magistrate. You can regard this as your one and only formal warning.'

Harden stood perfectly still, gazing from one to the other, his hands clenched into fists.

'Did you hear me?' she asked.

'Yes.' But he turned back to Jane. 'Think you're clever, don't you? Well, you can't stay here twenty-four-seven. The men I've hired will do their jobs later, that's all.' He swung round and glared at Arthur. 'As for you—'

The old man pretended to cower away. 'Don't let him hurt me.'

'I won't.' The officer looked at Harden. 'What has happened here tonight will go on record. I'll leave it to the sergeant to decide whether to take it further.'

Harden took one short step back. 'I can wait. It's the tree I'm after, not that old fool. Surely it's against the law for him to block our access to it? After all, I am working on behalf of the owner of these two houses and therefore of the verge here.'

'The verge belongs to the council, sir, not to the owner of the house.'

He looked at her as if this was genuinely a surprise to him. 'Mr Belkin told me otherwise, madam.'

'"Officer" will do.'

After a pause, he muttered, 'Officer, then.'

'Your employer would be better learning the facts and

you with him. And you can also tell him that all the trees in this street are registered as heritage, including these two. *No one* is allowed to damage them. They're not only protected by our town's by-laws but also by national legIlsation.'

Harden grunted something, strode back to his lorry and got in it, taking out his mobile phone.

'You're doing better at that feeble old man's voice, Dad,' Jane said.

He spoke in his normal tone this time. 'I've been practising.'

The police officer let out a choke of the laughter she'd been holding back with difficulty. 'I didn't hear you say that, Mr Keevil.'

'I hope the police are going to keep an eye on the situation here,' Jane said. 'It's been heard of before for someone to get rid of a historical artefact or treasure, then say sorry and pay the necessary fine. Those trees are over two hundred years old.'

The officer nodded. 'I have to enforce the law impartially, whatever my own views.'

'Yes. I know. But you coped very well just now and I'm grateful. I've been looking into a few things ever since I first heard about Belkin buying houses in our town.' Arthur gestured towards the builder's sign. 'I'd heard before about that chap and the nasty tricks he can play. He upset a friend of mine in Swindon when he was first starting up as a builder. I was very sorry when he bought land here. But not half as sorry as he'll be if he tries to destroy our heritage.'

Mavis joined in. 'We'll settle that man's hash one way or another, Officer. We've dealt with bullies and vandals before, starting many years before you were born. There were vandals even then who wanted to spoil our town and there weren't any by-laws to support us those days, but we still managed to stop them. The valley people will do it again as often as each new generation of scoundrels makes that necessary.' She nodded towards Jane and Les. 'There's a new generation learning how to do things and they're coming along nicely. The younger folk of today care about the environment not only out in the wide world but here in our town. It warms my heart to hear them talk. Essington St Mary will be all right after we're gone.'

'I hope so.' The police officer was grinning across at Mavis's chair. 'Do I see another set of chains on you as well, Mavis? You didn't have those last time.'

'I asked Arthur to make me some. They help keep us where we want to be and stop nasty oiks like that fellow from moving us away by force. What's his name again?'

'Harden.'

'Harden. I won't forget that this time.' Mavis cast another disgusted glance in the direction of the builder's van.

The foreman was still on the phone but was obviously keeping an eye on them as well. When he saw Mavis looking, he made a rude sign in her direction.

She and Arthur both smiled sweetly and blew kisses towards him, then Arthur snuggled lower.

'I'm going to take my usual afternoon nap a little early in case things get more lively later. Eh, old age can be annoying but I do much better with a nap, so I put up with it. Mavis love, can you keep watch for a while? Blow that whistle I gave you if you need my help. There are plenty of people around now to protect us.'

'Happy to do that, Arthur lad. I'm not into taking naps. I never feel sleepy in the daytime unless I'm ill.'

She looked round and sighed happily. 'Eh, this is just like old times, isn't it? I'm enjoying getting out of the house and doing something worthwhile, for a change. Library books are all very well, and they help to pass the time, but I like to be involved in real activities.'

'It's not quite like old times. Thanks to technology, we've got a few more tricks up our sleeves than we had then, and it helps make up for our physical weakness.'

'I saw you use your stick. Boy, didn't he jump!'

They both chuckled.

Nellie's husband turned to Jane and said in a low voice, 'They seem unaware of the danger, but I've heard Belkin uses violence as a tool if all else fails.'

'I think one of us had better stay around at all times till we've got defenders rostered here. This Harden fellow is already proving to be a nasty sod and for all their brave talk and gadgets, our oldies are physically vulnerable.'

Les patted his pocket. 'I've got my phone and I'll take photos as necessary. I've got one or two telling shots already.'

'Good for you. I reckon quite a few of us will need to stay here all night in case that baboon does try to cut down the trees later. Can you phone your Nellie and let her know where we're at, Les? She was going to hold an emergency committee meeting.'

'Yes, of course, Jane.'

'I'll not be gone long, but Dad and I came out in a hurry and I need to nip to the shops for some food and drink supplies. I reckon this is going to be a long day, and a long night too, perhaps. Our two oldies will need regular snacks and bottles of water.'

Her father had his eyes closed but he was clearly still listening. He wriggled into a more comfortable position and said quietly, 'Take your time, Jane. Me and Mavis have got it covered here.'

His daughter spoke quietly so Harden wouldn't hear. 'You're enjoying this, you old rascal.'

Arthur shrugged. 'I am. I don't want to sit around the house all day watching TV, but they took my driving licence away and I can't invade your life too often, so it's good to have something of my own to do.'

'It's my pleasure to help you, Dad. I care about our street too.'

He closed his eyes then opened them again. 'Has someone let the press know?'

'Nellie said she'd do that. She has a couple of good contacts. Let's see if we can get you on TV.'

He grinned at her. 'With my good looks, how can we fail?'

This time when he snuggled down, he really did look as if he was sleeping.

Chapter Fourteen

There had been no need for them to help protect the trees, so Ilsa said, 'How about a sandwich, Rob? I don't think we've seen the last of this.'

'Good idea. I definitely want to keep an eye on what happens because I agree with what these people are doing. I'm even prepared to go out and help fight off Harden and anyone else who tries to hurt those brave oldies. Besides, the trees are our valley heritage too, now that we live here. I saw them in blossom when I was visiting here as a lad and they're stunningly beautiful. I never forgot them.'

'I agree. I'm in for whatever help is needed, too.'

'Not till you're fully recovered, surely?'

'Another person standing there can be useful sometimes. The builder's employees won't know how feeble I am still.'

'Good thinking. I admire your attitude.'

'Though actually, I've felt better this past couple of days.'

'Maybe you needed people around you to push you to the next stage of recovery.'

'Maybe I did.'

An hour later, there was more shouting from outside and they jumped to their feet.

'We'll probably get a better view from the bedroom,' she suggested.

'Lead the way.'

They watched in delight, chuckling as the new foreman was routed by an old guy in a wheelchair.

'He may be old but he has a boy's mischievous expression on his face,' she said. 'I hope I'm still that lively when I'm his age.'

'I hope I am, too. Let's go outside and join in. There are a lot more people in the street now. At the very least it'll be a good way to meet some locals.'

'Great. Let's do it.'

So they went outside, hesitating at the edge of the group. The old guy looked as if he was taking a nap now but the woman in the wheelchair chained to the second tree, which was closer to their houses, beckoned them over and got them to introduce themselves to her and to the people standing around nearby.

Mavis shook her head. 'So you're right on top of the action, you poor things. Has he tried any nasty tricks yet?'

'Unfortunately yes.'

Mavis seemed happy to continue chatting and explained more about the background to what was going on and the history of the valley. 'Just watch and you'll see for yourself how people in this town rally round once they see a problem.'

'If there's any way I can help, don't hesitate to ask. I live here permanently as well now and I don't want to lose the trees, either,' Rob said.

Ilsa joined in. 'So that's two more volunteers you've got. I want to continue living in a pretty street and town, too.'

Mavis gave her a sympathetic look. 'It's going to be harder for you two, though, living next door to that fool of a builder. I bet he won't stop nagging you to sell to him.'

'I'm sure he won't.'

'If we can help you, the heritage group will. But there's something you can do for us already, if you don't mind. It's rather mundane but we're going to need occasional access to toilets, especially Arthur and me, and probably a few other older people. Bodies will be bodies, won't they, especially as they're getting on a bit. And me and Arthur will need someone to guard our wheelchairs when we're away from them using your facilities.'

She looked at Rob questioningly and when he nodded, she said, 'Good man.'

As easily as that, they found themselves recruited into the local team helping to defend the town's trees.

When they went back inside her house, Rob suddenly grinned at Ilsa. 'I did a lot of jobs to earn my way when I was a student, but I've never been an attendant at public toilets before or a guardian of wheelchairs.'

They both chuckled but then she looked at him more seriously. 'I'm glad you suggested going out to chat to them. It's good to get to know people from round here.'

'Yes. And you're still looking more alert.'

Not only that but her body was coming alive in more ways than one with such a good-looking man spending time with her.

But she wasn't ready to focus on that yet. Well, only a little.

Chapter Fifteen

Relieved that all the clearing up had been done, Amy handed over the keys to her former flat to the agent at the hour agreed. It felt strange closing the door behind her for the last time.

It was a bit late to travel to Wiltshire that afternoon and anyway, she was feeling utterly drained so took a room at a small motel she knew of for the night.

So much had happened in the last few weeks that she felt disoriented and had to force herself to concentrate because she needed to work out what exactly to do next and when to do it. However, after she'd sat down with a cup of coffee and her feet up on the bed, she began to think more clearly.

The first decision was easy enough: finalise the tentative arrangements for meeting her great-aunt. It seemed clear to her now that she needed to see where that led before she could decide what to do next.

She emailed Maggie at once saying her home had now

been sold and asking if it'd be all right for her to come for a visit in two days' time, arriving in the late morning. As she waited, she tried and failed to settle to reading a book. How long would it be before her great-aunt replied?

The response came only half an hour later and sounded so friendly it made her feel that her relative really did want to see her. That eased something inside her. The email had an attachment giving detailed directions for finding the house, which was apparently at the top end of Larch Tree Lane, the main street in the valley, and the turning could be easy to miss.

Maggie must have to give directions regularly to have instructions like these ready to go so quickly. Amy doubted she would have had time to put them together specially for her.

This meant that the preliminaries to an important step in her life had been taken care of, so she went to have a solitary evening meal in the café attached to the motel. She ordered a glass of white wine because she felt she ought to celebrate selling her flat in some way but she couldn't finish the meal or the wine so went straight to bed.

She slept surprisingly well for someone with no fixed abode and no real idea where the future might take her, and when she woke, she felt eager to set off. There was a covered tray on the shelf outside her room bearing the simple breakfast that was all they offered here. She ate the banana and spread jam on one of the pieces of stale toast, but couldn't face eating any more.

She signed out of the motel and drove to her storage unit as soon as it was light. When the roller door slid up, revealing the jumble of contents, she beamed at the sight of her painting equipment. That was the main thing she wanted to reclaim. She took her remaining household bits and pieces out of the back of her car, and put the easel and other art equipment into the space that left.

She gave them a quick pat and felt amused when she realised what she'd done. 'Idiot!' she mocked herself. Only, it was like greeting old friends to see them again. She bought a cup of coffee from an automatic machine at the end of the row of flats and sat in her car, sipping it slowly and listening to the news on the radio.

When she started work again, she took out a few cherished possessions, smaller things like books and her favourite outfit for going to fancier social events and found room for them in the car as well. She put the other scattered possessions back into storage and locked the roller door. Done!

By that time, it was nearly noon so she set off for Wiltshire, grabbing a quick meal at the first motorway services she came to.

She was still feeling deep-down tired and was glad to find a small motel just outside Swindon to stay at the following night. She'd take a quick look round Essington St Mary in the morning before going to visit her relative at the agreed time.

To her annoyance, she slept badly and when she got ready for the meeting the following morning and checked out of the motel, she was surprised at how nervous she was feeling. Well, she had very little experience of relatives or, for that matter, of life in grand country houses.

As she sat in her car, she took out the glossy book of

the sort often called a 'coffee table book' that she'd found in a charity shop. It was about historic country houses of England and looked as if it had hardly been used. She'd flicked through it half-heartedly in the shop and been surprised to find that Larch House was included, so had bought it. There was only a colour photo of the front elevation and a brief potted summary of the house's origins, but it was a relief to gain some idea of what it looked like.

She'd stared at that photo a few times and now studied it again before she set off. Unlike the small indistinct photo she'd found in a newspaper article online, this image showed a pretty house that the author had called 'a pleasant little country manor'. That didn't sound nearly as frightening as somewhere larger would have done, but she still felt nervous about the coming meeting with its owner.

After strolling round the centre of the small town, she stopped on the pavement outside the bookshop, tempted into buying a couple of novels from the tray of 'specials' to one side of the shop entrance. She kept looking at her watch, wondering if she should set off now, but if she did she'd get there far too early.

She scolded herself for her nervousness: *Calm down, you fool! This woman isn't going to bite you.*

But she couldn't calm down, just – could – not!

She strolled round the town, loving the fact that it was a mixture of building styles and eras, and also presumably a mixture of people. She was glad it wasn't a dormitory town with lookalike boxes for living in crammed together and hardly anyone around during the daytime. At this time of day there were all sorts of people visiting the shops in Essington St Mary, from older folk to mothers (and occasionally fathers) pushing prams with babies or toddlers in them.

At last, it was indisputably time for her to set off. She drove slowly up Larch Tree Lane, seeing a few short streets leading off the main road and when she got beyond the built-up area, there were occasional pieces of open land between some of the houses she passed, not big fields, just gaps peopled by grass, trees, animals and shrubs.

She missed the turn-off so it was a good thing the instructions said that if you got to a gateway with huge larch trees on either side of it, you'd gone too far. Well, there were the trees, larger than any larch trees she'd ever seen before, so she must have passed the gateway.

She braked and saw the top end of the street ahead, clearly a cul-de-sac, so checked the instructions again. These said to go back down to the next gateway on the same side as the trees, which was more visible when you approached it from the top of the street.

She found the gateway easily this time and turned in to it, moving along a drive lined by beautiful mature trees with bright green spring foliage.

At her first sight of the big house, she stopped the car to stare, exclaiming, 'Oh!' in a soft voice. Larch House was far more beautiful than it had looked in the glossy photo and it seemed welcoming. She couldn't quite work out why, it just did.

The instructions from her great-aunt said to follow the drive round to the rear entrance of the house because people rarely used the front door these days. When she did that, she found herself in a roughly square gravelled area rather like a large courtyard. It was formed by two sets of rather tumble-down outbuildings, one opposite and one at a ninety-degree angle to the house itself.

The back door opened before she had even decided where to park and two smiling older people came out to greet her. The woman must be Maggie and there was also a man who had his arm round his companion's shoulders in an openly loving way.

Amy pulled up next to two parked cars and got out, turning round straight into a hug from the woman.

'I'm Maggie and I know I'm your great-aunt but it makes me feel old even to think of that, so please call me by my name or just Aunt. This is my fiancé, James.'

Amy was immediately hugged by the man as well. It felt weird but lovely to be greeted so enthusiastically by complete strangers.

Maggie smiled warmly at her. 'I had no doubt you were Amy the minute you got out of your car because you look like a Hatherall with that hair and those dark eyes. Wait till you see the family paintings. Some of them could be your siblings. And I should have started by saying "Welcome to Larch House", because you are very welcome indeed to the family home.'

Another hug followed this statement.

The man grinned and put his arm round his fiancée again. 'She's an inveterate hugger. If you can't beat 'em, it's easier to join 'em.'

Amy felt herself relaxing still further. 'I'm happy to join 'em. I've been a bit short of hugs in my life.' She was surprised that she'd said that, considering they were both strangers, but they'd made her feel genuinely welcome already and she'd relaxed a lot.

'Good. Not good that you're short of hugs but that you'd like some more. We'll gradually make up for the shortage. Now, do you want your luggage bringing in?'

'Heavens, no. Only this case. I had to clear things out of my home and put them into storage to make it look bigger to prospective buyers. It worked but now that I've moved out permanently, I want to keep my art equipment and some other bits and pieces with me. They can stay in the car while I'm here. The rest of my furniture and a few household items are still in storage in Newcastle.'

'What do you paint?' Maggie asked.

'Landscapes mostly. Oils.'

'I'll look forward to seeing some of them if that's all right with you.'

'Maggie's into painting too,' James said, 'but she does watercolours. She's done some gorgeous flower paintings. Artistic skills must run in the Hatherall family. I can't draw a straight line for love nor money.'

Her great-aunt smiled. 'You can bring your art materials inside later, Amy dear. They'd be quite safe out here but you might want to use them because we're hoping you'll stay for longer than a day or two. There are several unused bedrooms where you can set up to paint, one opposite the room I've put you in, as it happens.'

Amy stared at her, trying to hide her surprise. Was Maggie already assuming a longer stay? 'Thank you. I, um, hadn't expected such a pretty house.'

'I think it's pretty but then I've never lived anywhere else, so what do I know? It's just . . . well, not only my physical home but my heart's home too. I'm so looking forward to showing you round.'

She pulled her guest's hand into the crook of her arm and took her into the house. This was a way of walking that a friend of Amy's had favoured too and it brought a welcome sense of familiarity.

In fact, she had felt instantly at home here and had relaxed with Maggie and James more rapidly than she'd ever done with any strangers before. Even as she thought about that, her companion gave her another warm, happy smile.

'Make yourself at home here, Amy dear. You are, after all, the only other Hatherall of the senior line left.'

'Am I really? Well, thank you for your warm welcome.'

She not only felt at home here, she had instantly taken a liking to these two.

And to the house. It was as if it was another person, standing there smiling a welcome at her from its many twinkling windows.

Chapter Sixteen

They walked through a huge, old-fashioned kitchen and James went across to fill the kettle while Maggie took her to the doorway at the far side.

'This is the main entrance hall.'

A 'wow!' escaped before Amy could stop it and she simply had to stand still to take it in. The hall was as big as her whole flat had been and it had oil paintings on the walls of people in historical costumes from various periods.

'Family portraits. I'll explain who exactly they are another time.' Maggie gave a dismissive wave of her hand, then realised what her companion was staring at so stopped again with a slight smile, giving her more time to take it in.

'That is so beautiful,' Amy said in a hushed, reverent tone, gesturing to a huge stained-glass window with two or three groups of medieval figures standing under trees and among flowers. It went up one side of the staircase to the next floor and shed glorious coloured light across the hall.

'It makes me want to catch those glowing colours of light in my hands and put them away safely for dull days,' Amy said.

Maggie nodded. 'I feel that way too sometimes. I never tire of that window, even though it's a bit of a fake, because it's eighteenth-century not medieval.'

She continued to move across the hall again and stopped in another doorway, saying unnecessarily, 'This is the library.'

'Oh, how amazing!' Every bit of wall in the huge room was lined with shelves crammed with books and there were cushioned window seats inviting you to sit and read as well as a big sofa near the fireplace.

'Just take books out if you want to read them. I keep some sticky notes on this little table by the door to mark the spot for when one returns a book. My father spent his whole life creating this library, filling in the gaps of what he said were important basic subjects and arranging the books *properly*, as he called it, so I like to keep it as he'd have wanted.'

'Good idea to mark the spot.' Amy chuckled suddenly as the incongruity of something struck her.

'What's so amusing?'

'I bought a couple of cheapie books from that little bookshop in the town, in case I needed something to read. I don't think I'm going to need them here, though.'

Maggie smiled in sympathy. 'Oh, you can't have too many books. There's even what my father called a "reading for pleasure" section. He wasn't at all a literary snob.'

'Good to hear that. We had to study some miserable literary books at school and the teacher scorned popular tastes in fiction. Nowadays I only read for pleasure or to learn about something I'm interested in.'

'Me, too. If a story doesn't grab me, I put it back on the shelf and tiptoe away.' Maggie tugged her guest onwards. 'Come and look at the formal drawing room. It's a lovely room but we rarely use it in winter because it takes so much fuel to heat. It's been quite mild lately so we've used it a few times. I always feel it lifts your spirits to sit surrounded by beauty.' She gestured. 'There are other smaller rooms scattered haphazardly about the ground floor but we don't use most of them, except for the one we call the office, the kitchen and the "cosy". Feel free to explore and poke your nose into any of them once you've settled in.'

'The rooms you've shown me feel lived in, not merely for show,' Amy said.

'They are lived in. Larch House is a home first and a manor house second, but even so we're never going to need most of the rooms. Well, after my father died, there was only me and occasional visiting friends. I was thinking of starting a B&B, but now, I have James and you. Two people close to me for the first time in my life. That feels so wonderful.'

Any could relate to that. 'I thought I was completely alone in the world when my mother died but she left a letter to tell me about you. I was delighted to find out I did still have a close relative.'

'It means you're not alone now and nor am I.'

She got another quick hug, then Maggie stepped back. 'I'll show you upstairs now and you can see the bedroom I'd suggest you use – though there are others if you'd prefer a different one.'

Fancy having enough rooms to offer guests a choice, Amy thought. She had only ever lived in small houses and flats, usually with two bedrooms, one for her mother and one for herself. When she'd moved out to live on her own, she still couldn't afford a big place and had chosen her unit mainly because the living room had a large window that gave a good light for painting.

Upstairs here there were three *corridors* of bedrooms leading off the landing.

Maggie took her to a room at the far end of one. 'I thought this bedroom might be suitable because it has a bathroom next to it – a rather old-fashioned one with no shower but hey, it's clean.'

'It looks fine to me.' But Amy was drawn to the view and walked over to stand looking out of one of the two huge sash windows. 'This is absolutely gorgeous. I'll be delighted to have this view to look out at.'

Maggie beamed. 'There! I knew somehow that it would suit you. And there's an unused room opposite that you can use as a studio. You don't have to rush away, do you? You can stay for a while?'

'I don't want to inconvenience you.'

Maggie let out a gurgle of laughter. 'I'm not domesticated enough to be fussy about the housework. Nor do I intend to wait on you hand and foot, so you won't be much inconvenience to me at all, I promise you.' She looked at her guest uncertainly and added, 'You don't have a home of your own now, do you?'

'No. I haven't felt to have a proper home for a few years.'

'I thought not. You can tell, somehow. So make a home here, at least for a while. I have various social engagements and so does James, so you'll be left to look after yourself a lot of the time.' She went a bit pink and added, 'Actually, James and I are getting married in three weeks' time, so I'd love you to come to the wedding. It'd be absolutely wonderful to have a close relative present for the ceremony.'

'Don't you have any other relatives?'

'No Hatheralls except you. I have a distant relative who doesn't live far away, but Sheila doesn't feel like a Hatherall to me and never has, so I avoid seeing her if I can and I'm definitely not inviting her to the wedding.'

That was the first time Amy had heard her aunt say something even remotely critical about anyone. 'Dare I ask what's wrong with her?'

'She's hoping I'll leave the house to her when I pop my clogs, but I could never do that. She'd simply sell it.'

'Goodness!'

'Sheila's like that bit in *My Fair Lady* on her rare visits here: she's too charming for words. Only she doesn't fool me. She's not sincere. And that's all I'm going to say about her.' She gave Amy another of those quick hugs. 'Now you, on the other hand, felt like one of the family straight away and you say what you're thinking. As to you staying, if you've nowhere pressing to go, stay as long as you like, then we can get to know one another properly.'

Amy didn't hesitate. 'You've made me feel so welcome that I'd love to do that and I'd be absolutely delighted to attend your wedding.' She couldn't help turning to glance out of the window again, saying in a very quiet voice, 'It's so beautiful and peaceful here. Who couldn't like it?'

Maggie's voice softened. 'If you don't mind me saying so, I think you need some quiet time. You've just lost your mother, which must have been so difficult for you, and you've no settled home. I think you'll benefit from time for yourself to come to terms with it all.'

Amy could only nod. Such sympathetic understanding made her want to weep and she hated to do that in front of people.

'We can go back downstairs now and find you something to eat, or you can settle into your bedroom first and come down at your leisure.'

'I'll unpack, if you don't mind.'

'Not at all. And later on today or tomorrow, whenever you're ready, James will help you move the furniture round and set up a studio for you in the next bedroom. There's far too much in there. I don't know about you but I need a clear space around me to paint.' She patted Amy's arm and stepped back. 'Take as long as you wish to settle into this room, then come down and join us. I'm not doing a fancy lunch, only sandwiches, crunchy bites and fruit, so they'll keep.'

She was gone before her niece could say anything, leaving behind a sense of peace that felt so wonderful, tears came into Amy's eyes.

Of course, she walked back to stand by the window again. Would she ever grow used to having such a lovely woodland vista? It was a huge contrast to her last flat with its view of the car park and rear elevation of a small factory and its busy despatch area. There had also been a row of dustbins decorating one corner.

Her mother's little house had been nice but it had stood cheek by jowl with its neighbours. All the houses on that side of the street came with a row of tiny front gardens and a modest courtyard at the rear.

She walked slowly across the corridor to her future studio, which also had a lovely view from the windows, this time of a huge tree surrounded by a meadow of wildflowers to the left. Light flooded into the room if you held the heavy velvet curtains back, so somehow she must find a way to do that.

What a beautiful place to live and work! If she couldn't paint well enough here to turn professional, then she doubted she would be able to do it anywhere.

Her emotions seemed in a tangle and tears began rolling down her cheeks again. Though she hadn't heard anyone come in, when someone put her arms round her, she knew it was Maggie, who was making motherly shushing noises and holding her close.

'I came up to ask you something. Sorry if I'm intruding on your grief, only you looked as if you needed comforting. I can go away if you prefer it.'

'I don't.' She laid her head on Maggie's shoulder and hugged her convulsively. 'I did need comforting. I'm sorry to be so – so stupid when you're offering me a respite in such a beautiful place. I don't know what's come over me.'

'I think you're having a perfectly normal reaction to having gone through a stressful period and losing your mother. There were only the two of you, weren't there?'

'Yes. For most of my life anyway. Mum had a lot of friends but I didn't. I've never made friends easily like she did.'

'And your father?'

'He died years ago, when I was eight. I hardly remember him.' She realised they were sitting on her bed together but had no memory of how they'd got there.

'I had a very old-fashioned father, who didn't believe in expressing your love for another person in words or hugs,' Maggie said. 'Your grandfather left home to get away from him, but I stayed on because I felt the house needed me to keep it safe, and luckily the woman who cared for me did show her emotions. I always knew Patsy loved me. She died when I was just over fifty and I still miss her.'

'I envy you.'

'Yes. I was so lucky to have had her. She taught me to look after the house as well as how to get on with other people. Father would have let everything except the library rot away. And there was enough room here for me to get away from him. My father didn't really want to bother with anyone, only cared about his books.' She smiled reminiscently. 'He left me a well-stocked library and a well-stocked brain too, I'll grant him that. But I have no memories of him ever playing with me, just chatting over evening meals about his favourite books and authors.' She brushed the damp hair from Amy's forehead in another of those gentle, caring gestures. 'Do stay with us for a while, dear. I think you need the company of someone who cares about you. Just think, when James and I are married, I'll have two close family members to love. It seems wonderful to have a partner after all these years alone.' Her voice caught on the last words, but the tears in her eyes were clearly happy ones.

'Are you sure I won't be in your way? I mean if you're newly married . . .'

Maggie didn't let her finish. 'I'm certain. Besides, as I've said before, it's a big house so we'll all have the space to get away from one another. Even newly-weds must surely enjoy spending time with other people than their partner. I know I shall and James has made some very good friends near here already.'

Amy gave in. 'I'd love to stay longer, then. I didn't realise how much I needed to stop the world and get off it for a while. Thank you.'

'You're welcome.' Maggie kissed Amy's cheek and stood up. 'Come down when you're ready. Or if you're tired, lie down and rest. Whatever you need.' She gave her visitor another of those truly happy glances. 'It seems marvellous to have found someone to love at my age. A lot of people consider their lives are almost over at seventy but mine feels to be beginning again on a new path.'

Amy nodded and ventured another confidence of her own. 'I think the last few weeks have felt worse because I had a bad marriage a couple of years ago. It only lasted a few months. He was a bully who'd only been pretending to be nice when he was courting me. He wanted a housekeeper not a companion. He started hitting me within weeks of the wedding. I did hit him back, but he was so much stronger than me, he just laughed. He wouldn't go for counselling, so in the end I left.' She shrugged. 'I'm sure you must have heard such tales from other women. I envy you having James. He seems truly kind.'

'He is. And yet he's tough when he needs to be. Catch!' Maggie smacked a big kiss into her hand and pretended to throw it to Amy, then closed the door behind her.

It felt as if a kiss really had landed on her cheek.

* * *

Downstairs, James looked up from making sandwiches. 'How is she?'

'She's been weeping out the worst of her stress on my shoulder and now she's lying down. She sounds to have had a difficult time of it lately, on top of a bad marriage that only lasted a few months. Poor girl.'

'I liked her.'

She grinned at him. 'Good *potential* as my heir, then?'

'Yes. But don't tell her about that side of things yet.'

'I won't. It's my guess she'll fall asleep now so let's get our lunch because I'm absolutely ravenous. Then we'll potter and totter around the house till she joins us.'

He made a pleading sign, hands clasped in front of him. 'I've been longing for a piece of that apple pie. We don't have to wait for her before we cut into it, do we?'

'No, of course not.' She put a big piece on a plate and pushed it towards him. 'It beats me how you stay so slim when you eat so heartily.'

'Loving you keeps me trim. And you're just the right size for me.'

She let out a happy sigh and plonked a kiss on his cheek. 'You say the nicest things, my darling.'

It was over an hour before Amy joined them. She found them chatting in the kitchen, laughing together.

'There are the makings of sandwiches on the surface over there.' Maggie waved one hand in the direction of the window.

As Amy ate some sandwiches, they stayed to chat to her and James told her about the big news in the valley, the struggle going on to defend the heritage trees.

'Half the town has signed up to stand guard,' he said describing what was going on. 'Well, those without small children or family responsibilities. I'm going to put my name down for a night watch.'

'He has really good night vision,' Maggie said. 'I don't so I'll stay at home with you during the night.'

'You said even people in wheelchairs are joining in!' Amy exclaimed. 'That's amazing. What if things turn violent?'

'I think those particular oldies can hold their own,' James said. 'Arthur Keevil is a legendary fellow round here. I intend to check that they're complaining to their local member of parliament. People don't particularly like him but he has a duty to his electorate.'

'Singleton hasn't been very supportive about anything,' Maggie said. 'He'll be losing votes hand over fist if he doesn't help defend the town's heritage. That might wake him up a bit.'

'Or it might lose him the next election and I hope it does,' James said.

Chapter Seventeen

As Corin turned in to his drive, his mobile phone warbled at him and he sighed. He'd been looking forward to a peaceful evening with his wife. For a moment he was tempted to ignore whoever it was but as he came to a halt, he made the fatal error of glancing at it to see who the caller was. Deanna. He'd better take this.

He switched off the car and clicked on his phone to answer the call. 'Corin here.'

'It's me, Deanna. Have you checked the Essington council rules about permits and parking yet?'

Just like her to dive straight into business without the politeness of a greeting. 'No. I've had some urgent business of my own to attend to.'

'Ah. Well, Didier wants to continue our investigations so we need to know what sort of paperwork will have to be gone through to obtain the right permissions. If you can't do it straight away, shall I ring the council for you?'

'No, don't do anything in my name. If you need to find out anything more general, that's up to you, but I prefer to make contact myself for queries about my land so I'll only be paying attention to what the council tell me. Anyway, I know a couple of the councillors and understand their ways better than you do, so I'll probably get a more useful response. But there are only twenty-four hours in a day and I'm in the middle of something so I'll come back to you within a day or two.'

'Yes, but—'

'Sorry, Deanna, but not now. I've had a long, hard day and I need to tell Lucia about something else that's cropped up and then deal with it as a matter of urgency.'

He disconnected before she could answer, not bothering to say goodbye. Well, too bad. He had bothered to give her a brief explanation at least. Trouble was, he was already having second thoughts about working with her, and about the project too, come to that.

And someone he knew slightly had asked him why he was allowing people to put a development on his land.

A development? It was one café and so he'd told his acquaintance. Had Belkin's arrival in town made some people paranoid?

What was Didier up to, sending Deanna to scope out the bunker for a café? That puzzled Corin. The more he heard about the man, the less he was inclined to do business with him. And he simply couldn't see a man of Didier's obvious intelligence in love romantically with a woman like Deanna. She wasn't the brightest brain on the planet, as everyone in the family knew.

Anyway, far more importantly at the moment, a couple

of people he knew had texted him urgently to say that the situation in Hawthorn Close was worrying and it was looking as if the survival of the two very special trees at the end of the street was seriously threatened by the new and unscrupulous builder. Locals were going to mount an all-night guard on them for a while. If so, would he be up for helping out?

He didn't have to think twice or even discuss it with his wife because he knew what she'd say. He'd replied at once to tell them that he'd definitely be available to help and would join them in just under an hour.

He might be fairly new in the valley but he'd been made welcome here and he'd quickly decided that it was the nicest place he'd ever lived in, both for scenery and for friendly people.

Already the house he'd chosen felt truly home to both himself and Lucia. He was pleased with what he'd done to modernise it, had enjoyed using his skills as an architect on the sort of job he loved most: creating real homes. The huge conservatory had made a big difference to the living space and was now their favourite place to sit together in the evenings.

And there were now two modern bathrooms upstairs. The original one had been big enough to add a shower in one corner and they'd made a new en suite bathroom from the former fourth bedroom, which Lucia had described as too 'squinchy minchy' even for a single bed to fit into comfortably when she first saw it.

She too said frequently how pleasant it was to live in the valley. But with her being pregnant, he wasn't going to encourage her to take part in any all-night guard duties or vigils – or any daytime ones either with Belkin involved. He hoped she wouldn't push matters about that.

He didn't usually tell her what to do or not to do, but this time he said she and the child were too precious to risk.

She was waiting for him, ready to serve drinks, non-alcoholic tonight because he liked to keep her company.

He raised his glass. 'To mama and child.'

'To papa as well.' They clinked glasses.

She patted her belly instinctively as she joined in the toast, though the bump wasn't very big yet. 'I'm looking forward to finding out whether this little dear is a boy or girl.'

'So am I.'

He wished he could just sit and simply be with her, it felt so cosy. Tonight the kitchen smelt of one of her delicious but she said easy to make casseroles, so he gave her a thorough kissing by way of a proper greeting and after that he allowed himself a few minutes to chat to her.

He kept an eye on the clock and allowed himself only ten minutes tonight. 'We need to talk about something else. I'm afraid I have to go out again.'

'I think I can guess why.'

'Have you heard about the problems in Hawthorn Close, then?'

'Yes. Who hasn't? The whole town is buzzing with it.' She studied his face.

'How did you find out about that, Lucia?'

'A friend phoned to tell me. It's because of that new builder, isn't it? The one you told me you don't trust.'

'Belkin, yes. I've volunteered to go on guard duty again tonight to help protect the trees from his wreckers. Do you mind?'

She sighed. 'I'm not exactly happy about it but I guessed you might have to, not only on principle but because we own a house in that street now.'

'You're right. There's a whole group of people intending to turn up for guard duty tonight then continue keeping watch.' He told her about Arthur and Mavis, and how they were leading the defence from their wheelchairs.

'How wonderful of them!'

'The valley and its natural treasures are worth the effort. I had never even seen hawthorn trees that old before.'

She echoed his own thoughts. 'If I weren't in this condition, I'd be joining in the defence, but I don't want to risk anything.'

'Thank goodness for that. I was prepared to sit on you if necessary to stop you taking part.'

She grinned and stuck her tongue out at him. 'You could have tried and it would have been fun fighting you off.'

He looked at her anxiously. 'You won't risk it, will you? There might be scuffles.'

'No, I won't. But it's because I don't want to risk the baby, not because of you or anyone else ordering me around.'

He rolled his eyes. 'Would I dare order you around for real?'

She looked at him rather smugly and said simply, 'No.'

She was right. As well as loving her, he had more respect for her than to treat her as if she couldn't think for herself.

'Can we get tea quite quickly now, please?'

'It's ready. Jacket potatoes and chicken casserole all right?'

'If it tastes as good as it smells, more than all right.' His stomach rumbled as if to emphasise his need and they both chuckled.

Half an hour later, Corin was back in the car driving down Larch Tree Lane with tea-and-coffee-making equipment sitting in the boot to leave in his empty house. He didn't know what exactly to expect, only that he'd join his fellow citizens to protect Hawthorn Close any time it needed help.

As he turned in to the street, he found the small cul-de-sac lined with parked vehicles of all sorts. He had to slow right down to drive through the narrow gap between a vehicle parked sideways across the street in front of the third house just beyond Belkin's properties. Presumably it was half blocking the road to prevent anyone coming to attack the trees.

There were now combi-vans parked in the drives of the first two houses. They had the logo of Belkin's company on their sides and a couple of burly men were standing near them, scowling across at the locals.

Harden was standing there too, looking extremely angry. *Good*, Corin thought. *You've stirred the locals up, now you'll have to live with it.*

Several people were chatting to the two wheelchair occupants guarding the trees on the verges outside Belkin's houses. Others were sitting in their cars or on the garden wall of the block of retirement flats on the other side of the street. No mistaking that they were there to protect the trees. They all looked utterly determined and the occasional glances they threw in the direction of Belkin's vehicles were not friendly – nor did they look afraid.

Corin was able to park in the drive of the house he'd bought. When he got out of his car, he saw another vehicle standing nearby in the street. The driver was peering up and down and had his engine running, clearly looking for a parking place. Corin gestured to the space beside his car and beckoned to the man, who nodded a thank you as he rolled slowly into the drive.

After taking the supplies inside and locking his car, Corin went to join the people standing near the person who looked to be the leader of this struggle: Arthur's daughter Jane. He wasn't surprised to see her giving orders. Some people just have that aura of command and take over instinctively in a difficult group situation. Both Jane and Nellie seemed to share the leadership role.

He waited till she'd finished and walked over to her. 'Is there anything specific I can do to help, Jane?'

'Hi, Corin. Glad to see you here. Nothing is urgent at the moment unless those men try to cause trouble, in which case do whatever you can to keep them away from those trees. We shall need to draw up a roster for the week because we're all quite sure Belkin won't give up after one night of us blocking his access to the trees. I assume you'll be in on the ongoing efforts to stop him?'

'Of course.' He pointed to the men. 'Our new foreman looks to me as if he's plotting some action.'

'He'll probably get those men to try to push through our people to the trees. I doubt he'll expect serious resistance from older protesters, but he's in for a shock and won't get anywhere. Our people are very determined.'

Corin didn't feel as confident of that. 'It's going to be hard to block access with such big, strong-looking men involved. What if they do break through and hurt our people? It won't take much to chop a tree down or poison it, and how do we stop them if they're swinging an axe or holding a chainsaw?'

'They'll find us waiting and there's a police car parked round the corner on Larch Tree Lane and a couple of officers on foot were going to be stationed at the other end of our street in Magnolia Gardens to prevent access that way. And don't forget it's against the law to damage these trees.'

'Fat lot of good Belkin will care about that, if you don't mind my saying so.'

She shrugged. 'I'd guess that tonight he'll mainly be testing our defences and our determination. And we'll have to prove that we're capable of resisting these gorillas. Ah! Excuse me.'

He watched her move forward to greet some newcomers who turned out to be from the local radio station and thank goodness for that. The more publicity they could get, the better. After recording a brief interview with her, in which he thought she performed really well, one of them walked back to his car. Corin walked across to chat to the other, who'd stayed behind.

'Whose side are you on?' he asked.

'Officially, neither side.' The journo winked and added, 'But my aunt is over there among the protesters and my cousin's joining her later and she's made a very good case for their side of things.' He gave Corin a very serious look. 'Do you think you'll manage to hold Belkin off?'

'I hope so. We can only do our best.'

The man moved away, speaking to another woman he

seemed to know, who was visibly angry and waved her arms round a lot to emphasise what she was saying.

In fact, the usually peaceful street felt like a minor battle ground already and was humming with what he could only describe as nervous energy. He'd been in a couple of small skirmishes when supervising building projects in third world countries, so could recognise the signs and feel of it.

He hadn't expected to encounter that sort of situation here when he gave up charity work and settled in a usually peaceful valley, but some things were worth fighting for. He wanted his child to grow up in a peaceful environment where people worked together and lived sanely.

He studied the groups near the trees, but couldn't see many signs of resistance measures. Why were these defenders not taking more visible precautions? Putting up barricades round the trees, maybe?

He found out why shortly afterwards when Belkin's men suddenly made a rush towards the nearest tree, and were met with pepper spray. That had the attackers jumping back and cursing as they rubbed their eyes.

The defenders followed that by hurling some soft lumps of greyish material at them, lumps that released some sort of gloopy stuff as they hit the attackers' faces and hands.

Amateur that sort of defence might be, but it was surprisingly effective. Other defenders had got out of their cars at the first sign of trouble and had now joined the group. In fact, there were quite a lot of them gathered around each tree.

The attackers had retired to the house, presumably to clean themselves up.

The defenders settled down again, waiting to see what the next attack would consist of.

This time as the attackers started walking steadily towards them, an elderly man clutched his chest and crumpled to the ground.

Someone must have had medical skills because a woman began resuscitation techniques on him and the sight of her doing that once again stopped the attackers in their tracks. Even they wouldn't want to be involved in a death.

At that moment, a car with a local TV station logo on it pulled up and a cameraman jumped out and began filming. That sent the two men back to the first house in the street, which seemed to be used as headquarters. They were trying to hide their faces as they ran.

Corin moved closer, standing beside Arthur, who was watching carefully from his wheelchair, and nodding in a satisfied way.

'I was hoping the TV people would come and join in the fun.'

Some men picked up the oldie who had collapsed and put him in the back of a van. As soon as he was out of sight of the group of bullies, he sat up and grinned, holding up one thumb in a sign of triumph.

'You sneaky devils,' Corin exclaimed, also grinning.

'We wanted to keep them back till the TV people were here.'

Jane went across to join the TV crew, speaking earnestly to them for a few minutes, then nodding farewell and coming back to join her father, whom they'd also filmed in his wheelchair.

'That worked quite well. Hopefully we'll get a court

order tomorrow for prevention of violence by Belkin's men. I doubt it'll stop them because he doesn't pay much attention to the law. He's already gained a reputation for paying the fines imposed for illegal activities and carrying on with what he originally wanted to do.'

'Yes, I'd heard that about him too.'

'An injunction might slow them down a bit. And at the very least it'll make the financial penalty greater if they break the injunction. But if he brings more men in, we could be in trouble.'

Jane began walking back to the chair that seemed to constitute her headquarters and Corin went with her on his way up to his own house.

'I wonder how long we can hold them back for,' he wondered aloud.

'I gather Dad and his friends have a few other surprises in store. I hope you'll continue to keep watch with us.'

'Of course I will.' He frowned in thought. It was all very well taking them by surprise this time and tricking them with a mock collapse, but would these people continue to come night after night? And most of them seemed to be older. That was worrying because Belkin's men looked young and strong – and yes, he had to admit it, nasty.

Corin had a sudden thought as to how he could help make the defenders a little more comfortable and turned to Jane. 'I've had a small idea. Come across to your dad again so that I don't have to go through it twice.'

When the three of them were there plus Mavis, temporarily liberated from her wheelchair, he said, 'You know that I've bought the house Judith used to live in? Well, how about I make it available to your defenders for coffee, bathroom breaks and so on? Would that help?'

'Of course it would,' Jane said. 'Rob and Ilsa have offered to let us use their houses, but it'll disturb them a lot. If your house is free, we won't be disturbing any occupants. I thought you were going to let it, though?'

'Eventually. I want to do some decorating first so it can be used to help protect these trees in the meantime.'

'What if something gets damaged?'

'I doubt people would be so careless and uncaring. Anyway, I'll risk it.'

Arthur reached up to clap him on the shoulder. 'You're a good lad. You fit in well here already.'

'I hope so because I want to spend the rest of my life living in the valley.'

'It's a good place.' Arthur waved one hand towards the vans and group of surly men. 'When we've sorted this lot out, I'd like to come up and see how it's all going at the Marrakin.'

'You'd be welcome any time, Arthur.'

Chapter Eighteen

Corin turned to leave but Arthur tugged at his sleeve. 'Have you thought what to do about that underground bunker yet?'

'I have a relative who's thinking about setting up a café there. I need to find out what the local rules are before I come to any sort of decision.'

Arthur pulled a face. 'It'd make a rotten place for a café, if you ask me. I'd not like to sit underground for a casual meal or a snack. There would be nothing to look at outside the windows. You'd just be hemmed in by blank walls.'

And just like that, the old man put his finger on the worry that was hovering at the back of Corin's mind. The idea of a theme café had sounded like a good one at first, but he had begun to wonder and now, at Arthur's words, he felt suddenly *sure* it wouldn't work.

'That's what I wanted to talk to someone knowledgeable about. I think you're right. Is there anyone round here that

I could discuss the bunker café idea with?'

'Surely those two have some plans developed already?'

'No, I don't think they have. They are, what would you call it, one-horse ponies. They only know what they've read. The original people involved in places like that during the war are mostly dead now.'

Arthur nodded. 'You should talk to Ben Thorson. He's over ninety so doesn't go out much but he'd welcome a caller any time. He's still alive in the head, smart as ever, our Ben is. There'd be no one better to talk to about an idea like this.'

'Really? Why should I consult him in particular?'

'Because he was involved in setting that bunker up in the first place.'

'No! How amazing.'

'My friend Ben was probably only the office boy or some such, it's so long ago, but junior staff often see more than their bosses realise. He's proud of what they did "just in case" we didn't win the war. That bunker had a very serious purpose concerned with the defence of the realm, though he won't say what. I reckon he'd hate to see it jollied up into a fancy café playing at being at war, and actually, so would I. It feels disrespectful, somehow. Though I know that isn't often a sought-after attribute these days.'

Corin looked at Arthur gratefully. 'Nonetheless, you've given me something to think about. Thanks for the tip. Ben's knowledge of the bunker might be very useful indeed. I can't think what to do with it. And I'm really grateful for your advice, too.'

'Ben's the one who really knows, though. And, come to think of it, he has a good knowledge of the sort of tourists who visit our valley as well. He used to run a café in the town. He moved on from it after a few years, said it was hard work and he didn't want to spend his life making cups of tea.'

'That experience makes him sound even more useful. Thanks.'

'You're welcome. Now, let's concentrate on getting through the night without those sods breaking through to our trees. They're three very strong-looking chaps.'

It seemed a long night to Corin. But he wasn't going to let anyone spoil this lovely street, if he could help it.

Arthur greeted a skinny stripling of a lad at one stage and the two of them whispered about something for quite a while.

It'd take a lot of very determined people to save the trees, though, and Corin doubted it could be done against such odds. It was his guess that Belkin would send in even more men tomorrow. From what he'd heard in architectural circles, this guy was totally lacking in morals when it came to getting his own way, which was how he'd made his money relatively quickly.

Jane was working on a roster to have enough core people staying in the street both day and night to defend their trees. She was pleased to see new people, fresh from a good night's sleep, trickling in to relieve the first group of defenders, who were looking weary now.

Jane's friend Nellie took over running things for the day but they were all concerned to see that Harden and the two men had gone into the first house.

To their further dismay, Jane was proved right and two new men took their places. She was worried about how determined Belkin seemed to be. You'd have thought he could have found better places to start a new development than this street. There must be something else behind it. But what?

Belkin popped in for a while, then left again. The two men spent the day mostly outside, watching the protesters and chatting.

No one trusted any of Belkin's people one single inch.

When he was released from guard duty, Corin simply left his house open and asked Nellie to let newcomers know they could use his bathroom and the coffee-making equipment in the kitchen. All he'd ask was that they would be prepared to wash out any mugs they used.

That done, he left to go home and change.

He was feeling in desperate need of sleep now but if this project of Deanna's wasn't viable, he felt obliged to let her and Didier know quickly. He had almost made up his mind that it wouldn't be viable, but would speak to this friend of Arthur's first, just to be certain.

Once he'd had a shower and changed into clean jeans, he gobbled down the bacon sandwiches Lucia had made for him, drank a cup of strong coffee to keep himself awake and went off to visit Ben Thorson. If Arthur placed so much trust in this man, he must be worth speaking to.

The old man's cottage was at the other side of Magnolia Park from Hawthorn Close, but you had to detour round some houses as well as the park to reach it by car because the public's access to the park was only on foot, and council officials were the only ones with keys to the huge wrought-iron gates at the far side of it from Hawthorn Close that allowed vehicles into it for maintenance work.

The old man lived in one of a group of bungalows provided for elderly people who needed some help with household cleaning and shopping but were otherwise perfectly capable of looking after themselves.

Corin was invited in by a pleasant woman who said she was Ben's granddaughter, doing a quick tidy-up for him. As he shook his host's hand and took the chair indicated, she said she'd bring them a pot of tea and then get off home.

Ben's face was even more wrinkled than Arthur's but he too had a pair of bright, alert eyes and an infectious, boyish grin. Some people never grew old mentally, Corin thought, and it showed in their eyes particularly. He hoped he'd look that alert in forty more years' time.

He explained that he needed to know more about the underground bunker.

'Why would anyone be interested in that old place these days?'

'I own that part of the valley now and someone is thinking about leasing it from me and opening a café there, one with a World War Two theme, to be shown by murals and mock bomb shelters.'

Ben scowled. 'They should fill it all in and be done with it.'

'Why do you think that?'

'Because they don't really know what they're doing. If I remember correctly, some writer or other once said about the past that it's a different and alien country to the present generation. Eh, who was it? A man, I think.'

'Was it L. P. Hartley?'

'Yes, that's the chap. And he was right, too. I've never forgotten his words, even if I forgot his name. Today's folk can never truly understand what it was like in Britain in the past or how it offends some people when others try to re-create it, especially when they do it wrongly.' He was silent for a moment or two, then looked up. 'What's more, I don't think that after an initial interest in the novelty of it, folk will think it pleasant to sit underground to do their eating and drinking. There will be no view, no people walking past.' He shook his head vigorously. 'No, when they go out for refreshments and a convivial meeting with friends, folk like somewhere interesting to hang out. Isn't that what they call it these days? Hanging out?'

'These people who had the idea thought school trips might go there as well as café customers if it had a war theme. It would bring the past to life a bit for the kids, surely?'

Ben let out a scornful snort. 'That's as may be, but how will they make enough money to run a café full-time out of a few school trips? Most parents won't pay lavishly for trips and some of them can't afford it at all, can they?'

'I'm wondering about that myself.'

Ben leant forward, speaking earnestly. 'Look, lad, I ran a café for years after the war, and I made a decent living from it, so I know what I'm talking about. That sort of themed setting won't pull in many regular customers in a small place like our valley. And what about you?'

Corin looked at him in puzzlement. 'What do you mean?'

'As the owner, you'll be left with it on your hands when these folk pull out of running it after the first year, as I'm sure they will. I doubt you'll even make back your set-up costs.'

'You're right and I agree with you. The trouble is, I've got that bunker standing empty and it'd cost a fortune to fill it all in safely. I really would prefer to find some use for it.'

'I always thought the only thing it would be good for after the war ended was as a long-term storage area – well, it would if you were to put another entrance on the far side, block off some storage space and get permission to make a small car park nearby. That shouldn't cost you a fortune because there wouldn't be much to do inside the space. Lockers and cupboards could be bought second-hand, or brought in by your clients for their own stuff.'

Corin looked at him, struck instantly by the sense of this. 'That sounds much more do-able. And after the first year or so it'd probably make a small ongoing profit for me.'

'I reckon it would. There isn't a long-term storage facility in the valley at present. There wouldn't be a huge demand, mind, but I've heard people complain about the lack. It would only need to be opened part-time, too, and I agree that it'd likely make a small profit for you – and for someone you could rent it out to, who'd run it as a business.'

When Corin took his leave, he thanked Ben very sincerely for his help. What a sharp, clever brain his host had.

When he got home and told Lucia what Ben had suggested, she agreed instantly. 'His analysis makes a lot more sense to me than Deanna's wild optimism. Let's invite her and Didier to come round and tell them we've changed our minds about it all.'

'Hmm. I'll tell them on the phone, I think. It'll be quicker and with a bit of luck they'll take my refusal on board without paying us another visit and boring me to tears.'

She burst out laughing. 'Deanna does rabbit on a bit, doesn't she?'

'Does she ever stop talking, do you think? I'd guess Didier is much more interested in the financial facts than she is, and was I mistaken or did he look at her in irritation a couple of times?'

'I noticed that too.'

'She's never been known for her good sense and has had other sudden enthusiasms, but I'm sure he'll accept a refusal without quibbling.'

Lucia looked thoughtful. 'There's something not right about this whole situation and his involvement. I can't work out what, I just feel sure there is. And also, I'm glad you're not going to be allowing them into our lives here.'

'I haven't often heard you talk like that about someone. You didn't take to Didier, did you?'

'No, I didn't, for all his smarmy ways. Can't you wait and tell her tomorrow? You're looking so tired.'

'I'd rather phone her straight away and get it off my mind, then I'll go to bed for a few hours before I join the watchers again. You're right. I'm exhausted but what we're doing in Hawthorn Close is so worthwhile.'

Deanna listened to him in silence, then protested and insisted she could make it work.

'Sorry, but I'm not going to go into it. It'd cost me too much in set-up expenses.'

'Talk to Didier about it. He'll be able to put things better than I can.'

'I'm not talking to anyone about business developments at the moment. We have a difficult situation on our hands in Essington and that's much more important to me.'

'But—'

'I have to go now, Deanna. I didn't get any sleep last night.' He put the phone down without waiting for her to speak again and turned to Lucia, unable to suppress another yawn. 'I'm going to bed now.'

'Just one quick thing before you do that. How about I take over discussing the idea of a car park and storage rental facility with someone at the council?'

'Would you? Are you sure you want to do it?'

'Yes. I'd enjoy having a project to work on at home, actually. I'm having a baby, not going into mental hibernation for nine months. Now that this house is more or less sorted out, I'm already fed up of sitting around at home reading novels or occasionally meeting people for coffee and a natter. I like to do *useful* things.'

Another huge yawn stopped him replying and she laughed. 'Go and get that sleep, darling, and leave me to make a start on investigating the storage idea. I'll keep you abreast of developments, don't worry.'

'OK.' He plonked a kiss on her nearest cheek and went up to bed, not stirring till she woke him to eat a meal before he went on guard duty again.

Chapter Nineteen

When Amy got up that first morning in Larch House, she went straight to the window to enjoy the view. It did something to her, that lovely view did, made her feel more relaxed and hopeful too, she didn't know why.

Then she caught sight of the time on the small clock ticking quietly to itself on the mantelpiece and gasped. It was nearly nine o'clock and she was usually up and busy by seven thirty at the latest.

But what had she to be busy about now? She smiled as it sank in that she could do whatever she wanted with her days, including lie in bed if the fancy took her, though that wasn't likely to be a regular occurrence.

It'd be good to stay here at Larch House a little longer and attend the wedding. And she'd been longing to set up a studio and start a new painting. She could set up a temporary one quite quickly, then take her time and work steadily for a few days.

She'd been seeing one particular scene in her mind's eye for weeks now, based on a place she'd driven through on one of her solitary country outings in Northumberland. She'd parked at a lookout near the top of a hill and the scene across a valley had been so lovely, she'd taken several photographs.

But of course she wanted to add her own touches to the composition; she nearly always did. Sometimes, placing a figure or animal in a scene, or a beautiful tree seemed to set it off better, bring it to life and give those looking at it a starting focus. She usually got a better feeling for exactly what was needed in that sense later on, once she'd captured the main scene roughly on canvas. She'd even dreamt of some scenes and found her focus that way, though she hadn't told anyone about that or they'd think she was weird.

Perhaps she was weird. What did it matter now? She didn't have to fit in with any group or manager.

She caught a glimpse of herself in the mirror. Her clothes looked so plain. She needed – no, wanted – to wear something brighter and more cheerful.

When she went downstairs, there was no one in the kitchen and one of the cars was missing. Had her great-aunt and James gone out already?

'Oh, there you are,' said a voice behind her.

She swung round. 'Hi, Maggie. I slept in, I'm afraid.'

'Sleep in all you like. Don't forget that you'll need to rest and take time to recover from your loss, my dear. And you sounded yesterday as if you need a few hugs to help you on your way, so here's another one.' She came across and drew Amy close for a few moments.

That felt so good, Amy had no hesitation in hugging her great-aunt back.

When Maggie pulled away, she said, 'Now, what do you like for breakfast? James is an eggy person but I prefer cereals or toast. I'll get things out for you today, so that you'll know how I organise the kitchen, then I'll leave you to prepare your own breakfast in peace.'

'I usually just grab some toast while I'm getting ready to go out to work but maybe I'll indulge in one of my favourites this morning: scrambled eggs on toast. Would that be all right? Do you have enough eggs?'

'Of course it would be OK. We get our eggs from a nearby farm so they're really fresh and we can always get more. They have a kiosk at their gates.' She shot a quick glance at Amy. 'You don't look to be fully functioning yet so perhaps you'd just like a cup of tea or coffee to start with, then I'll show you around the cupboards and leave you in peace. The newspaper is over there if you like to read with your meal. We'll have plenty of time to chat later. We don't have to tell each other our entire life stories at once.'

As she moved towards the hall door, she stopped again. 'If you need me, I'll be doing my monthly clear-up of the library. I dust the main areas and pieces of furniture, but I don't even try to dust all the books and bookshelves or I'd be there for several days. It'd be like the Forth Bridge used to be before the really long-lasting outdoor paints were invented: finish one end of the bridge then need to start again painting at the other end.'

'I'm looking forward to exploring the library. I love reading.'

'Good. Enjoy your meal.' She walked out again.

Amy made a pot of tea. It felt really decadent to drink her first cup while she read the newspaper. Then she cooked her breakfast and ate it slowly, enjoying every mouthful.

After clearing up, she glanced at the newspaper again and lingered over it when she found an article on an exhibition of oil paintings that had been held in London. What mainly interested her was that it gave details about what had been the best sellers and the approximate prices made by them. Landscapes seemed to be doing quite well.

Would her own paintings ever be shown and sold to the public? Oh, she did hope so. She didn't hanker after earning a fortune from them but she wanted to prove she was good enough to earn a living by painting. And she wanted to give people pleasure as other artists' paintings had given her over the years.

She cleared up the kitchen, then went back upstairs to brush her teeth, after which she couldn't resist going into the room opposite her bedroom, which Maggie had suggested she use as a studio. Someone had brought up the rest of the things from her car, James presumably. He must have done it very quietly because he hadn't woken her.

Most of the furniture would have to be cleared out to give her the space she needed for her easel and other equipment. She was quite capable of removing the smaller items but wasn't sure where to put them, so went downstairs to see if she could find her great-aunt to ask about that.

She hesitated by the kitchen door as the two of them looked so comfortable together. 'Will I be in your way if I make myself a quick cup of coffee?'

They both smiled and Maggie said, 'Nope. We've nearly finished putting the groceries away. It's just instant coffee so you could make us all a cup while you're at it, if you don't mind. Black, no sugar for both of us.'

'Did you sleep well?' James asked.

'Wonderfully well. And thanks for bringing up my things from the car. How did you get the keys?'

'You'd left them on the kitchen table.'

'Oh, my goodness! I must have been more tired than I realised.'

She suddenly remembered the leftover groceries among her things and mentioned them. 'They're not perishables, mainly tins and packets. Shall I add them to the stuff in the pantry?'

'Yes, please do. Thanks.'

'You must have taken them upstairs with the rest, James. I'll bring them down now while we're waiting for the kettle to boil.'

That task was soon accomplished, then they sat down to drink their coffee and have a chat.

Afterwards, Maggie said, 'All right if we come up and help you sort out the furniture from that room now, Amy? Many hands make light work and I'm dying to see how you arrange it all and what you'll be working on. My studio is up in the attic and I can't seem to keep it tidy but you're welcome to visit me at Chaos Central any time.'

James chuckled. 'That's a perfect name for it. She doesn't have the tidy gene where her art materials are concerned.'

She pretended to slap him, then continued, 'Well, you have to work quickly with watercolours so you can't always take time to tidy up. My room was formerly the housekeeper's sitting room. I used to use one of the bedrooms as a studio but when James moved in here, he suggested the attic was a much better space if we cleared part of it out. He was right and I love it up there. I'll show it to you later.'

Setting up Amy's studio together turned out to be fun.

She had never had other family members to share tasks with in this casual way and loved the give and take. They all had opinions about what might or might not work, and some lively discussions ensued. They were in complete agreement, however, about removing all the bigger pieces of furniture.

It took the three of them to carry the old-fashioned metal bed frame up to the attic, it was so heavy and awkward. Other unwanted furniture had been dumped in one corner up there too.

They peeped into Maggie's studio, which was indeed chaotic, but her great-aunt insisted that she knew where to find every single item that was used regularly.

Once they'd removed all the furniture Amy didn't want, Maggie nudged James. 'She'll need to be on her own now, to work out how she wants to set up her painting equipment.'

She smiled across at her great-aunt, grateful for that understanding. 'Thanks.'

'Remember, anything from that pile of furniture in the attic is available for your use if you need another chair or whatever.' Maggie then grabbed James's hand and tugged him out of the room.

When Amy went across to close the door a couple of minutes later, she heard a muffled noise and peeped out to see what it was.

The other two were kissing one another at the far end of the landing. Wow! They weren't holding back. She couldn't imagine her own mother behaving like that. But then her mother had never even dated after her father died.

As Amy went back into her studio, she sighed wistfully. It must be lovely to have a partner you loved and trusted. She didn't think it'd ever happen to her again, and if the possibility arose, she wasn't sure she'd dare rely on her own judgement about men. Not after her horrible experience of marriage to someone she'd mistakenly thought charming.

Pity.

By lunchtime, Amy had done as much as she could. She needed to buy some more art supplies before she could make a proper start on her painting. She'd brought a prepared canvas with her already, thank goodness, and a couple of smaller spares too but none of them was suitable for the painting she'd set her heart on creating.

She suddenly realised how ravenous she was, couldn't remember the last time she'd felt this hungry, so went down to the kitchen. There she found Maggie sitting at the table, working on her laptop.

Her great-aunt looked up and blew her a kiss. 'How's it coming along?'

'Really well. I'm so excited about having a proper studio, but I need to buy some more art supplies before I can start. Is there anywhere in town that sells them?'

'There's a quirky little shop run by a woman called Blossom, who calls herself a neo-hippie. It sells stationery, second-hand oddments of clothing and art materials, and a few other things too. There isn't a big range of art supplies, but she carries most of the basics. It's a wider range than you might expect to find in such a small shop, actually. I suspect she's an artist herself. There will probably be enough to give you a start. Otherwise she'll get things in or you can order them online.'

'I'll do that, too, once I've set up a new internet connection, but I like to support local shops.'

'I agree. As for the internet, we can add you to ours, if you like.'

'Are you sure?'

'Of course I am. Unless you're going to need to make gigantic downloads, that is?'

'No, definitely not. Going online is interesting for some things, but I have a real-world life that's far more important to me. Staying here will give me a rare chance to concentrate on my painting. I'm really grateful for the opportunity. You're being so kind.'

That won her another smile and a deprecating shrug.

When she'd given directions to the shop, Maggie added, 'If you see a lot of people milling around near Hawthorn Close, which is on the left just before you get into town, it'll be the protest about the trees.'

'Protest?'

'A builder is trying to knock down some magnificent hawthorn trees and a lot of people are up in arms protesting. It's bad enough that this Belkin creature is going to build some of his shonky houses in our valley, but we don't intend to let him destroy our trees. He's not supposed to touch them. Those hawthorns are officially heritage-listed and are over two hundred years old, stunningly beautiful when they're in flower in the spring.'

'I'm on the side of the protestors about that sort of thing!'

'So am I.'

Amy set off, driving slowly down the hill so that she could look around. There were several cars parked on the left just before she got into town, and a couple on the right. When she slowed right down for a quick glance into the nearby side street, she saw a surprising number of people standing around and cars parked everywhere. Well, good luck to them!

She carried on into town and found the shop easily. It looked as quirky as Maggie had suggested, even in the way the window was set out, with one or two toy animals peeping at you from behind piles of goods in such a way as to make you smile.

Its owner was an older woman with an untidy bun on top of her head, in which a couple of pencils were stuck as well as a hairpin with a sparkling ball on the end.

She frowned as Amy entered. 'I'm afraid I was just about to shut up shop.'

'Oh dear. I really need some art materials.'

'Are you staying in the village?'

'Yes, with my great-aunt Maggie at Larch House.'

'Oh, that's all right, then. I know Maggie. She comes in here regularly. Just take what you want and leave me a note to say what it is and how much it comes to. There are some scraps of paper in that holder. You can pay me next time you're in town or phone and give me your credit card details. Oh, and put the latch on the door as you leave, if you don't mind. I shan't be back for a while as I have to do some sentry duty for the protest.'

'Maggie told me about the trees.'

'Yes. We're all furious about that horrible builder.' She caught sight of the clock. 'Must go. I'm meeting a friend there. Hope you find what you want.'

Not such a peaceful little town, after all, Amy thought as she turned to study the shelves. Was anywhere in the world ever totally peaceful?

She spent an enjoyable hour checking all the art materials and piling what she needed on the counter, not worrying about what it cost because she wasn't short of money for necessities now. And her art things were necessities.

Then she caught sight of some retro clothing, second-hand by the looks of it, but clean and not badly worn. In fact there were quite a few hangers crammed into a small alcove near one corner. She couldn't resist going through the items and when she found some pretty skirts and tops that looked about her size, she locked the shop door and stood behind a stand of books to try a few on.

A couple of gypsy skirts and three tops fitted her perfectly so she added them to the purchases. They must have come from the early seventies and were a vivid mix of colours.

She wouldn't ever need to wear her work clothes again, she thought in delight. She'd hated the black business suits she'd had to wear for the office and that colour didn't flatter her. With her dark hair, she'd always felt like a funereal crone in them.

As she made her way round the shop, she unlocked the door again before checking the final shelves. It'd be good to know what else was being sold there for future reference.

She paused as it struck her that she was acting as though she'd be staying round here permanently. Well, why not? There would surely be a small house that she could afford.

An older man walked in as she was about to write a note about what she'd bought, but he looked respectable so she left him to look round till she was ready to leave. He gave her a quick nod and selected some pencils and a refill for an expensive ballpoint pen.

He came back to the counter and pulled out his wallet

to pay so she said with a smile, 'I don't work here so I can't take your payment, and the owner is at a meeting to protect some heritage trees. She told me to select what I wanted and leave payment details because she knows my family. Do you know her?'

'Er, no.'

'Well, you could leave cash and a list of what you've bought. I'm sure she'd be all right with that.'

There was something rather arrogant about the way he was looking at her, running his eyes quickly up and down her body. It always annoyed her when men did that, so she gave him a very direct look of disapproval and ran her eyes up and down his body. He flushed and hastily turned his gaze elsewhere.

Only then did she push a piece of scrap paper across the counter and say, 'You can write on this.'

'Thanks.' He scribbled a note and put some money down, then hesitated. 'How's the save the trees movement going? Have you heard?'

'I gather it went very well yesterday. They stopped the builder destroying the trees.'

'Did they really?' He gave a scornful sniff. 'I don't call that going well. Such a fuss over some scruffy old trees that are probably a danger to passers-by. The protest will come to nothing. It's jobs people need, not trees.'

She looked at him, surprised at his confident, know-it-all tone. 'From what the shopkeeper said, they're stunningly beautiful trees when in blossom and are over two hundred years old. No wonder they've been heritage-listed. They're apparently quite a feature of the town in spring and tourists come to see them.'

He stilled, frowning slightly. 'They're heritage-listed? Are you sure about that? I was told that was a myth put about by the greenies.'

'I don't see why the owner of the shop or my great-aunt would lie about it to me, and actually, I agree with the protesters. I think people should preserve old trees. The locals are so up in arms about it that a lot of them have signed up to spend the nights on guard duty as well as the days.'

He gaped in shock at that, then shook his head as if dismissing what she'd said. 'It'll only be a few stupid greenies showing off.'

'More than a few. I drove past the street on the way here and it was absolutely full of cars and people. It's getting that builder a very bad name in the valley, which won't be helpful for his business. I've only been here a couple of days and I've heard nothing good about him.'

His frown deepened. 'Are you sure about people planning to stand guard at night?'

'Very sure. My great-aunt is furious about what he's doing. She and her partner have signed up to help.'

His voice became sarcastic. 'She's an expert on trees, is she?'

'Well, she owns a small estate at the top of Larch Tree Lane, so she probably knows quite a lot about managing trees because it has extensive grounds. And apparently the trees in Hawthorn Close are special to most people who live round here. Both sides of the street are lined by them and they bring a lot of tourists to the area in spring as well as giving locals huge pleasure. Some people even time their weddings so that they can be photographed with them. I should think they increase the value of properties in that street, too.'

He was still frowning and said slowly, 'I didn't realise they were so special.'

'Don't take my word for it, go and have a look. The street was crowded when I drove past it on my way into town. That builder is making plenty of enemies. My aunt says he'll have to physically remove people to get to the trees and there are even people in wheelchairs standing guard, as well as a police presence. It'll look really bad to eject oldies and people in wheelchairs, don't you think?' She hadn't liked the scornful way he'd dismissed what she'd said, so added, 'The local press has been there already and my great-aunt thinks it'll probably hit the national headlines too. Sadly, I heard it's no use appealing to the local member of parliament for help. Apparently he doesn't care about the environment and rarely shows his face in town anyway.'

He was positively glaring at her now. Muttering something under his breath, he slammed down a couple of banknotes on the counter. He didn't bother to close the door as he left and it started banging to and fro so she had to go across and shut it.

What an unpleasant man! Probably a friend of the builder from the way he'd talked. Or maybe just grumpy. Or both.

She finished writing out her list of purchases, locked up the shop and drove back up the hill. When she saw even more cars parked on Larch Tree Lane near the entrance to the side street, she pulled over and stopped to stare along the side street again. There were more people there than there had been when she drove into town.

But even though she wished the locals well, she wasn't

going to join the protesting. She had enough on her plate sorting out her life.

She was about to set off again when she noticed the grumpy man from the shop standing near the entrance to the street, staring along it. That made her so curious, she stayed to watch him. He didn't attempt to go into the street, just continued to stare along it, his head turning from side to side. When he turned to go back to his car, he was scowling again and muttering something. She could read lips well enough to see that he was cursing about 'those damned trees'.

On a sudden impulse, she got out her phone and snapped a quick photo of him. She'd mention his interest in the tree affair to Maggie and see if her great-aunt knew who he was.

He got into a gleaming black car, which must have cost a fortune. She didn't even recognise the make. He narrowly missed another vehicle as he pulled out onto Larch Tree Lane, but didn't slow down at all. In fact, he was driving quite fast as he set off down the hill towards the town. He didn't seem to care about anyone or anything except himself.

She set off up the hill again, a bit annoyed with herself for wasting time on him. She should just delete his photo and forget he existed. She'd probably never meet him again.

Only, she couldn't help wondering who he was. Such a well-dressed man and driving an extremely expensive car.

Why did the way people were defending the trees annoy him so much? If they were as lovely as Maggie had said when they were in bloom, not to mention ancient and rare, they were worth preserving, surely?

Chapter Twenty

Terence Singleton was amazed and extremely annoyed to see how many people had gathered in Hawthorn Close to protest. There were even big, professional-looking signs on cards pinned to the top of poles being waved about by a few people.

The signs said HANDS OFF OUR TREES and SAVE OUR TREES. Stupid fools. You couldn't halt modern changes to the world and stay living in the past. Unfortunately, housing was always a hot topic politically.

He'd been over in Paris last weekend with a friend and had come back to vague rumours of some problem concerning those damned hawthorn trees. Only, unlike that rather dishy woman he'd been speaking to in the shop, Des Belkin had dismissed this as a minor protest that would soon fade.

He should have asked her for more specific details, Terence decided, only she'd scowled at him. Some women were so stupid, didn't even like you looking at them these days.

He'd have to keep an eye on the situation, though. In his position as the local member of parliament, he had to pay attention to his image. Only, the business deal he and Belkin had been working on together had seemed more important at that time.

Either the situation about the trees had changed rapidly or Belkin had been trying to pull the wool over his eyes. He wouldn't be surprised if it were the latter. From what he'd just seen, it looked as though this protest was turning into far more than a minor disturbance. The people making up that crowd had looked genuinely angry and they'd been quite well dressed, too, not scruffy student types, to his further surprise and dismay.

He'd seen Arthur Keevil among them and his own annoyance had increased a notch or two at the mere sight of that man. They'd crossed swords before, but that had been years ago. You'd think that at his age Keevil would have stopped rabble-rousing and be drooling over his dinner in some quiet corner of a care home. But no, there he was, sitting in a fancy wheelchair encouraging people to annoy a new business that was going to bring housing, money *and* jobs into the valley.

Terence had also thought this business deal would give him some good publicity as they approached next year's elections, which would be a very important time for him.

He stood next to one of those old-fashioned lamp posts the heritage folk had also made a fuss about at one stage. Hoping no one had noticed him there, he scanned the crowd for other local troublemakers, yes, and saw them too.

He didn't go into the street because he didn't want to be recognised and harassed, let alone get involved in this debate before he'd been properly briefed and his PA had worked out a strategy for him to tackle this. The trouble was, he had other fish to fry at the moment, including a very angry wife who had not been invited to go with him to Paris. He'd better buy her a bunch of flowers on the way home.

He'd definitely get in touch with Belkin first, though, and tell him to do something ASAP to defuse the situation. He wasn't helping fund and set up building developments in the valley if the builder was going to annoy the local populace and pull him into it too.

It was one thing to make money, another thing altogether to become the target of troublemakers on your own territory and lose votes.

He walked back to his car and got into it, having to brake suddenly as he was about to drive off when some idiot in a ramshackle four-wheel drive nearly crashed into him.

As he set off, anger was still simmering through him like a stream of molten lava. Damn Arthur Keevil for causing trouble again and damn Belkin for not reading the mood of the locals more accurately.

That was no way to grow a business or attract future financial support from Terence.

Murad had been watching the goings-on in Hawthorn Close from the front bedroom of his new rental home, using binoculars for part of the time. He was under strict orders not to intervene unless the situation got out of hand. If the two sides continued to face one another without damage to persons or property, he should just keep watch and note down who was doing what.

He and Vicki were involved in efforts to trap bigger fish in the official net than these protesters. He'd have liked to intervene on their side and order those rough-looking men to go away. He didn't want the decent people of Essington getting hurt, especially those magnificent oldies in wheelchairs, and the world needed more trees not fewer.

Vicki would be back from her course in the morning and he'd be glad to have her around again. She was better at interacting with these people than he was, though he did his best and was improving all the time, he felt.

She'd helped him fit in when he first joined the special unit and he'd helped her understand why people from similar backgrounds to his were likely to act in certain ways.

In the meantime, he continued to keep watch and take careful written note of anything important that happened.

Well, he did until he fell asleep. He'd intended to stay awake all night, but somehow he dozed off sitting at his bedroom window and leaning against the corner of the wall and windowsill. You learnt to sleep when you could in his job but sometimes your body made it difficult to stay awake when you wanted to, especially when you were working on your own.

He was annoyed with himself when he woke up with a crick in the neck and nearly slipped sideways off the chair, but luckily nothing much seemed to have changed outside. The street was quieter and the locals seemed to be taking it in turns to walk around with lanterns, while other lanterns shed pools of light on each of the trees in question.

One of Belkin's men kept moving around the crowd as if he was keeping watch as well, a scowl wrinkling his features. He received dirty looks from everyone he passed.

Two people were standing near the trees, making it plain that they weren't going to be taken by surprise, and good luck to them. The wheelchairs were empty at the moment.

Murad was thinking of suggesting that his parents come to live in this valley when they retired in a year or two. The more time he was here, the more he liked it. They'd fit in, he was sure. He'd been unusually well received, not greeted with suspicion because of his different racial and religious background, so he'd be sorry when he got posted elsewhere, which was inevitable in the long term.

Amy left the protesters to it, mentally wishing them well, and set off again, driving slowly back up to Larch House.

As she lugged her bags of purchases inside, Maggie smiled at her from where she was stirring something on the stove. 'Get what you wanted?'

'Yes. Well, most of it. Enough to make a good start. I'll need to phone the owner tomorrow to pay for what I bought because she was rushing off to join the protesters when I arrived. Once she found I was staying with you, she told me to serve myself and lock up when I left.'

'Blossom is a dear, always very relaxed about her business. I reckon she enjoys the company of her customers as much as selling to them.'

'After she'd left, a man came into the shop and bought some bits and pieces. He was a real grump and the way he eyed me was sexist and old-fashioned. I kept an eye on him to make sure he left money for the things he took but he didn't leave his name.'

'Well, at least he bought something.'

'Yes. On my way back I stopped to look at the protestors in Hawthorn Lane and d'you know what? He'd parked nearby and got out of his car to watch what was going on. But he was standing under a tree just outside the street and it seemed obvious to me that he was trying to avoid being noticed.'

'That's strange.'

Amy pulled out her phone, fiddled with it and held it out to show her companion. 'I took a photo of him lurking. Do you know who he is?'

Maggie came over to look at it. 'Ha! That's Terence Singleton, our local MP. I've never voted for him. I can't stand the fellow. Talk about smarmy and insincere.'

'He might be smarmy if he wanted something from you but he wasn't smarmy with me.'

'He hasn't been seen much around town recently. He usually spends as little time as he can in his electorate, except during the month or two before an election. Unfortunately a lot of the sheeples will believe anything and he makes wonderful promises.'

'Sheeples? I don't know that word.'

'Sheep-like followers who can't think for themselves.'

'I like it. I'll add it to my vocabulary.'

Maggie handed the phone back, her frown returning as she continued to think aloud. 'I wonder why he was lurking there. I wouldn't have thought he'd care one way or the other about saving those trees.'

'Well, there were a lot of locals there so perhaps

someone's asked his help as their MP.'

'I doubt it. His scorn for greenies is well known. It's more likely that he's getting worried about the voters taking against him. I wonder . . .'

'Wonder what?'

'Exactly what he's doing in town when the election isn't till next year. I don't trust him or his brother, who is one of our town councillors. I don't know which of them is worse, Terence or Peter Singleton.' She shrugged. 'Anyway, who cares about them? Why don't you take your things up to your studio and enjoy unpacking them? Tea will only be half an hour or so. I'll call you when it's ready.'

'Thanks.'

Arthur had caught sight of someone standing in Larch Tree Lane, someone who'd stayed there for quite a long while, likely watching what was going on in Hawthorn Close. He frowned and squinted, but couldn't see well enough at this distance so grabbed his daughter's sleeve.

'Don't make it obvious that you're looking but take a quick glance and tell me who that chap is at the end of the street under the lamp post, Jane love.'

She took a casual look and sucked her breath in, exclaiming. 'It's Singleton. What's that nasty rat doing here? There isn't an election due.'

He chuckled. 'Don't hedge about – do you like him or not?'

She gave her father a mock punch. 'I feel the same about him as you do, and well you know it.'

'Ah. I thought it was him but couldn't be sure. My eyes aren't what they used to be. What's that sod spying on us for? I'm sure he'll not be there because he wants to help us. Is he going to bring the law down on us for some imaginary reason to stop us, do you think?'

She looked at him in puzzlement. 'Why would he do that? He's got no reason to want us to be arrested and anyway, we're not breaking any laws. I'd not have thought he cares two hoots about these trees.'

'All he cares about is money. I wouldn't put anything past him. He tries to hide it but I've been wondering for a while whether he and his brother are working behind the scenes with Belkin, helping him get building permissions that are borderline, so that he can move more of his operations to our valley, where the land is cheaper. If so, Singleton will probably have realised that this development is upsetting people. It'll probably come as a surprise to him. A greenie he isn't!'

'The land from two houses isn't enough to call a development, surely?'

'It will be starting to look like one if they can get hold of a couple of the other houses in the street and put all the plots together.' He paused to scowl darkly. 'I had a thought in the middle of the night. Singleton's brother might even try to nudge the council towards compulsory purchase of the nearby houses.'

'He'd better not. There would be outright rioting at the town hall if he tried that. And I'd be in the front row of the protesters, Dad, I promise you, even if they arrested me.' She frowned and was silent for a few moments, then said, 'And there's the park nearby.'

'It's heritage-listed too, and so is the little snicket that leads to it from the end of the close. I helped fight for that.

People love going to Magnolia Park on fine days, especially the oldies and those with small children. Eh, and those two magnolia trees are flourishing.'

They stared at one another in horror as the implications of that sank in.

'He wouldn't, surely?' Her voice was a half whisper. 'He's our MP. He's supposed to *help* us, not take away our amenities.'

'Singleton's like Belkin. He'd do anything for money. Only he keeps quieter about his ventures. I wondered at first why they were making such a big effort to purchase the houses on this street, then it all began to fit together. They could squeeze a lot of new houses round here if the land from Magnolia Park was added to that in Hawthorn Close. Not many people remember it but the council tried to do that once before,' he added. 'We had a good JP then who helped us prevent it. She's dead now and we've got that new fellow, Parkin. He's an incomer. I don't know whose side he's on or what he'd do about our heritage.'

She was silent for a moment, then said in a near whisper, 'Surely they haven't got the numbers on the council to subsume our park? It was left to the town on condition that it was never built on.'

'I wouldn't put anything past that trio, Jane. Maybe they've managed to nobble another couple of councillors. Ah, Singleton's driven off now.'

'We'll bother about him tomorrow, then. Time we got you home to bed.'

'I'm staying.'

'You're not. Leave the night watches to the younger

folk, Dad. You know what the doctor said at your last check-up.'

He breathed deeply but agreed to let someone drive him home. 'Leave my wheelchair where it is. It's chained up so no one's going to be able to run off with it and our helpers might like to sit on it when they want to have a rest. I don't mind them doing that as long as they don't fiddle with any of the controls. I use my old wheelchair round the house anyway. This one's too big for some of my doorways.'

She gave him a quick hug, feeling sad at the frailty of his shoulders these days. 'I'll tell Nellie about that when she takes over from me.'

'I'll be back to sit on this one first thing in the morning, mind. You'll not stop me then.'

'Of course not, as long as you get a good night's rest. And in case you think I won't be able to tell, it shows in your face when you don't sleep well, Dad.'

'Sometimes, Jane, you're too sharp for your own good.'

'For some weird reason I care about you.'

He reached out to squeeze her hand. 'You're a good daughter. The very best.'

He let her make arrangements for some neighbours to take him home. But when they'd left him there, he went into his bedroom and got on his phone to his old friend Ben Thorson.

He'd protested at first when Jane insisted he get a mobile phone, but now he didn't know how he'd manage without one.

He and Ben had a long and productive discussion and came to the conclusion that Ben's great-grandson was the best one to help them do any small jobs that were needed.

Norry was a smart young fellow and was also good at finding things out. He was so bright that if you polished him he'd sparkle, as Arthur's mum used to say. Norry was particularly good about IT stuff and had taught Arthur and Ben a lot about what digital tools could do, had changed their minds about all sorts of things, in fact.

When you got to the end of your life, it was good to know there were youngsters like Norry growing up to love your home town and take over the reins of local life.

The two men discussed the details, then Arthur ended the call, leaving it to Ben to contact his great-grandson about their current concerns.

He wasn't surprised when Ben rang back ten minutes later, just as he was getting into bed, to say his great-grandson would be delighted to help them further and would get his friends in to help them too, if necessary.

'See how you like that, Singleton,' Arthur muttered as he snuggled down in bed. He could sleep peacefully now.

He felt quite sure something helpful would come of this little investigation of theirs now that Norry had joined in. That lad knew more about modern stuff than oldies like Arthur ever would be able to now.

The two surly men and the foreman bedded down in Belkin's vans, taking it in turns to keep an eye on the local fools. They left the back door of the van open so that they could jump out of it in a hurry if they were needed.

Belkin had turned up around midnight and parked next to the vans, reversing to and fro till his car was ready to be driven straight out. This made the people keeping a watch on the protesters become suddenly more vigilant.

But after having a brief word with them, he went straight into the house and wasn't seen again, so they gradually relaxed.

Rob, who had been chatting to people, getting acquainted with some more of his fellow townsfolk, went across to see Jane around midnight. 'They haven't gone away, have they? Do you think I'll be needed during the night or should I grab a few hours' sleep and come back on watch in the morning? I'll do whatever you think will help most at this stage.'

'I doubt you'll be needed tonight because there are plenty of other people staying around to deter them. I think Belkin was hoping the numbers of those keeping watch would go down drastically during the night.'

'They don't look to me to have gone down much, though some people have brought sleeping bags or garden chairs.'

'I should guess he's expecting the numbers of people here will shrink as the days pass. They won't do. Nellie and I will make sure of that. Those trees are very special indeed, and our townsfolk are really proud of them. So Belkin can damned well think again about knocking them down.' She breathed deeply and glared at the two vans and large black car parked on the bare ground that had formerly been the pretty gardens of the first two houses till the plants were all bulldozed.

'So it'll be all right if I get some sleep?'

'Definitely, Rob. Anyway, your house is in the close and you'll hear if there's any real trouble. I told your neighbour to go to bed a while ago as well. Ilsa is still looking rather run-down.'

'Yes, but in a strange way, the trouble seems to be

making her perk up a bit. Who knows what can jerk a person out of convalescence? I reckon she was depressed as well at having been so ill for so long.'

She gave him a sly smile. 'You like her, don't you?'

'Yes.'

'And she likes you too.'

He gave her a quick glance. 'You think so? I confess, I've been wondering.'

'I know so. I can always tell. She's nice. If you really like her, don't let her get away. Women are still slower to take the initiative in these budding romances, so it'll be up to you.'

He smiled, not denying that it was a budding romance. 'I won't let her go. I can't remember getting on so well with a woman for a long time. It's partly because I've been too busy with my work, I suppose, but it's not just that. You have to meet someone who ignites that spark. Ilsa is . . . well, rather special and she definitely ignites my spark. See you in the morning, then.'

As he strolled the short distance along the street to his house, he decided not to get undressed in case he needed to rush out to help the defenders.

How far would Belkin go in pursuing this? Would he bring in a bigger group of thugs tomorrow? And why the hell was that man so keen to move his next development to Essington St Mary? There was no obvious patch of unoccupied or undeveloped land in or near this town on which to build a new housing estate.

He looked out of his bedroom window. He could hear the low murmur of voices, see some of the defenders moving around every now and then, while others were sitting in cars or lying around on verges.

There were some very decent people keeping watch and, like them, he didn't want the atmosphere in this valley being drastically changed by an influx of strangers moving into cramped, dormitory-style developments. He might have only just come to live here but already he knew he wanted to settle permanently and was hugely grateful he'd been left the pair of semi-detached houses.

A few people thought this valley old-fashioned and were openly scornful about it, but he considered the way people lived here to be *sane*. That was the best way of describing it if you asked him. Sane.

Ants might enjoy living on top of one another; people didn't usually thrive in such conditions.

Chapter Twenty-One

Belkin woke with a start as the moonbeams shining through the curtainless window shifted across to his face and disturbed him. He couldn't work out for a moment or two where he was, then realised he was in one of the houses at the Hawthorn Close development.

He was annoyed with himself for falling asleep lying on an old extending outdoor chair he'd brought with him. He'd intended to keep a close eye on things to see whether they went as he expected during the night and if they didn't, he'd be making a few changes to his tactics.

Jerking himself and the chair into a more upright position, he stared at his watch. One o'clock in the morning. Hell of a time to be so wide awake.

And hungry. He was definitely hungry.

He went across to stare out of the window. There were still people and lights everywhere. Those stupid locals might be planning to stay all night, but they'd soon get tired of keeping watch when they should be sleeping. He gave it a couple more days before numbers started to decline markedly.

He'd had a rather similar situation a couple of years ago and the protests had quickly fizzled out. It was annoying to have to hang around and wait for that to happen, because time really did cost money, but these days the police were a lot quicker to pounce on anyone hurting the meek little idiots who made up most of society.

He could do without this sort of interference just at the moment, though. Each day lost was costing him a lot of money and he was going through a rather tight patch financially. Most important of all, he didn't want anything to upset the bigger investor who had dipped a toe in the water, so to speak, with this project.

He was short of credit until more of his previous group of houses sold. Unfortunately, slow-downs in the economy also affected sales of new houses and he couldn't do much about that. But sales would pick up as the economy speeded up again. They always did.

He saw a woman pat one of the trees as she walked past. How stupid could you get? All this fuss for a bunch of plants. He glared across at the tree she'd touched. Talk about a ridiculous waste of time.

He made a sudden decision. Whatever it took, he'd do. Whatever. He needed to get things moving more quickly, wasn't putting up with this for long.

He reached for his thermos, thumping a clenched fist down on the windowsill when he realised he'd drunk all the coffee.

Picking up his phone, he rang his wife. It took the bitch a

long time to answer and her voice sounded sleepy. She was worse than his first wife for falling asleep on him.

'What? Oh, it's you, Des. Are you all right?'

'Of course I am. I need more coffee, though, and something to eat. Put some goodies together, and make sure they include my special chocolate biscuits.'

'But the doctor said—'

'Hang the doctor. I need my chocolate. Bring some refreshments here as soon as you can because there aren't any twenty-four-hour shops open at this time of night in such a dump of a town.'

'You want me to get up and do that now?'

'Didn't I just say so?'

'But it's the middle of the night and I was asleep.'

'Well, it'll be the middle of the morning by the time you get here if you don't get off your backside and make me something to eat and drink. And bring something for Harden and a couple of men as well. Ordinary biscuits for them, though, not my choccy bickies.'

He clicked to end the call without giving her the chance to say anything else and stood up, going to use the facilities, shabby as they were. Good thing he'd decided to keep the water connected and the electricity switched on till they actually knocked this hovel down.

After that, he went to stand just outside the front door.

The minute Harden saw him, he came across. 'Do you need anything, Mr Belkin?'

'Not from you. I fell asleep for a while. Anything happen in the last hour or two?'

'No, sir. I half expected Arthur Keevil to order an attack on our men, but he went home.'

'He left his daughter here, though, didn't he? She's just as bad. Dracula in a skirt, that one. Keep a careful eye on her.'

'Yes, Mr Belkin. I am doing.'

He was rather pleased with Harden, whom he'd promoted recently. A bit of guidance and the man would make a useful foreman. Bit squeamish but he'd soon learn that you got nowhere in business without a bit of effort.

It was over half an hour before Des's wife turned up but she'd brought some sandwiches as well as the biscuits, and some tea-and-coffee-making equipment to leave in the house, so he forgave her.

'Well done. You can go home now and leave it to us men. You'll need to bring more supplies for making tea and coffee tomorrow, because the men will need some drinks too and it'll cheer them up at low cost to us. But only bring food for me from now on. We'll send one of the men to that shop that's just down the hill to get stuff for the others. I set up an account there when we first started work and that way it'll be tax-deductible.'

The rest of the night dragged past and to Harden's dismay, Belkin kept coming out to see how things were going. And he got grumpier as the night dragged on.

At one point he said sourly, 'We didn't make much progress yesterday. I wasn't going to stay but I've changed my mind. I want to get the feel of the situation so that I know exactly what to do next and how far to push things to get rid of them.'

'I gather from what I've overheard that they'll be bringing in a fresh lot of people in the morning,' Harden said glumly.

'That Keevil woman is known for her efficiency, damn her.'

'I certainly didn't expect this many to stay for the whole night, sir.'

'No. Neither did I. You stick around out here and I'll just have a little nap inside the house.'

Harden watched him go and then stood there wondering whether there was anything else he could do. He couldn't think of anything at the moment, not without hurting someone, and anyway, his men were outnumbered, but he knew his boss would blow a fuse if he saw him sit down and close his eyes.

Belkin watched his foreman through the front window for a while, wondering whether the man had enough experience to do this job. But they'd had to leave his more experienced foreman in charge at his main development because Chas was good at selling houses as well as organising and supervising the work. He seemed to know exactly how to treat the customers, well, most of the time. Some of them could be difficult to deal with whatever you did or said.

Pity there had been so few of them looking round the show homes lately. But it wasn't just him; all the builders in the county were complaining that sales were slow just now.

He yawned and made himself more comfortable. He'd just allow himself another little nap.

He was woken by the sound of a car outside at this end of the street and found to his surprise that it was light already. He stood up, stretching as he peered out through the front window again. At least you could see the street clearly now he'd had all the bushes and plants in the two gardens knocked down.

Oh, hell! Talk of the devil. Someone was just dropping Arthur Keevil off again and he was looking more alert, as if he'd slept well. Why couldn't he have a stroke like Belkin's father had done? He stopped and pointed towards Belkin's car, saying something to his companion.

Damn! He shouldn't have left it in full sight of the road, should have parked it round the back. He saw the exact moment when Keevil registered whose car it was, and gave it a big broad smile and a rude sign with one hand.

I'll wipe that smile off his face before we're through here, Des vowed to himself. *See if I don't.*

Harden came into the house and said unnecessarily, 'Look who's come back, sir. I didn't expect to see Keevil again this early.'

'I'm tempted to launch an attack now just to see him hobble for shelter.'

His foreman looked at him warily. 'The men are still asleep in the vans, sir. They'll need to wake up properly before we ask them to make any move towards the trees. And they'll want something to eat first, too. Perhaps you and I should discuss tactics and work out what's best before we actually start doing anything. Yesterday's plan failed miserably.'

'Those idiots fooled you easily with that chap pretending to have a heart attack. Tell the men not to back off again, whatever happens, even if it's a real heart attack.'

There was a distinct pause before Harden said, 'Yes, sir.'

'Are the police still stationed at the end of the street?'

'Not at the moment. But they've only just driven away. I'd guess it's a change of shift and the new duty officers will soon turn up.'

'Well, keep your eye on the end of the street and watch out for the police returning, then let me know.'

'Yes, sir.'

Belkin went back to staring out, still talking and thinking aloud. 'I don't want it to take more than a day or two longer to wear down these morons, though we'll have to tread carefully if the police are going to hang around. We don't want them poking their noses in.'

He continued to watch people moving around, smiling at one another. What the hell had they got to smile about?

Some of them were talking to the female who owned the third house, which he was still determined to buy. One month, that's all he'd give her. No, two weeks and then he'd really have a go at her.

A steady stream of people was going into a house further up, the one Drayton had snatched from under him. Presumably they were going to use the facilities. He'd got Drayton on his list to deal with in the near future, too. The sod wasn't going to get away with sneaking in with a ridiculously generous offer for the house and upsetting Belkin's long-term plans.

If he was able to buy the next few houses for development purposes, it'd make a big difference to how the prospects looked here when he gave his presentation to the council about the need for more houses in the town and the possibilities of building a lot of new homes in Hawthorn Close. After all, these were all older buildings, ripe for replacement, and he'd remind them strongly of that. None of the younger folk wanted to buy houses in that style of architecture these days.

It had annoyed him big time to hear that Carswell had

put tenants into the fourth house when he'd paid good money to get rid of the other tenant. And what's more, that sod had known how to deal with that banned fire-starter material that Belkin had bought at great expense. It had worked so well the first time he'd used it and he had enough left to use a couple more times.

He was going to get hold of those houses by hook or by crook. There was always a way and sometimes you had to take risks. 'You can't stop progress,' he muttered. 'And you shouldn't even want to, not if you had any sense. Which was why some of us made our fortunes and others stayed poor.' He'd only just started making his fortune, though, still had a long way to go.

He remained grumpy because his wife hadn't brought the ham sandwiches he liked best. He sent one of the men to buy food for his workers at the nearby café, and sheer hunger drove him to eat a sandwich containing the same sort of the low-fat cheese and salad muck she usually ate.

It wasn't long before the man returned empty-handed and came into the house looking annoyed.

'That café owner refused to serve me because of the trees being threatened, Mr Belkin.'

'But I'd set up an account there!'

'I mentioned that, sir, but he said he was closing it forthwith.'

Belkin held back his anger only with difficulty and handed the chap some money. 'Go and find a place that will sell food to us for cash, then. But be sure to get a receipt.'

Outside, Harden walked about, keeping an eye on the protestors but not going too near them, not with the dirty looks they were casting in his direction. Their numbers seemed to him to have increased slightly. Where had all these people come from?

His employer might have bitten off more than he could chew with these trees. Stupid, the way he was going on about them. He could have just left them where they were and got on with building the new houses. Later on, a couple of accidents or a few squirts of poison would have killed them off quite easily.

He heard footsteps behind him and swung round. His heart sank to see the boss coming out to him again, red in the face with anger.

'While that fellow is out buying food, you can arrange for the JCB we usually hire to be brought back today, Harden. I'm not going to spend all week hanging about. A JCB will make short work of those damned trees.'

Harden looked at him, hesitated, then said, 'You were worried that someone might get hurt if we did that.'

'Well, I'm fed up of paying men to sit around doing nothing, and if those idiots get hurt, it'll be their own fault. Look, there's another damned car turning in to the street. We'll definitely have to use the JCB and end this problem permanently. The sooner it arrives, the better.'

'Yes, sir.' But Harden was getting more and more unhappy about the way things were going. On top of it all, his wife was furious with him for taking this job because some of her friends weren't speaking to her on account of the trees.

Now, he was beginning to worry about something else as well. He didn't want to be arrested because someone had been injured. He drew the line at injuring people.

He ventured a gentle suggestion. 'The numbers of

protestors will go right down after a few days, sir. Wouldn't it be better to wait and keep the JCB in reserve for then?'

'No, it bloody well wouldn't. I want to get on with this job. I've got other fish to fry.'

He had such a furious look on his face that Harden stopped trying to talk sense and waited for the man to return with more food.

The fellow took far longer than expected, but at last he came striding into Hawthorn Close carrying two big carrier bags.

'I had to go to three other shops before I found someone who'd sell to us. How do they know who we are?'

One of the other men had come across, licking his lips as he eyed the food. 'They've put information on the internet about what's going on here, including all our photos.'

His companions gaped at him.

'You should use the net more,' the man told them. 'Keeps you one step ahead.'

'I don't like the thought of people splashing my photo around,' Harden said slowly. 'I don't like it at all.'

'Nor do I,' the man next to him said. 'But you can't stop them now everyone's got a smartphone.'

Harden sighed. 'I'd better tell the boss about it.' He was not looking forward to doing that.

However, Belkin just shrugged. 'Sticks and stones.'

'It doesn't feel good when even the shops are boycotting us.'

'If you can't do the job and want me to appoint another foreman . . .'

'No, sir. Of course I don't.'

Belkin smiled – well, some might call it a smile but Harden

thought it made him look more like a tiger about to pounce on its prey, an elderly, sick tiger not a vibrant, younger one, though.

'The JCB will sort it all out for us later today. You'll see. Just get on with arranging to hire it. No, on second thoughts, leave that to me. I've dealt with Tugwell before.' Belkin went back inside.

Don't let anyone get hurt, Harden prayed as he grabbed one of the sandwiches and a can of lemonade. *Please don't let anyone get hurt.*

This felt bad. The boss didn't seem to realise how much more carefully you had to tread these days. He was too used to thrusting his way through life.

Well, these days there were folk with phones everywhere and you simply couldn't get away with doing some things openly. Once they'd snapped a photo of you doing something illegal, they'd tell the world and you would be in trouble.

What if someone got seriously hurt? That thought didn't seem to upset Belkin but it was a step beyond what Harden ever wanted to get involved in.

Only, he was earning more as a foreman than he'd ever earned before, and his wife was really pleased about that. It'd be hard to go back to a labourer's wages and intermittent work only, plus putting up with her complaints about money.

But that would still be better than ending up in prison.

A woman had been sitting cross-legged on the ground at the verge, hidden by the hedge of Number 3. She was tidying herself up after a night on guard but paused in brushing her tangled hair when her attention was caught by the conversation being held on the other side of the hedge.

She listened carefully and in growing indignation, staying there until Belkin went back into the house because she didn't want him noticing her presence. Then, just as she was about to stand up, a man strode across and joined that slimy toad of a foreman.

She smiled broadly when she heard about the shopkeepers refusing to serve the builder's men. Good for them.

Once she was sure everyone had moved away, she finished tying back her hair, then went and reported what she'd heard to Nellie, who was acting as coordinator of the protest while Jane got some much-needed sleep.

'Well done for keeping still and not letting them know you were there. Shows Belkin doesn't know his enemies if he thinks we'll give up meekly. Spread the word about what you heard and I will too. It'll help keep the people here on their toes. Not that most of them need it, but it never hurts to reinforce people's hatred of your common enemy.' A few moments later, she added, 'I wonder which shop eventually sold to them. We need to find out and gently suggest they don't do it again.'

'I'll see if my daughter can ask around when she does her shopping today. She can't join us because the baby's too little, but she'll be glad to help in other ways and will spread the word about what's going on here any time you like.'

'Good for her. You go and ask for her help and I'll discuss this with Mr Keevil. He's a cunning old devil.' She smiled. 'But charming with it. My mum always had a soft spot for him.' She brushed away a tear at the thought of her mother not being there any longer, then pulled herself together. 'More importantly, Mr Keevil has still got all his brain cells intact, however weak his body is getting.'

Chapter Twenty-Two

Rob woke early and saw from his landing window the faint outline of Ilsa moving around her kitchen next door. So he switched on his coffee maker and went across to invite her for a cup of the properly brewed stuff and some croissants that he'd pulled out of his freezer last night. If that didn't tempt her, nothing would.

She beamed at him and not for the first time he thought what a gorgeous smile she had. And was it his imagination or did she have more colour in her cheeks today?

'I'd really appreciate that, Rob. I'm still a bit short of food supplies. I might have to take a quick trip to the shops today, if I can get in and out of my drive safely. Can I fetch you anything?'

'Yes, please. We'll make a list as we eat and I'll walk beside your car till you get to the end of the street.'

'You're very kind.'

'My pleasure.'

There was another of those moments of silence that were starting to happen between them, where they stared at one another as if trying to understand each other's soul.

When they went outside her house, inevitably they both stared next door, where Belkin's men were lounging around near the lorries.

'Damn them,' he muttered, then led the way through the small gap he'd made in the low fence to get to and from his place. He was hoping they'd be using this way through quite a lot.

She shivered visibly. 'I wonder how long he's going to keep those brutes there? I don't even like to go out and sit in my garden now.'

'I should think it'll take more than a week to convince him that people are serious about saving those trees. And we'll only be able to do that if enough protesters keep turning up to stand guard. Sadly, these protests do usually taper off and I think he's counting on that.'

She frowned in thought and it was a minute or two before she spoke again. 'I don't think these people will do that. They seem to care very deeply about their valley.'

'I hope you're right. It's easier to care about a place when most of the locals are so nice. It isn't just the houses, it's the neighbours and people's attitudes to the world generally. Though there are occasional nastier types everywhere.'

'I agree. Yesterday evening I overheard two people wondering what Belkin might have in mind for the long term.'

'I've been wondering about that too. He's making a remarkable amount of fuss about two trees and a couple of building plots. From what I've heard, his Swindon development is far bigger than this one.'

They were both silent, then she said, 'It does seem strange. Even if he got your properties and mine, it'd still only give him five blocks of land on the close.'

'It's puzzling. That's surely not enough to be worth all this trouble to a man like him?'

'What other source of land is there nearby, then, Rob?'

They both frowned and fell silent, then she gasped. 'Are you thinking what I am? There's that nice little park at the other end of the snicket.'

'He'd have to get the council to change the local regulations to get hold of it, and could they do that legally? I heard someone saying it had been left to the town with firm conditions. It'd take years to get enough people on the council to even try, surely?'

'Unless he's found a loophole in the local laws.'

They both stood thinking about that, then he said slowly, 'I'm feeling more and more suspicious of his long-term plans.'

She shivered. 'He's such a horrible man. And this neighbourhood is so pretty. I hope no one will ever be able to build houses on the park.'

'There are a lot of people doing more than hope. That's why there are so many protesters.'

Arthur's main worry had resurfaced. Someone had heard that a JCB was to be delivered today and used on the trees. The thought of that worried Arthur more than anything else. Would their defences be good enough to keep it away from the trees? There were the protesters to think about, too. He didn't want anyone getting hurt.

He phoned his friend Ben and luckily Ben's great-grandson had just turned up and wanted to speak to him.

'Did you find anything out, Norry lad?'

'I found out quite a few things, Mr Keevil, but I'd rather not talk about them on the phone. Can you come over to Grandad's to discuss it?'

'Is it urgent? Or can it wait till this evening?'

'I think you should know about it now and take steps to deal with it as soon as you can.'

'Oh. Right. I'll get someone to drive me round to Ben's, then.' He ended the call and beckoned to Jane, telling her what he needed.

'Maybe you should go home after that, Dad? It's afternoon now and only a couple of hours till you'd be leaving anyway.'

'Depends what Norry has found out. I might be needed here if there's something major planned for tonight, and if so, you *won't* stop me staying. I'd not put anything past Belkin. He hasn't gone away and left things to his foreman today, has he? No, and he even slept here last night. That's not like him. So something important must be keeping him here.' He shook his head, feeling more and more upset about this whole situation. 'Jane, love, I think I should go and see what young Norry's found out straight away. We're going to need every bit of help we can get, and knowledge is power.'

She surprised him by plonking one of her rare kisses on his cheek. 'I'll find someone to drive you over to Ben's. And Dad?'

'Yes.'

'Take care how you go.'

It made him feel good, that kiss did. She wasn't usually one to express affection publicly. Well, he wasn't either. Maybe it was about time he did while he was still on the right side of the grass.

He turned round, walked back to her, gave her a big hug and kissed her cheek. 'Eh, you're a lovely daughter.' It made him chuckle to see how pink she went.

After that, he left his fancy wheelchair behind, trusting his own legs and walking stick to get him the short distance from the street into the car giving him a lift, then went into Ben's house the same way, even if he did have to go slowly.

Eh, he'd read somewhere and never forgotten it: *Old age gives no quarter*. It was right, too. You could slow down the effects of old age but you couldn't win in the end. By hell, he'd not go meekly, though.

He grinned and added mentally, *As Belkin will find out*.

Corin poked his head into the kitchen, where Lucia was just slipping his anorak on. She'd pinched it from him recently because it would still fit easily round her stomach, which was starting to increase in size now. She said it was more comfortable.

He'd buy her a dozen anoraks if she wanted them.

'You're sure we'll be able to go round that house we bought in Hawthorn Close without being disturbed by the protests?' she asked for the second time.

'I told you: our side's guards are out in full force, more people than I'd ever have expected, that's for sure. And our visit will seem to increase numbers still further, so will be a good thing, not a bad one.'

When they turned in to the street, the car was stopped

when he got level with the third house by a man with a pole who seemed to be acting as a guard to prevent anyone driving further into the street.

'Oh, it's you, Corin. We kept people off your parking place on the drive of your house.'

'We've come to check a few things out in it for when we put tenants in.'

'You'll have no trouble finding some. It's a nice house and a sought-after street. The house has been so useful. There's been a trail of people in and out. It's really kind of you to let us use your facilities there. Some of us have provided more toilet rolls, soap and paper towels, and we're checking that people making coffee there don't leave a mess. We're grateful that you provided the makings for hot drinks as well.'

'It's a cause worth contributing to. Thank you for keeping my parking space clear.'

He drove the short distance to Number 6 and got out to move the two red traffic cones they were using to keep his space, though he was happy for someone else to park in the space next to it on his drive.

When Lucia got out, she stood by the car, staring up and down the street in amazement. 'I hadn't realised how many people would get involved in the protests.'

'It's good to see, isn't it?' He'd only let her join him after phoning Jane Keevil to check that things were quiet, but he'd not told her that.

'It's wonderful to see people pulling together.'

They went inside and began checking out each room and taking notes, because when this protest was over, he wanted to get the place ready to let as quickly as he could.

It was a commodious residence with four bedrooms, so should rent out quickly, even though its interior was rather old-fashioned. He wasn't going to remodel bathrooms or do more than touch up the paintwork and make sure everything was in working order.

He couldn't rent out the house, though, till there was a long-term resolution to what Belkin was doing.

And even then he was going to vet any would-be renters very carefully indeed. He didn't want the builder planting anyone there ready for another attempt.

Arthur got out of the car slowly and carefully, as he did most of his moving around these days, and used the walking stick to keep his balance as he went towards Ben's front door.

It opened before he got there and Norry stood grinning at him. 'What kept you, Mr Keevil? Were you running round doing errands?'

He gave the lad's shoulder a quick squeeze. 'Cheeky devil.'

They went through into the sitting room and he took his usual place on an old maroon armchair. Like the ones in his own house, the furniture here had higher seats that were easy for older folk to sit down on and stand up from.

'What's so urgent, then?' he asked.

Ben gestured towards his great-grandson.

The lad's smile vanished. 'You were right to think Belkin had some bigger plans than just knocking the old houses down and building on those two pieces of land. And what's more, either he has a backer for his plans, or he's working for someone else. I haven't been able to find out which it is.

The other person has influence locally, it seems, but no one is even saying his name out loud, and I've even wondered if there are a few people involved.'

Arthur let out an angry growl. 'We need to find out who the main backer is, then. The ideas man or leader or whatever you want to call him.'

'Or her.'

'Yes. Or her. How did you find out that Belkin is plotting with these others?'

'I hacked into his email system. Luckily for us, he's skimped on how the online security was set up and he's also careless about how he uses it. I don't think he understands the risks of modern technology. Or maybe he's simply not a man who looks after the details properly.' His expression grew more solemn as he added, 'From what they're saying, Belkin has got someone on the local council who's going to help them change the by-laws.'

Arthur whistled softly in surprise. 'They said that openly?'

'I told you: not openly exactly. They said it online because they think their emails are secure and they're not. It'll likely be our dear MP's brother.' Norry looked more solemn than ever as he added, 'What's worrying me is that Chad Jones has just been in a serious accident and might have to resign from the council because it'll take him a while to recover.' He looked even more serious as he added, 'It sounded to me from a couple of Belkin's emails as if this wasn't an accident, though I have no way of proving that.'

There was dead silence and the two older men exchanged horrified glances.

'How did it happen?' Ben asked his great-grandson.

'It seems Mr Jones's car brakes failed and it had only just been serviced.'

'Someone from the valley risking a life? What is the world coming to?'

'This other person whose name we've yet to discover sent an email that sounded angry that the accident had been so serious. He'd apparently wanted only minor damage done to Mr Jones.'

'Is Belkin a potential murderer? Why would he really go to those lengths?'

'Well, in a later email there were threats that Belkin would be the next to find himself in trouble if he didn't pay up what had been agreed.'

'Hellfire! What's going on behind the scenes?'

After a pause, Arthur said slowly, 'I've heard from other sources that Belkin is short of money, but I thought it was due to the general downturn in house sales. We have to find out who he owes money to.'

'What about our beloved member of parliament?' Ben asked suddenly. 'Do you think he could be involved?'

Arthur had a quick think, then shook his head. 'I'd not have thought he'd do anything to hurt people physically.'

Ben looked across at him sadly. 'This is getting more serious than I'd ever expected, Arthur lad. Who knows how far they'll go if they get desperate?'

'Yes. We'll have to press on, see what our Norry can find and keep our own eyes open too. And at the same time we have to win our battle for the trees. It'd take another two hundred years to grow replacements to that size. You and I will be lucky to last another ten years.'

He didn't stay for a cup of tea, just got Norry to drive

him back to Hawthorn Close in his old rattletrap of a car.

'Are you sure this won't break down on us, lad?'

'The engine is in good order, Mr Keevil. I've brought it up to scratch myself. I haven't had time to see to the bodywork yet, but I will.'

When they got back, Norry pulled over to the side of Larch Tree Lane and looked at him. 'I'll keep my eyes and ears open, I promise. When is the JCB being delivered?'

'I thought they would send it this morning but I can't see any signs of it.'

Arthur got slowly out of the little car. He turned to say, 'Well done, lad,' then walked slowly along the street.

He'd thought that if they all pulled together, in the end they'd stop Belkin destroying their trees, but he was now wondering how far the builder was prepared to go.

In the meantime, he went and sat in his wheelchair and let his stupid heart calm down again.

Chapter Twenty-Three

Terence Singleton was feeling increasingly worried. Rash actions that involved him in any way whatsoever always upset him. He was a firm believer in taking your time, thinking through every detail of a course of action and even then doing the very minimum necessary to solve or appear to solve a problem.

This approach had worked very well for him so far. The duties of his role as a member of parliament could often be solved simply by promising to *try* to do something. If you failed, you were suitably apologetic and if things went well, you took as much of the credit as you could grab.

Best of all, he'd found ways to earn more money through the insight he gained as an MP. Knowing things the general public didn't could be useful, though he'd rejected as many offers of business deals as he'd accepted.

Having money in the bank made him feel good. Well, it usually did. He was getting increasingly concerned about the situation in Hawthorn Close because Belkin was handling it badly, in his opinion. He wished he'd not got involved.

Couldn't the fool leave the trees where they were and let them 'die' later of allegedly natural causes? There was still time to backtrack on that. But no, Belkin had fired up and been damned rude when that was mentioned as a possible course of action. The fool seemed determined to rush in heavy-handed.

Terence wished he'd kept out of it, however lucrative it might turn out to be. All he could do for the moment was continue to keep an eye on the whole situation in the valley. He'd try to find a way to pull himself clear of it. He might have grown up 'dirt poor' as the saying went, but that had taught him a lot. He hadn't stayed poor, had he? And he hadn't got caught doing anything that would upset people.

Being the MP to this valley's constituency was as perfect as life could get. This place had stayed delightfully untouched by major developments and was now ripe for harvesting. He'd spent years keeping an eye on the situation and had thought it was time to invest a little, so had accepted Belkin's offer of a share in his new enterprise. He wished he hadn't. The trouble was, how did he now get out of it? Belkin simply didn't have the money to buy him out.

He arranged for the two of them to meet in the far corner of Magnolia Park, where the recycling bins had been installed by some stupid green zealot in the council works department. There were rarely many people around in that area after the teatime rush to dump things, however, so it could be a useful place to meet. He was carrying one of those flimsy new paper carrier bags with him full of rubbish to toss into the appropriate bin and walk away if anyone else came there, so that there seemed a genuine reason for his presence.

The paper carrier bags were like the ones used just after the war. Strange how they'd come into fashion again. The bottoms dropped out of them if you put anything too wet in as they had all those years ago.

He didn't waste time on chit-chat when Belkin arrived but fixed him with a very firm gaze and said, 'I strongly suggest you leave those trees to die "naturally". It'll take longer but it'll have the same result. What's the rush?'

The builder stared at him as if he was crazy and rattled off a series of figures about the extra costs a waiting game would create, costs that worried Terence because they suggested that Belkin was short of operating capital and might even ask for further investment to prevent going under. Had he got in over his head financially?

He tried to forestall this by saying, 'Waiting is a necessary expense and we'll just have to wear it. We don't want people finding out about our long-term objectives, do we?'

'They won't. People are too stupid to see beyond their noses.'

'Most are, but some aren't. And there are enough of the latter around to cause trouble. We could—'

'Look, Singleton, I've been making make good money as a builder for the last few years and it wasn't by going the long way round. Time *is* money in the building industry.'

'But what if one of the protesters gets hurt by this JCB you're bringing in?'

'They'll get out of its way. You can't mistake a JCB when it's trundling towards you.'

'Accidents can happen at any time. People who're protesting don't always take care what they're doing. If there's an accident, the police will be brought in to investigate.'

Belkin glared at him. 'I keep telling you that this small protest is a storm in a teacup. It'll soon blow over. They always do.'

'In that case, I'd prefer to take my money out of this investment.'

'No can do. The money is out being used and won't be available for a while. Console yourself with the fact that you're going to make a really good profit eventually.'

'Then I must insist you take more care how you deal with this.'

'You can't insist. Just stay out of the day-to-day work, which you assured me you preferred to do, and leave me to handle this. Now, I can't stand here chatting. I have things to do, even if you don't.' And with a roll of the eyes, he walked briskly away.

Singleton didn't call him back. He could tell a brick wall when he met one and didn't intend to beat his head against this one. He was furious about his advice being ignored in such a cavalier fashion, though. He'd have to take some precautions of his own from now on.

He tipped the contents of the carrier bag into the wastepaper recycling bin in case anyone was watching and walked slowly away, still worrying. Belkin was wrong.

There was no such word as 'always' as far as human beings were concerned. People could be extremely unpredictable. The protest might or might not continue vigorously.

What's more, there were some very old people on guard duty in front of those trees and they would be far less likely to be capable of getting out of the way of a JCB quickly enough.

He must either find a way to handle Belkin or get rid of him.

The builder would not find that he accepted the situation meekly. Terence would rather lose his money than be caught out doing something dodgy.

As Singleton walked off round the corner, Murad let out a muffled groan of relief and stood up from where he'd been crouching behind one of the bins. He eased his shoulders and legs. Bit of luck that he'd been crouching down sorting out his recyclables when the other two men met.

He'd risked peeping out and it had been obvious that they were here to talk to one another, not deposit rubbish. Singleton might be carrying a crumpled paper carrier bag but it had hardly anything in it and Belkin wasn't making any pretence of bringing anything to throw away.

Murad eased his shoulders again. It had been very uncomfortable crouching in the narrow space behind the bottle container and not a perfect place acoustically. He'd been able to listen to much of the discussion but hadn't caught everything they said as clearly as he'd have liked because of occasional traffic noises nearby. But he'd caught enough to feel he'd chanced upon a useful lead to the bigger problems behind the scenes in the valley, problems that they were investigating slowly and carefully.

Was Belkin really going to order his men to use a JCB on the trees and let it shove protesters out of the way? It could hurt someone badly if they fell under the front and were caught beneath its treads.

He shoved the rest of his own stuff quickly into the appropriate bins and hurried back to his car. He and Vicki had better be in a position to intervene if the protesters seemed at risk.

Damn! That would really blow their cover.

Chapter Twenty-Four

Amy felt like taking an hour or two off so drove into Essington to see if she could find an outfit suitable for a wedding. She didn't want to wear one of her business suits, didn't even like to see them now and had left them in her suitcase. But she couldn't go to a wedding in casual clothes and she wanted to look her best for her great-aunt's special day.

The love between Maggie and James was like a shining beacon of happiness. It made you feel good just to see it. And it felt as if they'd welcomed her warmly into their space.

She easily found the little dress shop Maggie had told her about and liked the way a single outfit was elegantly displayed in the window. That dress wouldn't suit her but it was pretty and whoever had arranged it had excellent taste. She hadn't realised till she saw it how very much she was longing for feminine clothes.

She pushed the door open and a woman looked up from unpacking boxes.

'Welcome! I do apologise for the clutter. I don't usually greet people with a messy shop but these have just been delivered and one of my customers is waiting impatiently for her new outfit.' She pushed the boxes carefully to one side. 'How may I help you?'

Amy explained her needs, ending, 'I don't want anything remotely like a business suit. I've had to wear them all too often during the past few years. I've still got several that are too good to throw away though I can't see me ever wearing one of them willingly again.'

'Ah. Maybe I can help you there. I own a second-hand clothing shop just down the street as well as this one. If your suits are in good condition, you could deposit the unwanted ones there. You'll get a credit for use in either shop when they sell your clothes, your choice which shop.'

'Wow, that would be great. I'll bring them in another time.' Another vindication of her mother's old motto: *Don't throw anything away that you might use some other day.*

'Great. I'm Leona, by the way.'

'Amy. Pleased to meet you.'

'To get back to the reason you came here, I have some typical wedding outfits but I'm guessing from what you've said that you'd like something casually pretty rather than formally elegant.' She stood thinking for a minute or two and studying Amy's appearance, then said, 'Ah!' and led the way into the back room, still talking and gesticulating. 'The ones on this rack are labelled *Party Outfits* and it's usually the younger folk who buy them. There are a couple that might suit you and your lovely dark hair for a wedding.'

She pulled out a summer dress in a colour Amy could only describe as 'restrained scarlet' and held it against her customer, turning her with one gentle hand to face a full-length mirror. The fabric had a faint ripple pattern in paler shades of the same colour.

'The colour suits you and I'm betting the style will too. Why don't you try it on and find out?'

Amy gazed at it. She couldn't remember ever owning such a pretty dress let alone one so brightly coloured. The dress was simple, with a bias-cut frill round the bottom of the skirt, quite a low neckline and slightly puffed elbow-length sleeves.

'You don't think it's too young for me?'

'Definitely not. But try it on so that you can get the full effect. I'll tell you the truth about how you look, I promise, and I'm a good judge.'

Amy went into the cubicle, changed into the dress and was lost. She didn't even need the proprietor's approval to buy it. It fitted perfectly and did indeed suit her colouring, bringing a subtle warmth to her cheeks that cosmetics could never achieve. Although it was simple, there was something about the shape of the skirt, the way it fell from her hips and swayed as she moved. It screamed 'elegant', although she didn't really understand exactly why.

She went into the shop to show Leona, who said, 'You tell me what you think first!'

'It's gorgeous.'

'I agree. I knew it'd suit you.'

Amy didn't even ask the price. 'I'll take it.'

'I'm not trying to push you into buying more clothes, I swear, but if this is a type of dress you don't usually wear, do you have some sort of jacket or wrap that will go with it in case the wedding day is cool?'

'No, nothing.' She hesitated but it had been so long since she'd indulged herself and she didn't want to spoil the effect of that dress. 'Do you have something suitable?'

'Yes.' Leona went across to a row of hangers and unhooked a wrap a few shades darker than the dress with threads of glittering red just above the fringed ends. It would probably suit one of her other outfits too, it was so subtle a shade.

Amy didn't feel guilty, couldn't do because this was such a perfect outfit for her aunt's wedding and for use afterwards – if she ever developed a normal social life again.

But she would be wearing it first and foremost for herself, because it made her feel 'right'.

When she got back and tried on the outfit to show Maggie, her great-aunt beamed at her. 'Gorgeous clothes and almost perfect as an outfit.'

'Almost?'

'You need a necklace. One as simple and elegant as the dress. There's one in the box of family jewels that I think would look lovely with that outfit, a gold chain with a delicate ruby pendant in an art nouveau setting.'

'I can't borrow something so valuable.'

'Why ever not? Please don't refuse. It's only sitting in the safe at the moment and jewellery is made to be worn not hidden. Besides, you're the only family there is apart from me, so of course you can borrow it – any of the pieces, in fact. We Hatheralls don't own this jewellery, we're simply the custodians for each new generation, who can enjoy wearing it and then pass it on.' She took a deep breath and added something it hadn't taken her long to decide. 'You'll be the next custodian, anyway.'

'What do you mean?'

'Who do you think will inherit Larch House? Not my cousin Sheila, that's for sure.'

Amy gaped at her. 'Do you mean what I think?'

'Unless you have any objections to being the heir.'

'But you hardly know me.'

'I felt I knew you straight away. And you're the only Hatherall of the senior line left apart from me. Don't tell me you didn't love Larch House on sight. Your feelings for it show in your face.'

They stared at one another, then Amy burst into tears.

Maggie gathered her close. 'What's wrong, darling? Tell me.'

'Nothing whatsoever. I'm just so – happy. I've never felt to belong anywhere as I do here.'

Her great-aunt gave one of those delightful gurgles of laughter. 'That's all right, then. Phew, what a relief! Cry as much as you like as long as those are happy tears. I won't have to change my will. But though I'm telling you now that you'll be the heir, I intend to live till a ripe old age, so I hope you won't be getting the place for a decade or two.'

Amy stood looking round, still unable to believe that she could ever own this glorious house.

Maggie made a sweeping gesture with one hand. 'There's no reason you shouldn't continue to live here, however. Heaven only knows there are plenty of rooms to spare.'

It was Amy's turn to pull Maggie close and give her a big hug. 'Thank you. I still find it hard to believe but I can't think of anything that would make me happier. And I feel it's a *home*, not a mere house.'

Someone applauding made them break apart and they saw James standing by the outer door. 'What is this, a love fest?' he teased.

'I've told Amy about her inheritance.'

'And that made you both cry?'

'Can't you recognise happy tears, darling?'

'If that's the case, I'd better join in.' He went across to pull Maggie close, then they both tugged their visitor into a three-way embrace and he said, 'Even I can see that you've fallen in love with Larch House, Amy.'

'Yes, I have.'

'Then I think we should do as Maggie suggested and set you up with a completely self-contained flat so that you can live independently, following whatever pursuits you please, until we're out of your way permanently.'

Maggie added softly, 'That way you'll have both the independence and the sense of belonging you need, dear.'

Amy shook her head in amazement. 'I can't get over how much space you have here. Fancy being able to offer me a flat to live in, just like that.' She snapped her fingers to emphasise her surprise, then her expression grew serious. 'But you must let me pay for the conversion. I have enough money to buy a house of my own, so it seems only fair.'

'Whatever. We'll look into that after the wedding and if you do put money in, it'll be arranged legally, so that you own a tiny share of the house already. I don't think it'll cost a huge amount to create a flat, though. The corridor you're currently occupying would make a good one if we closed it off at the landing, don't you think. You'll need a sitting room, kitchen and spare bedrooms for when you have friends to visit.'

'I don't have any close friends left.'

'But you'll make some new ones, I'm sure.'

As they all moved apart, James turned to Maggie. 'We need to talk about our wedding, darling. Something's cropped up.'

'Should I leave you to it?' Amy asked.

'Heavens, no. I'm not going to reveal any deadly secrets.' He turned back to Maggie. 'I don't know how word got out but a couple of guys I worked with regularly overseas, who are really good friends of mine, have heard that I'm getting married and are assuming they'll be joining the festivities. Do you mind if we invite them? I know you haven't met them yet, but one of them saved my life a few years ago, and I'm quite close to them both. They'll probably be coming to visit us regularly and the one who's married will welcome you and me. You'll like his wife, I'm sure.'

Maggie nodded and gave him a rueful smile. 'I confess I've been thinking about one or two other people I've known for a long time and worrying that they'll be upset if they're left out.'

He nodded. 'Not to mention my family, who really ought to be invited, though my son may not be able to get away from the farm easily.'

'Also, I've just heard from an old friend. Rachel has asked for my help, nothing to do with the wedding but I'd like to put her up for a while. She used to live round here and we played together as kids, but she went to live in Cornwall with her second husband a few years ago. Sadly he died recently and the house goes to his children from his first marriage. They've never been exactly welcoming to his second wife so she's looking for a place of her own and they haven't invited her to go on living there when it's handed over, so she's thinking of coming back to live in this area.'

They exchanged rueful smiles.

'John Donne was right,' James said. 'No man is an Ilsand.'

'No woman, either. We can't avoid inviting your friends or mine. Rachel wants to come here a few days before the wedding. She doesn't know about us being together yet, it's happened so quickly. I'd really like to invite her to stay for a few days. If she still likes it in the valley, she'll look for somewhere to buy. She says she has more friends in the district than she ever did in Cornwall.'

'Well, you can't refuse to give her shelter, can you? Man proposes, life disposes, eh? So much for our small, simple wedding.'

'I don't mind really. As long as we get married and no one expects me to wear a white blancmange of a dress. The wedding still doesn't have to be terribly formal, surely? We can keep it simple.'

They gave each other one of 'those looks' again so Amy said quietly, 'I'll go and change back into my everyday clothes again.' She smiled as she went upstairs because she wasn't sure either of them had actually noticed her leave.

She wished sometimes that she had been that close to a partner. Instead she'd married a man who'd seemed charming but had turned out to be a really nasty type if he didn't get his own way.

She'd deeply regretted rushing into marrying him, but

knew she'd been manipulated into it. Well, at least she hadn't been stupid enough to stay with him when he turned out to be rough with women.

And what was she thinking about him for? He was out of her life now permanently and good riddance to him.

She paused to stroke the gleaming wood of the beautiful old door before she went into her bedroom. She loved this house so much already, couldn't believe it would be hers one day.

It occurred to her abruptly that she really ought to provide the family with an heir.

Well, she didn't need to do that straight away so could see what the future brought.

Ilsa felt uneasy and kept moving round her house, checking what was going on outside. Her home was uncomfortably close to the two houses Belkin was preparing to knock down and any time she was on her own she felt on edge.

She stared out of her front window at intervals, both worried and glad that there was an increasingly large group of people gathering in the street. From time to time she walked through the house to look out of the back windows at her own patio.

When she saw Belkin come out to the rear of the nearest of his two houses, she wondered what he was doing there, so stayed at the rear to make sure he didn't do any damage to her garden.

He began walking up and down the back, so she took a couple of quick steps back, hoping she was out of sight behind the curtain. Why was he pacing about? He kept looking at his watch, as if waiting for someone but no one arrived.

After a while he brandished both clenched fists in the air as if angry at the world and strode back inside Number 2.

It had only taken a couple of weeks for the empty house to start looking neglected and ready to fall down, yet he hadn't had any actual demolition work done on it. It was the exterior that had borne the brunt of his efforts so far after he'd had the gardens cleared and flattened. Every single plant was gone now.

Who had he expected to come and meet him? She was fairly certain he didn't have any friends in the town, and anyway friends wouldn't come round at a time like this.

Only, if someone was arranging to do a dirty trick for him, which she fully expected of that rat, they might be able to sneak into the back garden without being noticed through the remains of the hedge that had once separated the first two houses. With crowds surging here and there, rearranging themselves haphazardly, a person could stay in the background quite easily and not be noticed.

When Rob came across to join her from the back of his house, she was glad Belkin had gone inside and hurried to let her neighbour in before the builder saw him.

Once inside, Rob pulled her to him for a hug and a quick kiss, and that was lovely.

'What a mess all this is,' she said as they moved apart. 'I'm on edge all the time at the moment. Fancy a cup of coffee?'

'Later perhaps. I've just had one with Murad and I wanted to discuss something with you.'

'Go on.'

'He and Vicki are worried about the ordinary people caught in this mess. They don't want to reveal that they're police, but they may have to intervene if the situation grows violent. They're particularly worried about those two oldies in wheelchairs.'

'They'd call for back-up, I suppose.'

'Yes. But what Vicki suggested was that you and I should keep watch on the rear of Belkin's properties, which would relieve them of one job. Your house is ideally situated for that. And if we stay away from the windows, they're hoping he won't realise he's being watched. What do you think? Will you let your house be used for that and join me in keeping watch?'

'I think that's an excellent idea. I've been looking out at the back from time to time anyway. He keeps coming out and looking round as if he's expecting someone.'

Rob gave her one of his teasing smiles, pressed one hand to his chest and put on a mock soulful look. 'So you can put up with my company for a while?'

She chuckled. 'I'll put up with your company any time.' Then the joke turned into reality as he put his arms round her. He was a lovely, touchy-feely person.

His voice came out slightly husky. 'What a time to meet someone you're attracted to! I'd rather do my courting in more peaceful circumstances.'

She looked at him in shock. 'Courting?'

'An old-fashioned term, but the idea of pair bonding never seems to go out of fashion, whatever name people give it. Once this is over, could you face seeing me every day?'

'Sounds wonderful. I enjoy your company hugely.' She

twined her arms round his neck. 'But I do think a bargain like that should be sealed with a kiss.' She took the initiative this time and demonstrated.

When they came up for air, he plonked a quick kiss on the tip of her nose. 'Consider the bargain sealed. Now, we'd better get on with our task.' He studied the room. 'If we pull the table further across and put it near the window, with a few things like cereal packets on top of it, it'll help hide our presence.'

They did that, then stood back and Rob said, 'I'm hoping something will come out of this chaos about the trees to make Belkin give up plotting to take over the whole street.'

'He won't manage that, surely? Not with most of the locals against him?'

'Vicki has got the impression that he won't give up easily. And he's already got a foothold in the council too via Singleton's brother.'

Ilsa glared in the direction of the first two houses. 'Well, he's not having my house, whatever he does. Oh, look!'

Belkin came out of his house, stared from side to side, then picked up a stone from what was left of the former rockery and hurled it towards Ilsa's house. It missed the window but hit the wall close to it.

Anger filled her. 'How dare he?'

'Wait a minute. Got a camera handy?'

She picked up her phone and brandished it. 'If you stay here out of sight, he'll think I'm alone and be more likely to do something else nasty. I'm going outside and I'll let him see me taking a photo of him.'

'Be careful. I'm surprised he did that. Murad said Belkin

didn't usually play an active role in causing trouble. He gets others to do his dirty work. He must be too angry to think straight. I can't guess at any other explanation for that stupid action, certainly not a sensible one.'

'I'll show him!' She went out on to the patio and took a quick photo just as Belkin was lifting his arm to hurl another rock. 'Should make good proof if I have to put in any damage claims,' she called to him. 'You won't make me change my mind.'

He jerked in surprise and let the rock fall, staring round as if to check whether anyone else was around. 'You will change. I'll make sure of that one way or the other.'

'I definitely won't.'

He pretended to shoot her with an imaginary gun. She'd never seen any adult make that childish gesture with such a vicious expression on their face.

'What benefit could he possibly get from breaking my windows?' she wondered aloud as he went back inside Number 2.

Rob shook his head. 'He seems to have persuaded himself that he can wear you down. He's acting like a gangster in a very poor B movie. It's as if he's lost touch with reality.'

'Well, he's not getting my house,' she repeated.

Rob smiled at her. 'You know, you've been looking a lot better these past few days.'

'I've been feeling a lot better. It's partly down to meeting you. It's good not to be on my own.'

There was a sound from the rear and Belkin came out again. This time he didn't even look at her house.

But they watched him and saw his face brighten as a man pushed his way through the remains of the back hedge.

Chapter Twenty-Five

When the phone rang, Lucia picked it up, wishing she hadn't when she heard Deanna's voice.

'I need to speak to Corin. It's urgent. Really, *really* urgent.' She started sobbing.

'Hang on. I'll get him for you.'

She went to find her husband and held out the phone. 'It's Deanna and she sounds extremely upset.'

He took it from her. 'Corin here. What's wrong?' He set the phone to speaker mode and put it on a small table, gesturing to his wife to sit down and listen with him.

'Everything's wrong. It's Didier. He's been lying to me, *using* me.'

'Shouldn't you be talking to your mum or dad about that?'

'I have done. Dad says I must tell you about it as well before I leave.'

'Leave?'

'I'm moving out of the country for a while.'

'If things have gone so wrong here, it sounds a good idea to have a complete change of scenery.'

'Yes, but I need to tell you a few things before I go. First, Didier isn't at all interested in opening a café in your bunker. That's just a front. He's been using you as well as me. Actually, he's been working with that horrible Belkin creature.'

'*What?*' If so, he'd fooled Corin as well.

'They've got long-term plans for developing this valley and that includes taking over your land and some of the public land too.'

'How the hell do you know that?'

After a gulp and a moment's silence, she went on, 'He'd stopped being so nice and he said something that upset me a lot the other day about how stupid I was. Then when I asked what he really wanted in the valley, he said it was none of my business and if I had any sense I'd keep quiet about what he's doing. When he pretended he really did love me, I pretended to believe him and agreed not to say a word. But I know now that he doesn't love me and never did.' She sobbed again.

'How do you know that?'

'I overheard a phone call later. I think they're going to force people to sell their homes, first in Hawthorn Close, then somewhere else. He ended up by saying how much he was looking forward to getting rid of me once they'd sorted the first stage out.' Her voice grew solemn. 'I was so angry that later I went through the papers in his briefcase when he was out at a meeting to find out what was really going on.'

'Doesn't he keep it locked?'

'I know where he hides the key. I found too many papers to read before he came home so I photocopied them and put the originals back. I'll email a set of copies to you as soon as we finish talking.'

'That's brilliant. But how can he expect to take over people's houses if they refuse to sell? And he can't just take over public land.'

'He's intending to do it gradually, one sneaky step after another. Compulsory purchases of houses, change of council zoning, bribes, violence too, even. He was boasting about it on the phone. If he's got one big fault it's his own arrogance.'

'He doesn't have the power to do all that.'

'The local member of parliament is in the plot too, apparently. I don't exactly understand what he's going to do for them but Didier and Belkin are talking about pulling the wool over his eyes and simply using him till he's superfluous, then getting rid of him at the next election.'

This all seemed unreal, except it could fit together. 'I'd not have expected Belkin to plan something on that scale.'

'He's not on his own, Corin. And that Singleton fellow has a brother on the council as well as his own connections through being an MP.'

As this sank in, he said, 'Your father's right. You're best getting away. I'm really grateful that you told me about it, though. Do go on.'

'Dad said you'd be a good person to do something about it. He said you've been in some sticky situations and got yourself and others out of them.'

'I do my best.'

'I'm not staying around to find out. Dad agrees. He says I should take myself right out of the picture once I've told you.'

More sobbing, so he said gently, 'I'm sorry about this, Deanna. But better that you've found out now than later.'

'That's what Mum said, but it *hurts*, Corin. Anyway, that's it. I'm going to America for a while but you're the only one I'm telling and I'm not even telling you where. Dad's got some cousins there. He says they'll look after me.'

There was another silence, then she said, 'There you are, I've sent the copies of the papers to you.'

A few seconds later something pinged into his inbox. 'They've arrived.'

'I'll leave you in peace, then.'

'Just let me check that I can open them.'

He did that easily and stared in annoyance at the first one. 'They're through OK. Good luck in America, Deanna.'

'Thanks. Hope you have a lovely baby. Maybe I'll have one someday, only I don't seem to meet the right sort of guys for that.' She put her phone down without even saying goodbye.

He looked at Lucia, who was looking as astounded as he felt.

'Poor girl,' she said quietly.

'Yes. I'll forward the copies to you and then we can both have a quick read.'

An hour later, she came into his study.

He looked up. 'I was about to come and find you. Have you read enough to form any definite opinions?'

'Yes. Something long-term and nasty is being set up that will hurt a lot of smaller people in the valley if they get away with it. I know you've still got connections with people dealing with national security and crime, Corin. You should pass the papers on to them. They know and trust you, and even if it's not in their remit, they'll be able to pass them on to the right people to contact.'

'I think we've got someone closer to home who can help: Rob's two tenants are police officers. I'm going to call Vicki and Murad first because they're undercover here for some reason. It may even be connected with this. Stranger coincidences have happened.' He put one arm round her shoulders. 'I don't wish you to become any further involved than this, Lucia. You and the baby are too precious to risk involvement. And actually, you and I are not the ones who should be dealing with a major fraud scheme.'

He pulled away and picked up his phone again. 'If our two local officers are at home, I'll go and see them straight away and tell them what's come to light.'

To Corin's relief, Vicki answered the phone straight away.

'I need to see you, urgently. Police business.'

'I'm at home keeping an eye on the protesters. Can you come here or does this need police attendance at your place?'

'I can come there and tell you.'

'Then come straight away. Good thing you've got a parking place in the street. It's more crowded here now than it was yesterday. Can you come across the back gardens from your house to ours?'

'Easily. Oh, and I've got some digital files you should

see. I'll email them to you if you'll give me a secure address.'

He sent them off and drove down to Hawthorn Close, where he parked in front of his house. Taking his backpack, he went inside then crossed the rear patio to get to the house next door as unobtrusively as possible.

Vicki came to open the back door. 'Murad's reading quickly through that stuff you sent and has let out a few exclamations of surprise. Come inside.'

Murad waved one hand at him without looking away from the screen.

Vicki went across the room. 'I'll just leave the hall door open so that I can peep out occasionally to check what's going on at the front.'

Murad gestured to a dining chair. 'Do sit down. I've only skimmed through a few documents but I'm sure already that you're right and we do need to pass this information up the line. Actually, I didn't wait to ask you but sent it straight to my boss. I hope that's all right with you?'

'Of course it is.'

There was the sound of people arguing outside in the street and Vicki got up to peer out. 'There are one or two new people causing problems out there. I wonder who they are, goodies or baddies. We've got uniforms on under our tracksuits in case we have to intervene.'

Murad was looking worried as he peered out. 'I think Belkin's planted one or two rough guys in among the crowd. He's probably intending to stir things up.'

Corin grimaced. 'From what I've heard, he's used violence as a tool before. I checked with a friend when this trouble first started and Belkin's been lucky not to have been jailed a couple of times. He managed to wriggle out of it by pleading ignorance and paying hefty fines. I suspect he's trying to move into the big league of developers, but I don't think he's got the financial backing for that, or the mental capacity. He's too much at the mercy of his temper.'

'There might be big money to be made but there are big risks involved too,' Murad said.

'Trouble is, our dear local MP is going round saying there's a shortage of housing in the valley and some people on the council seem inclined to work with him to attract builders. But you don't solve a problem like that by creating the slums of the future and destroying the architectural gems of the past.'

Vicki said sadly, 'Or by ruining the most beautiful parts of the countryside. People need places to go where they can breathe fresh air and enjoy the greenery.'

There was another outburst of yelling from the street and Murad grimaced. 'In the meantime, things are rapidly approaching flashpoint out there.'

'And that man seems to be itching to touch a match to the fuse.'

Chapter Twenty-Six

Earlier that day, Belkin had at last managed to get through to Tugwells' Equipment Hire.

'I need one of those JCBs of yours again this afternoon.'

'Ah. I'm afraid they're both already hired out for today.'

Belkin didn't believe him. There had always been one free before. 'Then find one from somewhere else.'

'I can't produce one out of thin air.'

'You have other contacts round here. Get me a JCB or I'll not only take my business away from you permanently but put the word round everywhere that Tugwells' isn't a reliable firm to deal with.'

Silence, then, 'Well, I can't perform miracles and partway through the afternoon is the soonest I can get one to you, Mr Belkin.'

'See that you do it, then. And we'll keep it overnight. I have a couple of important jobs that need attending to.'

Mr Tugwell put the phone down, grimacing.

His son looked across the office. 'What's wrong, Dad?'

'Belkin wants a JCB ASAP. And I can't afford to lose his other business. But I don't like the thought of what he may be intending to use it for.'

'I heard you tell him our two were hired out but that's not true. There's one of ours standing round the back.'

'Well, I don't want to hire it to him, right?'

'He's causing a lot of trouble round the place. My friend Norry is up in arms about what he's doing in Hawthorn Close.'

'I don't like the sound of it, either.'

Joss stared at his father. 'You've got that look on your face, Dad. What are you plotting?'

'Not sure. I don't want you to be involved in it, though. It'd be too obvious who set it up. I need to speak to your pal Norry, and quickly. He's a smart lad. Can you ask him to come round but not to let anyone see him? He can slip through the old back yard.'

'Tell me why you need to see him. In case you're wondering, I care about those trees too. So do all my friends.'

His father sighed. 'I'll tell both of you together. Now, you take care of the front reception desk in the meantime. I need to think this through carefully. Nothing must be traceable to me, or to you.'

Norry was there in five minutes and Mr Tugwell asked whether he could create an incident in Hawthorn Close to distract people. 'Something for them to watch so that we can help protect the trees without Belkin finding out I'm involved.'

Norry stared into the distance for a moment or two then smiled. 'I think my cousin Jean will jump at the chance to help us. She's in the amateur dramatic society and she's very good-looking. Men always stare at her. But what are you going to do about the JCB?'

'I'm hoping you'll do it for me, Norry. My Joss would be recognised but you're a quiet chap, into computers and people don't even notice you most of the time. Don't think I don't notice that you usually stay out of the limelight.' He took a deep breath and explained, 'If the petrol cap isn't locked and we create a bit of a diversion, do you think you can get to the JCB without being noticed and pour some water into the petrol tank, Norry?'

They both gaped at him, then started to smile.

'Would water be enough to mess the engine up?'

'Yes. It'll stop it from firing.'

Norry beamed at him. 'Brilliant idea. It all depends on whether I can get near it, though. I'll certainly give it my best, Mr Tugwell.'

Joss stared at his father. 'It'll cost a bit to repair it afterwards.'

'I'll wear the cost happily. Call it Tugwells' contribution to saving our trees. Only I don't want my involvement generally known at the moment. A couple of my regular customers are on Belkin's side, unfortunately.'

Mr Tugwell nodded and thrust his hand out to Norry, who smiled as they shook hands.

'I'll go and set the JCB up, Dad?'

'Yes. And give him a bottle of that fancy water to take with him. Folk carry that round all the time.'

He watched the two lads set the JCB up. Was he doing the right thing?

He thought so, had to try, but you could never guarantee your plan would work out.

Belkin was in such a foul mood after the call to Tugwells' that his workmen gave him a wide berth if they could.

Harden watched uneasily as his boss walked up and down the ruined front garden, talking to himself and gesticulating. He'd never seen anyone he worked with behaving so irrationally. If it had been a woman, you'd have called her 'hysterical'. It worried him that his livelihood depended on this man.

After a few minutes, Belkin stopped nearby to stare at the crowds, still muttering to himself. Harden took a couple of steps away and knelt down behind a rubbish container, pretending to fiddle with the laces of his work boot, so that he could eavesdrop.

'There are even more people keeping watch today. Damn them! I need to teach them a sharp lesson. It'll help pave the way.'

Pave the way to what? Harden wondered.

When one big sign with *STOP BELKIN* on it came bobbing into sight at the end of a pole being waved by one of the protesters, the builder picked up a chunk of brick and hurled it at the man. He missed him and only just missed a woman standing nearby.

The men were sneaking glances at Belkin by now, muttering to one another at his increasingly bizarre behaviour.

When Belkin fumbled in his pocket and brought out his phone, he didn't even check whether anyone was close enough to hear the conversation.

Harden's heart sank when he heard him arrange to bring in two of the tough guys he'd employed occasionally before to threaten people. He stood up as Belkin ended the call and stared triumphantly at his foreman.

'I'm glad you were listening. Saves me explaining all over again. The two extra men will be here within the hour. They'll sort out how to take back *my* trees and land. The ones you've hired are utter wimps and no use to me.'

'They're experienced tradesmen and you need their skills.'

'Well, you may be right in one sense, but they're not what I need to do first. I'm going to get my verges back from those fools and knock down the trees. The locals won't know what's hit them! Your men are squeamish ninnies. The temporary ones will do whatever I consider necessary. And I expect you to give them every bit of support they ask for. *Whatever it is.*'

'Yes, sir.'

'Do not let me down on this or you'll be out of your new job as foreman before you've been in it a month.'

Harden didn't dare remind him that the trees and verges belonged to the council. But the threat made him realise suddenly that there was a limit to what he was prepared to do. He hoped it wouldn't come to losing his job, though. He was enjoying the extra money he was earning as foreman.

When the boss had gone inside and slammed the door shut behind him, one of the tradesmen, a man whose family Harden knew, sauntered across to him and said in a low voice, 'I'm beginning to wish I hadn't taken this damned job. It was only because you were working for him that I did. Well, I'm warning you now that I'm not doing anything that's against the law.'

'I haven't asked you to, have I? And I don't intend to either. But if you want to be paid for what you *are* doing, Bill, just keep your thoughts to yourself and pretend to agree. He'll calm down eventually – he always does – but I doubt anyone could stop him at the moment. I don't know why he's so set on getting rid of those trees quickly but he is, so that's that.'

'My mother loves those trees, especially when they're in bloom. She had some of her wedding photos taken in front of them. She'll go mad at me if I help damage them. So will a lot of other folk. They'll go mad at you, too.'

Harden was all too aware of that. His neighbour had already yelled something at him. 'I'm not rushing to obey his orders, am I?'

Bill slouched off to hang around with a couple of the workers out of sight of the boss. No use nagging them to do any work, Harden thought. There wasn't anything they could do till the problem of the trees was settled and their employer gave the go-ahead to demolish the two houses.

It cheered Belkin up visibly when the new men arrived less than an hour later.

It didn't cheer Harden up, on the contrary, because the newcomers weren't the ones he'd expected but large and brutish-looking with foreign accents. Where had Belkin got these two from? Harden would never have taken them on as workers because the very way they moved and looked at the people around them seemed to say they were dangerous and arrogant, and that could lead to trouble.

What would men like that do to any of the locals who got in their way? He shuddered to think of it. The other workers were keeping their distance from them, making no attempt to chat to them as they normally would with newcomers to the team. And he didn't blame them.

He frowned as he looked round. There seemed to be more people in the street today than yesterday, ordinary people he'd known from childhood, people who cared about their town. Oh hell! What a situation to be in!

The two newcomers stood at one side, chatting in their own language, whatever that was. If they had to speak to Belkin or Harden, they did so in heavily accented English. They kept a sharp eye on anyone who came near them, not bothering to hide their scorn for the protesters.

He saw one of them shove aside a young man who got too close, and do it so violently the lad fell over. Some of the bystanders helped him up and got between him and his attacker, thank goodness, so Harden didn't have to intervene.

What had been the point of doing that? None. But it just showed what sort of violent guys the strangers were.

This whole situation was getting worse by the hour.

When the JCB arrived, Belkin came out of the house again. 'Park that thing outside Number 2 facing the verge, then move away from it, Harden. Leave it ready to be driven forward towards those damned trees as soon as I give the word. Which means not parking anything else in front of it. Right?'

'We'll have to give people time to get out of the way,' Harden protested.

Belkin chewed the side of one lip for a moment, scowling at the protesters 'You'd better tell the men to move the JCB forward at walking pace only, then no one can say you didn't give people time to get out of the way.'

What was with the 'you' when it was Belkin giving these orders? Harden tried one final protest. 'Those oldies have their wheelchairs chained to the trees. How are they going to get away quickly?'

Belkin gave a nasty smile. 'The new men can use a bolt cutter. It will slice through that metal chain like butter. You'll be in charge of that job but don't do it till after I've left. We don't want kids getting their hands on the bolt cutter.' He looked at his watch. 'I'll be leaving in about fifteen minutes. I have to go to the bank. You'll be in charge while I'm away. In twenty minutes' time, tell them to take the JCB and knock down the trees.' He walked into the house.

Harden didn't like the sounds of this at all. He reckoned Belkin was setting this up so that he could blame Harden if things went wrong. No, thank you. Not going to happen.

Once his employer was indoors, he went across to Bill. 'He's intending to leave us to take the blame if anything goes wrong. *He* plans to go into town while we do the dirty work. After he's gone, I'm supposed to give the order to use the JCB to knock down the trees. He expects the protesters to get themselves out of the way.'

'Them two in wheelchairs won't be able to move quickly enough.'

'He's passing the buck, as usual. I've seen him do it before.'

'Hmm. Let's hope something stops him leaving.' Harden raised one eyebrow questioningly and his companion nodded.

That was enough. He didn't need to say anything else. They'd worked together long enough to guess what the other wanted or intended.

While he was moving the JCB into position, he saw Belkin peer out of the front room window, but at the same time he saw Bill speak to another man, who sent a dirty look towards the house and nodded.

The two of them did their best to keep out of sight as they moved to the driver's side of Belkin's car. After crouching down for a couple of minutes, presumably to fiddle with the tyres, one kept watch on the house while the other let down the tyres on this side. Then they walked quickly away again, smiling grimly.

A ripple of comments and a few laughs from the protestors made Harden spin round, wondering what had happened now. But it was nothing to do with him.

A young woman had turned in to Hawthorn Close pushing a big, old-fashioned pram. She bent over it, straightening the covers over her baby. Pretty, she was. In fact, very pretty indeed.

Nearby, Bill exclaimed suddenly, 'That's my cousin Jean. I'd recognise that pram anywhere. It used to belong to our grandma then our mum. Has she gone mad to bring her baby here at a time like this? What if there's fighting and the pram gets overturned?'

Harden saw more heads turn at his words and not only the protestors but Belkin's men were now watching closely as she bent over the pram again, showing a very nice pair of long, slender legs under an extremely short skirt. 'You should tell her to go away, Bill. This is no place to bring a baby.'

'I will.' He marched across to his cousin, grabbing the handle of the big, old-fashioned pram and stopping her from moving it any further forward.

Jean glared at her cousin. 'Let go of my pram this minute,

Bill Newman. It's a valuable retro artefact, that is.'

'I'll let go once you've wheeled it out of this street.'

'I'm here to join the protest.'

'With a baby in a pram? Don't be stupid. What if she gets hurt?'

'No one would hurt a baby,' she said loudly.

'There's only one way to make certain of that.' He tried to pull the pram away from her and she jabbed him with her forefinger so hard, he yelled, 'Ouch!' and let go for a moment, rubbing his chest.

By now even Belkin's workmen were grinning at Bill's efforts and nearly all the people at that end of the street were watching them.

As the argument grew louder, both cousins began bringing up old childhood grievances at the tops of their voices, and people were edging even closer, enjoying the repartee.

The two foreign bullies were watching too, making signs about her figure with their hands that were unmistakable in any language.

Norry arrived at the close and paused for a few moments near the entrance to smile at what was going on. Exactly what he'd asked Jean to do. He doubted whether anyone would notice him moving about with a pretty girl like her to stare at and insults flying between her and her cousin.

He gradually worked his way through the crowd till he was near the JCB and no one seemed to notice him, with such a show to watch.

The JCB was standing in a patch of shadow and there were no spectators near it at the moment and even those nearest had their backs turned to it as they watched the ongoing argument.

He looked down at the bottle of water he kept pretending to take sips from, grasping it tightly. This was his chance. Could he get away with it for long enough?

Only one way to find out. Taking a deep breath, he backed towards the JCB step by careful step till he was standing on the other side of it, even deeper in the late afternoon shadows.

As he stretched his arm out towards the fuel cap that Mr Tugwell had fixed so that it couldn't be locked, he prayed that no one would see him do this. He didn't want one of those brutes giving him a thumping. He wasn't big enough or tough enough to be any good at fighting. He always tried to use his brain to get him through life, not his body.

The two people arguing were still at it. The crowd laughed as Jean suddenly clocked Bill good and hard with her handbag and then had to struggle as he tried to take it away from her.

Norry tried to give the fuel cap a quick twist without having to move his whole body closer and to his relief, he succeeded and it came off easily. *Thank you, Mr Tugwell,* he thought.

He quickly started pouring the bottle of water into the top of the petrol tank. It seemed to take ages to glug its way down the hole. In theory, this would prevent the engine from starting.

As he tried to put the fuel cap back on, it slipped out of his fingers and fell to the ground, rolling further into the shadows. No way was he going to look for it. He reckoned he'd pushed his luck far enough. All he wanted to do now was get away from this part of the street as quickly as possible.

As he began moving, he tossed the almost empty water bottle aside, something he'd never normally do but he didn't want anyone to link him to the JCB.

He was sure his heart was beating double time as he edged along the dead remnants of the hedge at Number 1 and his pulse didn't start to slow down until he'd joined a group of people standing at the other side of the end of Hawthorn Close at the junction with Larch Tree Lane.

He tried to look casual as he stared round, unable to believe that he'd done it without anyone seeming to notice him.

Now they had to wait to find out if the engine would start or not. It seemed such a simple thing to have such a big effect.

He probably ought to have gone home if he wanted to be totally safe, because he couldn't be 100 per cent sure that no one had noticed him pouring in the water. But he couldn't bear to tear himself away until he'd seen what happened next. *Please be right about all this, Mr Tugwell!*

Harden watched Belkin come outside, carrying his fancy briefcase, and waited for the explosion when he saw his car. He didn't have to wait long.

The boss noticed the two flat tyres on this side immediately, stepped back and then looked at the other side of his vehicle, cursing loudly. He turned to yell at his foreman, 'Look at that! It can only have been done on purpose. It's got to be one of them sods who're protesting.'

Harden heard him add in a low murmur, 'They bloody

well deserve to be run over, that lot do.' He then turned towards his foreman, yelling loudly now, 'You should have kept an eye on my car, damn you!'

'You didn't tell me to and anyway, I can't do everything at once. No one can.'

'Well, I'm not giving them the chance to do any more damage to my property. Tell them two to get that damned JCB moving. And I hope it mows some of the protesters down.'

He didn't wait for an answer but walked into the house and slammed the door shut behind him.

Harden gestured to one of the two newcomers to get up on to the driving seat. He didn't want to see anyone get hurt, but he didn't want to lose his job, either.

As one of the two approached the JCB, he said loudly, 'When I give the word, knock down those two trees.' He added, 'But go slowly and *do not* hurt any of these people.'

The man shrugged. 'I try not to.' He had climbed nimbly up into the driving seat before Harden could explain about the two oldies chained to the trees.

He suspected there would be an out-and-out riot if anything happened to either of them, so prayed the man would take care.

Of course Belkin was still inside the house.

Chapter Twenty-Seven

Arthur had been keeping a careful eye on what was going on but even he hadn't noticed Norry move across to the JCB because he was in his wheelchair and there were several people standing between him and the vehicle.

But he did see one of Belkin's men climb up into its driving seat and his heart sank. He leant forward to grab his daughter's arm just as she turned to him, looking distressed. 'We've done our best but we can't stop a JCB. Get out of its way once it starts moving, Jane, and tell everyone else to do the same. We don't want any of our people getting hurt.'

'You'll need to unlock that chain of yours and let me move you out of the way, too, Dad.'

He ignored that, his attention on the JCB now. 'Eh, it'll be a sad loss to the valley to lose these trees. I never thought I'd see the day.'

He slumped against the back of his wheelchair and closed his eyes for a moment, feeling desperately sad, then opened them again and said sharply, 'What are you waiting for, Jane? Go round and tell people to move out of its way. When it comes down to it, lives are far more important than trees.'

He saw tears well in her eyes and added softly, 'At least we've done our best, lass.'

'I know, Dad. But I hate to fail. And I love those trees.'

He loved them too. They were like old friends to him. He watched the driver settle himself more comfortably in the seat of the JCB.

'Did you hear me, Dad? You'll need to get away from its path as well. Let me help you unlock that chain and move your wheelchair before I do anything else.'

'No. I'm staying right here.'

'You can't stay there.'

'I damned well can. They'll have to choose then whether to deliberately knock me and my wheelchair out of the way or not. If they do, there will be enough witnesses for the police to arrest them.'

'Dad, no!'

Arthur hardly heard her. Feeling sick to the core of his being, he watched the man reach out to start the JCB's motor.

Singleton parked his wife's car further down the hill and before he got out, he pulled an old beanie down over his ears and jerked the collar of his father's shabby old overcoat up round his neck. He doubted anyone would recognise him as their smartly dressed MP now. He normally prided himself on being well turned out.

He began to shuffle up the street, trying to move like an arthritic old man. He wanted to see what happened as it happened; somehow he had to. He felt helpless in the face of this coming attack on the trees, which was bound to injure protesters. It was stupid, so very stupid, did no good to anyone. The trees could be got rid of in other ways later on.

He shuffled on, making mumbling noises when one woman spoke to him, which seemed to satisfy her and stop her pestering him.

There was some sort of altercation going on between a youngish chap and a woman with a pram and nearly everyone had stopped to watch it. She must be crazy to bring her baby here – or more angry than he'd have expected even of a damned greenie.

The fellow on the JCB hadn't got it moving yet. He was watching them too, a half-smile on his ugly face. What was taking him so long? Had it broken down? He wished it would.

This mess was all Belkin's fault. The man was a fool, an utter fool and he'd been wrong to get involved with him. *Softly, softly, catchee monkey!* was a far better way to go through life, as he had proved time and time again over the years.

Surely even Belkin wouldn't allow the fellow in the JCB to hurt people who got in its way? Why, someone could get seriously injured – or worse. Terence felt sick at the thought of the lawsuits that might cause, and where they might lead.

And he'd been stupid enough to invest in Belkin's project! Too greedy. Oh, hell!

Bill took a firmer hold of the pram with one hand and reached in to uncover the baby. Maybe the sight of her little daughter would make his cousin think again.

What he saw made him gasp and pull the covers hastily over the little face looking blindly up at him then turn to stare accusingly at her. 'What have you done?'

She stared at him solemnly, then winked and pretended to knock his hand off the covers. 'Leave my baby alone, you brute!'

He stepped back slightly, not knowing what to do, but holding his hands in the air as though giving in. If people found out that this pram only contained a doll, he didn't think they'd be happy about how they'd been fooled.

'Let's pretend to make up and get out of here now,' she murmured. 'Norry said not to linger too long or those horrible-looking men might get suspicious. Even you didn't suspect till you uncovered my darling little baby, though, did you?'

'We'll make up and then I'll see you safely away from here.'

'I'm only going as far as the lane. I want to see what happens next.'

'What if someone else notices what you've got in the pram?'

She shrugged. 'What if they do? It isn't illegal to wheel a doll around town, is it? Children do it all the time.'

'Grown-ups don't usually pretend a doll is their baby.'

'Perhaps I'll start a new craze, then.'

He gave her a sudden hug and whispered, 'What Belkin's doing is wrong, very wrong. You and I are in absolute agreement about that.'

As they hugged again, the people nearest to them made a soft 'Ahhh' sound, thinking they'd made up their differences, and a couple of them cheered and shouted encouragement to 'stay friends'.

'I'll be fine now, Bill. You'd better get back to work if you want to keep your job.'

He stood utterly motionless as he realised something, then said slowly, 'I don't want to keep working for that man. I'm quitting as of this minute. I'm not working for someone who'll send a JCB to knock down valuable heritage trees and worse still, put people's lives in danger to do it. Those two oldies are still chained there, you know. Talk about brave.'

He took over the pram and Jean moved to one side, letting him push it now. After a couple of moments she slowed down and let out a huge breath. 'Phew! I feel a bit shaky now. I'm glad that's over.'

'You were lucky to get away with it for so long.'

'Yeah. But me doing it slowed everything down, didn't it?'

'It certainly did. Well done you.'

'I'm double glad you're not working for that man any more, Bill. I can't stand him. There's something thoroughly unwholesome about him.'

'I agree. He cheats and skimps on everything he can, not just quality of building materials but underpaying his employees. And any mistakes in wages are always in his favour. I doubt I'll ever get the money owing to me. Liz and I will probably have to dip into our holiday savings till I can find another job.'

'But at least you'll have your self-respect.'

'You can't feed self-respect to hungry children or put it on their feet when their shoes wear out,' he said glumly.

'Some things are more important than money, Bill. Let's stop over there. If we stand on the end of the wall that goes round the retirement homes, we should have a clear view of the street. I'm not leaving till I've seen what happens. I do hope no one will get hurt.'

'I hope so too.' He frowned but helped her get up on the wall, then joined her and stared across at the JCB. 'Why is that chap still sitting there? Why hasn't he started the damn thing?'

Chapter Twenty-Eight

Arthur continued to watch the man on the JCB as the minutes ticked slowly by. He saw him fiddle with the motor but nothing happened. He tried to start it again and this time the crowd were quiet enough that those close by could hear a faint clicking sound. But that was all.

'What's going on, Dad?' Jane asked.

'The motor won't start. Is it possible that something's gone wrong with it?' Arthur whispered.

'We could do with a bit of luck like that,' she said.

'I doubt it's pure luck. Someone must have got at it. Eh, if Norry's managed to do this, he deserves a medal.'

They saw the man on the JCB look towards Harden and make a beckoning gesture. The crowd had fallen completely silent now.

The foreman got up on the edge of the vehicle and after fiddling with some cables said, 'Try it again'.

Once again they could hear the starter motor turning

over, but apart from a faint sound almost like a cough, it wasn't followed by the sound of the motor starting up or indeed any sound from the engine.

People were nudging one another, listening intently and exchanging glances.

'There's definitely something wrong with the engine.' Arthur beamed at his daughter, pulled her towards him and gave her a big hug. 'I don't think we have failed yet, love. I think our trees are going to live for another day.'

When the man on the JCB turned the starter key yet again, with the same result, Harden finally accepted that something was wrong with it. He suddenly noticed something. 'You fool. What have you been doing to it, trying to siphon off some fuel? The petrol cap is missing.'

'I not touch it.'

'Let me check it.' Round the top of the fuel tank were small trails in the dust as if something had been spilt there. He rubbed his finger in one of the runnels, then licked it cautiously. No taste. Water? How could that be?

Belkin was glaring at him from near the front door of the house and called, 'What's that man doing? Tell him to start the engine.'

Harden knew it wasn't likely to work but he wanted to postpone the confrontation with his employer. What's more, he was totally and utterly fed up of being shouted at and blamed for everything that didn't go the way the builder wanted.

He gestured to the man, who tried it again and naturally nothing happened.

Harden caught his attention and pointed. 'Why is the petrol cap on the ground?'

The man merely shrugged.

As Harden went and picked the cap up, his foot hit something else, something bigger that went rolling away. 'What's that?' he yelled as he nearly fell.

'Is just empty water bottle,' the man said.

And then it hit him. It was empty because someone had poured the water into the tank.

That sank in slowly, then they looked at one another and the man had obviously figured it out too because he rolled his eyes. 'Need to clean out carburettor and fuel tank. Not nice job.'

Harden closed his eyes, wishing he were anywhere but here but glad suddenly that the sabotage had succeeded. He was sick to death of Belkin and his nasty ways.

He turned round to his employer and explained what had probably happened.

Belkin gaped at him. 'But who could have done such a thing? That JCB was driven into place by the man who brought it. No trouble with the engine then. And it's been standing there ever since.'

'I don't know who did it, sir. I didn't see anyone.' He didn't wait to be accused of not doing his job but went on the attack. 'Didn't you see anything? You were looking out of the window all the time, after all.'

There was no response to that.

As the minutes ticked past, Arthur watched the two men on the JCB intently and smiled as he saw it dawn on them what had happened. He even managed to read their lips, they were speaking so slowly.

'Harden's saying someone has poured water into the fuel tank. Norry was carrying a bottle of water.'

'A lot of people can't seem to manage without them these days. They're always taking sips, even when they're serving you in a shop,' she said scornfully. 'It reminds me of babies and their bottles.'

Arthur beamed at his daughter. 'That Norry is one smart lad.' He turned round to Mavis at the other tree and called out an explanation of what he thought had happened.

She beamed at him and of course a lot of other people heard what he said and an excited buzz ran through the crowd of protesters.

'I can't believe that lot have been stopped from knocking down the trees,' Jane said.

'Look at the expression on Harden's face. He knows what's happened.'

'We owe Norry a lot. Looks like he's saved our trees today.'

'Ben's family breeds good people.' Arthur smiled at her and added, 'And so does mine.'

He pulled her close and they gave one another a big hug, then relaxed for the first time in hours. 'Eh, fate's been good to us today.'

'What will Belkin try next, though?'

'Who knows?'

'Oh, oh! Here he comes. This is going to be fun to watch, Dad.'

'Great fun.'

* * *

When Belkin came storming out of the house, Harden took a deep breath and waited for him to start shouting. Sure enough, his employer began yelling at him, cursing him for a useless lump.

All of a sudden he'd had enough. E-bloody-nuff. He leant forward and shoved Belkin backwards. 'I quit.'

The builder jumped as if he'd been stung. 'Oh no, you don't. You haven't finished the job.'

'And I'm not going to. How can you stop me leaving?' Harden turned round and strode into Number 1. He came out a couple of minutes later carrying his worn backpack.

As he passed Belkin, who was still standing there looking stunned, he gave him a two-finger salute and continued walking to the end of the street, where he turned left down the hill.

Left standing on his own, Belkin opened and shut his mouth a couple of times, but didn't say anything else. He avoided the other men's eyes and went back into the house.

The foreign worker got down from the JCB and beckoned his companion. 'Waste of time staying here.'

They turned without another word and walked away from the chaos.

'Not a good boss,' one said.

'Not a good man.' The other tapped the side of his forehead in an age-old gesture.

'Shouts all the time, doesn't use brain much.'

'Hasn't got brain?'

They both laughed loudly, saw a pub and went in for a drink.

* * *

Terence had been watching and for all the seriousness of the situation, he couldn't help laughing at Belkin's outraged expression. Unfortunately that brought attention to him.

Before he could move away, a woman nearby peered at him more closely and said, 'It's you, isn't it? Mr Singleton? I can tell by the scar on your nose.'

A tiny scar from his childhood. How the hell had she seen that?

'You won't remember me but I'm Minnie Gale and we used to be in the same class at school.'

'Oh. Sorry, I'm afraid I don't remember you, though the name does sound familiar.'

'Well, I remember you. What are you doing here? You should be trying to stop incidents like this one, not skulking around and letting them ruin our street.'

He didn't know what to reply to that, so looked at her earnestly and said, 'I'm trying to find out what's going on before I do anything.'

Several people nearby had moved closer, listening unashamedly to their conversation. They now joined in, all trying to speak at once.

He held up one hand to stop them and forced a half smile. 'Perhaps we can let this lady explain to me what's been happening? I've only just returned from abroad, so that would be a big help.'

'What are we paying your wages for if you use them to gallivant all over the world instead of for helping us when we need you? You can't have been paying attention to your constituency if you have to ask about this mess.' She gestured towards the protesters.

There was another chorus of loud agreement and a man

yelled at them to be quiet and let Mr Singleton speak.

He forced another smile. What he thought of as his softening-up-constituents smile. 'I can only hear one voice at a time, my friends. The whole town seems to be up in arms about something, but I'm not sure exactly what.'

A man's voice repeated what the woman had said. 'You shouldn't have been out of the country, then; you should have been here, representing us, bringing the government in to resolve our situation.'

'You're never there when we need you.'

'I'm not voting for you next time if you don't do something to sort this out.'

'No, I'm not either.'

Those comments made him pay full attention to them.

'Shut up and let me tell him.' The woman who'd first recognised him started talking again, telling Singleton about the trees and the way the whole town was up in arms about their heritage being threatened.

He let her rant on till she'd run herself down, trying to keep his attentive expression in place. Fortunately, he'd practised it in front of the mirror till he could summon it up at will. She was even more troublesome than constituents usually were.

But he'd clearly been right to worry about what Belkin was doing to the trees causing more trouble than it was worth.

When she'd finished, he said simply, 'Thank you very much for your explanation. It's a good thing I came back earlier than I'd planned. I shall go and see this Belkin person tomorrow and ask him to stop doing this. I shall try my very best to save those trees, I promise you. They are glorious in the late spring, truly glorious.' He started to edge away. 'Now, I must get off home or my wife will start to worry.'

A short, bald man stepped in front of him. 'You always say you'll *try* to do something. And you rarely succeed. Try harder this time, Mr Singleton. A lot harder. It's your last chance if you're interested in getting re-elected next year.'

He saw the people nearby all nod and some echoed the words 'last chance'. Most of them did that, in fact. He was on full alert now. He'd been greedy, shouldn't have invested so much money in this project, whatever returns Belkin promised. Why had he broken his usual way of doing things?

Because his stupid wife had been complaining about money yet again, that's why. She wanted to move to a bigger house.

The man jabbed one finger towards Singleton and raised his voice. 'I'll be coming to see you tomorrow morning to find out what you've actually arranged to do to protect our trees. And I don't expect to be kept waiting, either. Eleven o'clock sharp I'll be there. And I'll be bringing a couple of interested neighbours with me.'

'More than a couple!' someone yelled. 'I'm coming too, Jim lad.'

'You were elected as our member of parliament. Do something about this mess. And above all, save our trees.' The spokesman gestured to the masses of green leaves with a few buds showing now.

Terence's heart sank. He nodded, trying to smile serenely but fearing he wasn't being very convincing this time. 'I'll tell my secretary to expect you.'

They let him walk away, but they watched him till he got to his car and they were not looking happy.

He felt nervous as he drove away from Hawthorn Close. This situation was far worse than he'd expected.

When he got home, he locked the front door behind him and leant against it, he felt that unsafe. How was he going to persuade Belkin to stop trying to get rid of those trees?

He couldn't see any other way of satisfying his constituents than by saving the two hawthorns.

Belkin was behaving more and more rashly, trying to expand his business too quickly. And he'd hinted that this was supposed to be part of a long-term project for a big housing development. That worried Singleton.

A lamp was switched on in a corner of the sitting room. Good. It meant his wife had gone to bed early. At least he didn't need to chat to her.

He got out the whisky and poured himself a big shot of it, then sat down and took a large mouthful.

How the hell was he going to set about saving the situation? He had to do something!

Chapter Twenty-Nine

Between them, Corin, Vicki and Murad kept watch on the protesters and especially on the thugs who'd obviously been brought in to deal with the situation in a more robust manner.

Like everyone else watching the events play out, they were relieved to see the JCB fail to start and when Belkin cursed and blamed them, the two foreigners simply walked away, leaving the people in the wheelchairs safe still.

'What's Belkin going to do now, do you think?' Corin muttered. 'He's just lost his hired muscles.'

'I doubt he knows himself. I suppose he's trying to work that out as we speak. I doubt he'll want to see his plans ruined,' Vicki said thoughtfully. 'But panic can lead to dangerous actions.'

'He won't have much choice but to do this himself if he hasn't got anyone to carry out his orders.'

'Who'd want to work for someone who shouts and

curses at you? Was he always this bad?' Corin asked.

'Actually, I don't think so. And you don't solve problems by yelling at them,' Murad said quietly.

Vicki couldn't imagine Murad yelling and shouting at anyone and yet he got things done. He didn't let any of the miscreants they dealt with mess him around, but he was always courteous.

The phone rang just then and Murad answered it. He waved his hand to attract their attention and then put one finger to his lips and put the phone in speaker mode.

The first thing they heard was him saying, 'Yes, sir. Unfortunately Belkin hasn't done anything against the law that we've seen.' He listened again and rolled his eyes at his companions but kept repeating, 'Yes, sir. Yes, we'll look into that. We'll do our very best, I promise you.'

When the call ended, he said, 'They're really eager for us to catch Belkin doing something against the law. I wonder why.'

'Your boss is being unreasonable if he expects you to arrest him without due cause,' Corin said.

Murad shrugged. 'They've got a court warrant and are now going to put a trace on his phone, at least.'

'Good. Tell them to keep an eye on Singleton's calls, too.'

'I don't think they've thought about him. He hasn't got a track record of being involved in crimes. In fact, he doesn't seem to do much at all, considering he's the MP for this area.'

'It wouldn't hurt to suggest strongly that they do keep an eye on him. I can't take to that slimeball at all, for all his smiles and promises. I don't think he's on the side of law and order.'

'I doubt he's on anyone's side except his own.' Murad made another call to his boss, spoke earnestly, then nodded and held up one thumb in triumph. 'He'll try and persuade the magistrate to issue a warrant for us to tap Singleton's phone too, but he's not very hopeful. He wasn't going to, but when I said we were wondering if Singleton was working with Belkin because we'd seen them together in an out-of-the way place, he changed his mind.'

Vicki went outside at the rear again and when there was a roar of approval from the crowd at the front of the house, Murad went to see what was going on there.

Corin went to stand a couple of paces behind him.

It looked very unsettled and Murad asked Corin to keep Vicki informed of anything that happened at the front.

He watched for a few moments then went to tell her, 'Harden's walking out of the close and he's not looking happy. He's brought a bag out of the house, quite a heavy one.'

Murad turned to stare at Corin. 'Do you think he might have resigned?'

'He might have. Perhaps Belkin has gone a step too far with him.'

'I certainly hope so. We officers are not supposed to take sides but I can't help agreeing with the locals here. Belkin is bad news.'

Even as Murad watched, Harden turned out into Larch Tree Lane and vanished.

'He's gone off down the hill.'

Corin smiled. 'Good riddance!'

Murad looked thoughtful and disagreed. 'Good man if he's resigned at what he's been asked to do.'

The situation seemed to settle down after that and nothing more caught their attention.

After a while, Vicki came in the back way. 'It's starting to get dark. I reckon we can knock off work now. If we keep our bedroom windows open, we'll be able to hear if anything sparks fighting out there again. I don't know about you two guys but I'm exhausted.' She turned to Corin. 'You're welcome to stay the night if you don't mind sleeping on the sofa.'

'Thanks but if you don't need me here, I'd rather get back to Lucia. I must confess, it feels very flat the way things have ended. I'd rather we'd had some proper closure. I'll probably see you two tomorrow. I'm still going to come back and help keep watch on the trees.'

Murad nodded. 'And we'll continue keeping a careful eye on this street. You know what? It still feels to me as if something's brewing under the surface.'

'I get that impression too. But what can it be?'

Terence kept only the lamp switched on in his living room and sat in the semi-darkness, sipping his whisky and gradually settling towards sleep. Since he and his wife no longer shared a bedroom, he could choose his own time schedule.

He was starting to doze off when his personal phone rang. He jerked fully awake again and glanced at his watch. After midnight. Who the hell could be calling at this hour? So few people had this number and that was how he liked it.

He took it out of his inner pocket. 'Hello?'

'Don't hang up, Terry dear,' a woman's voice said.

He didn't recognise her voice but realised with a sinking heart what use of this silly nickname meant. Only one group of people called him that.

'Just a minute,' she added.

There was a faint sound and then a man took over. 'Terry dear, are you alone?'

He stiffened. He recognised this second voice but had hoped never to hear it again. He'd have loved to slam the phone down, but didn't dare. 'Yes, I'm alone.'

'Good. No names, remember. Listen carefully. The time has come for you to pay us back for the help we gave you to get elected in those early days.'

He managed not to groan aloud. 'I'm listening.'

The caller laughed. 'You don't sound happy to hear from us. You surely expected this to happen one day? You were told it would cost you to get us on side.'

'Yes. I know. Go on.'

'We're a bit annoyed about something that's happening in your constituency and we want you to stop it.'

'Oh? What?'

'Belkin trying to get rid of the heritage trees.'

What the hell did that matter? Singleton shook his head instinctively even though his caller couldn't see him. 'I can't stop him. I did speak to him but he seems hell bent on knocking them down.'

'We'll persuade him to leave Hawthorn Close alone, don't worry. But we'll require your help financially to finalise the arrangement.'

'*What?*'

'You will need to pay the piper now, Terry dear.'

He didn't dare tell them no. You didn't order these people around. How much was it going to cost him?

'We'll get back to you in the morning. Do not go out till you've heard from us again.'

When the conversation ended, he poured some more whisky into his glass, far too wide awake again now to go to bed.

He didn't want to get involved in this, hated the mere idea of continuing to interact with Belkin and was wondering how much this was in fact going to cost him. He doubted it'd be cheap.

He wouldn't dare refuse to do what they told him to, however. He wasn't that stupid. He didn't know who they all were individually but he had guessed some of their identities. Important figures in the political world, whether they were MPs or not. And he'd figured out they'd been behind a couple of changes of legIlsation because he'd been told to vote against the party's usual position at one stage.

Early the following morning, he received another phone call from the same man, giving his more specific instructions. He didn't want to do this, but he didn't dare refuse.

And he hated, absolutely hated the thought of dipping into his savings to such an extent.

As instructed, Singleton phoned Belkin on the private number he'd been given.

He was greeted by, 'How the hell did you get hold of this number?'

'I was given it by some mutual friends.'

'Who?'

'We don't name these people.'

Silence, then Belkin cursed.

Singleton took over. 'You and I need to meet. I'll see you behind the second house in Hawthorn Close at one o'clock this afternoon.'

He'd chosen that venue because, given what he'd been instructed to do, he wanted to study the two properties due for demolition more carefully.

'I'm too busy today. I'll meet you tomorrow.'

'No. You're not too busy. You've been told to do a business deal with me today and if I report to our friends that you're refusing to meet me, you'll be in very bad trouble indeed.'

He heard Belkin suck in his breath and knew he'd hit the target there. He didn't know what hold they had on the other man, but it must be something important.

'How the hell are you involved with that lot, Singleton?' Belkin asked suddenly. 'No one's ever seen you do anything dodgy.'

That was because he tried not to get involved too deeply with problems in his constituency. He was, if anything, a paid vote that they could utilise whenever they needed to push something controversial through.

'All you need to know is that I work with these mutual friends occasionally.' They were in no way friends, but Belkin wasn't to know that. 'They're more powerful than you realise so if you want to continue in business, you'll do as they say. I'll meet you at one o'clock in the garden behind Number 2.'

He ended the call without waiting for an answer.

It was going to be a vile day. Before he saw Belkin, he had the meeting with the group who'd cornered him the previous evening. Troubles never came singly, did they?

At eleven o'clock, Singleton's secretary came to tell him that a group of constituents had arrived to see him and wouldn't take no for an answer.

'I already knew these people were coming but forgot to tell you. Sorry.'

She frowned at him and he knew why. He usually avoided seeing such nuisances when they turned up in groups.

'It might be a good time for you to take a lunch break. Do you mind going early?'

'Not at all, Mr Singleton.' She showed the constituents in and got a couple more chairs because there were six of them, three men and three women. Baldy still seemed to be in charge.

He took his time settling down behind his desk, waiting till he heard the sound of the outer office door being closed before turning to them with a careful smile.

'Never mind the chit-chat,' Baldy said. 'Tell us exactly what you're going to do about Belkin to stop him spoiling our valley. You should have intervened before now, you really should.'

'You'll be glad to hear that I've arranged to go and see Mr Belkin later today.' He waited for their approval but it didn't come.

'And? What are you going to ask of him?' one of the women said in a very sharp voice.

'Ask of him?'

'Yes. Are you supporting us on protecting those trees or will you let him continue to work against us?'

He never liked to promise any specific outcome. 'I shall, of course, do my best to persuade him to leave the trees be.'

'Not good enough,' another man snapped.

'I can't perform miracles.'

The bald man took over again. 'It seems to me you aren't confident of being able to do anything definite for your constituency. We don't even know which side you support in this.'

'I hope to make him see sense.' That was as vague an objective as he could think of.

'Well, how about this for making sense? If you come back without an agreement that he will leave our trees alone, I'll personally stand against you at the next election – as well as making your working life miserable in the meantime.'

'And I'll put money into his campaign,' the woman said.

'I assure you that I shall do my utmost,' he said hastily.

'You need to stop him knocking down our trees. Nothing more, nothing less. We'll wait here if you don't mind to find out what you've achieved.'

'Please make yourselves comfortable in the waiting room.' He wasn't letting them occupy his office. To his relief they went out and sat down, discussing someone going out for takeaways.

What worried Singleton in addition to the obvious was whether these constituents had been sent to harass him by the people he feared. It wouldn't surprise him if they'd done it to give him an added incentive.

But he had always intended to do exactly as they'd told him. Unlike Belkin, he wasn't stupid. Indeed, he considered himself very good at gauging people's power.

The main problem he saw was that he suspected Belkin was developing a serious medical problem, probably something to do with mental health. His sudden furious rages were not helpful to the situation and were at times bizarre.

* * *

Belkin was late for the meeting, which didn't surprise Singleton. But he'd deliberately come early and strolled round while he waited for Belkin to arrive, taking a good look at the outsides of the two houses he'd been told to buy.

There was one man on duty there, keeping guard, but he looked vaguely familiar. When he was greeted by name, Singleton clapped him on the back and said how nice it was to see him again. After that there was no trouble being allowed to take a quick look round inside the houses.

What a mess Number 1 was in! But was it badly damaged structurally or was it just slovenly chaos? He'd get advice on that before he decided what to do with it. Number 2 was dusty and a few fittings seemed to have been ripped out of the kitchen, but it looked to be relatively easy to fix.

Expensive, though. He sighed.

When Singleton came out, the man was still there. 'I'll be taking over here shortly. Want a security job with the firm I use when you lose this one? We pay well.' He named an amount and the man beamed at him.

'Happy to work for you, sir. I'm still waiting for my last week's wages from the present owner.'

'How shocking. Consider yourself hired. I'll tell you when to take over. It'll be in a few minutes and I'll need you to witness Mr Belkin's signature on a document before you do anything.'

'Yes, sir. Just call me over when you need me.'

It didn't take Singleton long to look at the gardens, which were both a total disaster. They'd been deliberately flattened then driven over by numerous vehicles. Even the trees at the edges had been chopped down. Belkin being stupid again.

He'd have to have the gardens completely re-landscaped. More expense. But he'd have to pay out to recoup some of his money.

By the time Belkin drew up and strolled round to the rear of Number 2, Singleton had decided to pay him even less than he'd been told to do.

He waited for the other man to stop near him, then immediately took over. 'I've been told by mutual acquaintances that you need to sell these houses.'

'I don't *need* to. I've been ordered to do it, as you damned well know. But I'm not giving them away. And I'm having those street trees cut down before I leave. Those locals are not getting the better of me.'

Singleton was amazed that he'd still care about this minor point. 'I have only one price to offer, and unfortunately for you, it's less than you expect.' He named it and enjoyed the shock on Belkin's face.

'*What?* You have to be joking. These houses are worth twice that even as they are.'

'I never joke about money. And they're only worth what someone will pay for them. Basic finance rule, that. If you don't accept my offer and sign the preliminary agreement at once, then you'll have to explain yourself to our mutual friends.'

There was a pregnant silence, then Belkin said in a slightly less aggressive tone, 'Surely there's some room for manoeuvre? I paid more than that for the houses and I've spent a lot of money on them.'

'You've spent money on destroying them, Number 1 especially. I find that strange.'

'Preparations for the demolition. I was about to start on preparing Number 2.'

'Well, you won't need to now. But I can't afford to pay more than I've said. And our friends have given me the go-ahead and agreed that it's a fair price in the condition the houses are.' He stretched out his arm and stared at his wristwatch while Belkin fidgeted and waited for him to continue. 'I'll give you five minutes to think it over, then if you don't agree to sell, I'm leaving and I'll be phoning our friends straight away.'

'You might find yourself in trouble later if you don't give me a fair price now,' Belkin threatened in a low voice.

'I'm recording this conversation.'

He watched Belkin look surprised, then open and shut his mouth.

'Our friends won't like to hear your refusal or your threat.' He looked down at his watch, waited for the second hand to tick its way round to the top again, then said, 'Four minutes'.

Belkin let him reach five minutes without saying another word, let alone agreeing, so he turned away. 'I'll leave it, then.'

The idiot even waited till Singleton reached the edge of the garden before yelling in a harsh, angry voice, 'Damn you! I'll accept it.'

Singleton pulled out the folded piece of paper he'd prepared and filled in the details of sale price quickly, then called the security guard to come round to the back and witness the signatures.

When that had been done, he looked at his watch. 'You have exactly five minutes to clear your possessions out of the house. After that, this place will be watched twenty-four-seven and you will not be allowed into either the premises or the grounds.'

Belkin's face turned almost purple and he looked ready to explode with rage but he managed to regain control of himself.

Singleton walked with him to the front of Number 1 and said to the man who'd gone back to wait there, 'Changeover time for the property will be in five minutes precisely. Will you please escort Mr Belkin inside to collect his possessions now, watch what he takes to make sure he's entitled to it, then see him off the premises completely. After that, he is not to come back into either the house or the garden.'

'Yes, sir.' The man looked as if he was enjoying this. Perhaps he'd been shouted and sworn at too.

Belkin rushed into the house and came out again six minutes later with a shabby briefcase and a big rubbish bin liner full of something or other.

Singleton didn't mention that but watched Belkin drive off, then looked across to the street trees. He might as well get this over and done with before he went back to his office. He didn't like Arthur Keevil but they now shared one common aim, at least.

He didn't care one way or the other about trees, but they would raise the value of the two houses he'd just bought whether he sold them as they were (his preferred option) or knocked them down and built new, modern houses. No, they'd have to be reproduction period houses to fit in.

What a nuisance all this was. And oh, the cost! But he owed these people and had promised to do as they asked 'one day' in order to pay them back for their help in getting elected.

Chapter Thirty

Arthur had slept badly last night, was wondering what nasty tricks Belkin would try today to get at the trees. He was feeling as if every one of his years was sitting heavily on his shoulders as he settled into his place.

When he saw Singleton walking round the two houses, he wondered what he was doing there. He didn't expect any support from their MP. Everyone knew that the only person that man cared about was himself.

He watched Singleton go into each of the two houses, then vanish round the back of Number 2. There was no sign of him walking away down the street.

Then Belkin arrived and went round the back as well.

What were those two up to, meeting like this? But Arthur could see no way of managing to hear what they were saying.

Shortly afterwards, Belkin came storming round the front, clearly in one of his rages. He seemed to be angry a lot of the time these days. He went into the first house, accompanied by the guy who seemed to be on guard there today, while Singleton waited outside.

When Belkin came out a few minutes later he was carrying a briefcase and what looked like a bin liner full of bits and pieces. He glared across at Arthur and Mavis sitting under their trees, scowled at the MP, then got into his car and drove off.

Well, well. What was going on here?

Once Singleton had got rid of Belkin, he walked briskly across to the old man in the wheelchair, hoping his expression hadn't given away how annoyed he felt about the need to pacify the locals.

He stood in front of the wheelchair and forced a smile. 'I'm the bearer of good tidings today, Mr Keevil.'

'Oh? That makes a change.'

'I hope it'll mark the start of better relations between us. I've just signed an agreement to buy these two houses from Belkin.' He waved one hand towards them, amused at how shocked Keevil looked by this. 'That means the pressure will be off you about the trees.'

The old man seemed lost for words, then said cautiously, 'Is this some sort of joke?'

'No. I don't want Belkin building his tacky little houses in my constituency so I've made him an offer he can't refuse.'

'Why should you care?'

He decided to tell the truth – well, mostly. 'I own one or two investment properties near here and his tacky little houses would lower the value of my houses. And I enjoy being the MP for this area, so I don't like anyone causing trouble here. Moreover, stopping this stupidity about the trees should win me more votes next time.'

'Well, those reasons I can believe,' Arthur allowed. 'And it'll definitely win you more votes.'

Singleton managed to keep his smile steady. He wouldn't have cared if they'd been knocked down as long as it had made him a lot of money as an investor, especially if he'd been able to give up work earlier on the proceeds. But as it turned out he had no choice, and would probably be losing money, so he might as well benefit from the goodwill this would generate locally and keep his property prices up.

He'd have a photo taken of the trees next time they were in blossom in a few weeks and put it on his publicity material to remind the locals of what he'd done for them.

'If I may offer one piece of advice, however?'

Arthur looked at him cautiously. 'Yes?'

'Don't stop guarding the trees yet. Belkin isn't doing well in his business and has had to sell this project to me. He isn't best pleased at that. From what he said to me, it's my guess he'll still go after those trees as a parting gesture.'

'Hmm. Thank you for the hint. Again, I believe you. It's the sort of thing he would do. May I ask why you told me that? You and I have never been on good terms.'

'I prefer a peaceful life, at home and in my constituency, and you were nearby, easy to chat to before I leave today. Besides, I don't like to see stupid gestures, whoever makes them.'

Arthur nodded and looked thoughtful.

'I'll leave you to get on with your day.' Singleton nodded and walked away. He had nothing in common with Keevil and no desire to chat to him or any of the other protesters.

Unfortunately, he had to get back to his office to inform the group of constituents waiting for him there what was going on, damn their impudence. He hoped they'd be placated by him making an offer to buy those houses and promise not to go after the trees. His backers had insisted he must make that clear.

The trouble was, the protesters were a very determined bunch. As a gesture of goodwill, it might be worth letting them know that Belkin still intended to go after the trees as a parting gesture.

On the whole, though, Singleton was expecting to gain more supporters as a result of what he'd done or promised to do today. Hopefully some of them would vote for him from now onwards.

But oh, he wished he didn't have to deal with the two houses. Life was too short to fiddle around with that sort of thing. Were they worth renovating or should he just have them knocked down and build others in their place?

No, he doubted that would please people. He'd have to bring someone in to check them out. That'd cost money too.

Nothing came free in this life. But he was paying a high price this time for the support years ago that had enabled him to win this seat in the election.

Still, being an MP had helped him to amass a nice little fortune over the years so he could afford this, even if he did consider it an annoying waste of time.

The group of constituents was still waiting at his office, but at least his secretary had got them cups of tea. She was a sensible woman. It never hurt to soften people up with refreshments, as he'd taught her.

He smiled across the room at them. 'I have good news for you.'

'Oh? Surprise us.'

Did that bald guy never speak politely?

'I found that Belkin had overstretched his resources so I offered to buy those houses myself and he accepted.' Ha! That surprised them.

'What are you going to do with them?' one woman asked.

'Find out whether they're worth renovating and if so, do it. Then I'll put them up for sale. I have no desire to change careers and become a builder.'

'And the street trees?'

'Will be left untouched.'

'Can we believe you about that?'

'Yes. They'll enhance the value of my properties.'

'Ah,' the leader said. 'They will too. It's a good start, I will admit. We shall watch what happens with ongoing interest, Mr Singleton.'

'I hope you'll be pleased with what I do. Now, I really must get on with my day.'

They nodded and walked out.

'I'll get you a coffee, Mr Singleton,' his secretary said.

'With a shot of whisky in it, just a small one. It's been a very stressful day so far. I don't want to see anyone else. And on second thoughts, I think I'll just go home early and have my whisky there. You can leave early too.'

The following night was peaceful but Arthur told Jane and Nellie what Singleton had said and they arranged to have a careful watch kept over the trees. Nothing happened, thank goodness.

The day after that, however, Norry got word from a friend that Belkin was planning something for that night.

Would that horrible man never give up trying to spoil their valley?

Arthur let Norry plan the defence. He was growing weary after the disturbed nights and the worries would not be removed from his shoulders till he was sure Belkin wouldn't try to do any more harm. And how did you judge that?

When his daughter insisted he go home and have a good night's sleep, leaving any action needed to the younger generation, he didn't argue.

Jane took his place in the wheelchair, as Norry had instructed, pulling a shawl round her shoulders and a blanket over her knees, trying to look like her father.

Midnight passed and nothing happened, then suddenly someone let out a soft hiss of sound in warning. The night turned menacing and men crept forward from between the two empty houses, clutching what looked like axes.

Norry was hiding nearby with a friend and when the men got closer, they bobbed up to intercept the would-be attackers, but allowed the men to avoid them quite easily and make a sudden rush towards the trees.

But Jane had been prepared for exactly this and wanted them to take this path. As she blew a very shrill whistle, other defenders rose from the shadows to tackle the invaders.

They were well outnumbered but were experienced fighters and still tried to get to the trees. It took a while to drive them away and two of the defenders were injured, with deep cuts.

There was consternation when it was discovered that one of the trees had received a gash. An older woman famous for her gardening skills ran out of the shadows when she heard that, using a powerful torch to examine it.

'This is only a minor cut, thank goodness. It'll heal over.' She tied her own long scarf over it and patted the tree as if it was a living being.

'Come over here!' someone yelled suddenly. 'See who I've found.'

Arthur swung round and saw them drag a man out from near Ilsa's fence at Number 3. He struggled desperately and it took three of them to hold him. Then suddenly he stiffened and fell.

He didn't get up and after a moment's shock, the defenders shook him. When he didn't respond, they carried him under the street lamp to examine him properly.

One of the men called, 'It's Belkin. We were only pulling him out of hiding. We didn't hit him or anything.'

Jane ran across and knelt beside him. She'd seen that twisted look before.

'I think he's had a stroke. You're a nurse, Peter. See if you can find a pulse.'

He came and checked the still figure, then nodded. 'He's still alive, but he doesn't seem conscious. We need to call an ambulance.'

When it arrived, the paramedics examined him then said, 'It's a bad stroke. Who knows if he'll recover?'

They drove off and people gathered.

'Serves him right,' one woman said.

* * *

When Murad heard this, he called to Vicki to join him at the front of the house. He explained quickly what had happened, ending, 'I saw the whole incident and they definitely didn't thump him. I'd think I'd better go and check him officially, though.'

'It'll blow your cover.'

'I don't have much choice.' He moved forward towards the group that had gathered.

To his relief, one of the police officers from the end of the street had got to the group before him and Peter was a nurse, so Murad was able to leave it to them and slip back to join Vicki.

They watched as an ambulance came and took the body away.

'I'll phone the hospital later and see how he is,' Vicki said. 'But the valley would be a better place without that horrible man.'

'If he dies, who'll inherit his estate?' another wondered aloud.

'His wife perhaps. She's his second wife, always looks cowed.'

'Does he have children?'

'I don't think he does.'

'I'd better go home and tell my father,' Jane said. 'I won't shock him with a middle of the night phone call. I don't want him having a heart attack as well from worry.'

'Great old chap, your father.'

She smiled. 'I think so.'

The following morning, she rang the hospital and found out that Belkin had passed away during the night after a second stroke.

After that incident, the days passed quietly but Arthur still insisted on a watch being kept, still joined them for a while each day.

When would they ever feel their trees were safe? Jane sometimes wondered.

Before Singleton could do anything about the two houses, he received an offer to buy Number 2, which was clearly in better condition than its neighbour.

The offer was made through a lawyer and was a cash buyer, apparently. Who would want an old house in such terrible condition? he wondered.

The council had hurriedly put a caveat on the houses saying they could only be replaced by other single dwellings that suited the architectural style of the street.

But the buyer apparently intended to renovate the original house if at all possible.

The sale was agreed and the formalities were set in motion. It'd be several weeks before everything was settled.

And then it leaked out that the anonymous buyer was an old friend of Arthur's who had made a fortune overseas.

He was jubilant about that, assuring everyone that his friend had been born and bred in the valley and would fit in perfectly.

When Singleton came to see him again, he greeted him cautiously but more warmly than last time.

'I thought you should know: I've signed a contract with Corin Drayton to supervise a huge renovation of the house at Number 1 and extend it a little. He'll make sure it fits in here and that the tree on the verge is not damaged in any way. In fact, he's going to put a sort of cage round it. I even have a potential buyer provisionally signed up to buy it if it's as well done as we expect. And the trees were one of the things that sold it to him.'

Once again, Arthur believed him and for the first time he began to feel that his beloved trees might be truly safe.

'So you won't need to keep watch over the trees any longer.'

'Good. But we will keep our usual watch for the first signs of them flowering.'

Arthur watched Singleton walk away with a wry smile. If there was ever a case of someone doing the right thing for the wrong reason, this was it.

When he got to his car, Singleton sighed. He'd still lost a good deal of money, but not nearly as much as he'd thought he would. And he'd kept his position as member of parliament for the valley, not had to resign.

He even had hopes of getting re-elected at the next general election. But he'd tread very carefully from now on.

Chapter Thirty-One

As the days passed and nothing else disturbed the peace, the inhabitants of the valley settled down back into a more normal way of life.

Well, life became more normal for some. Having been denied a quiet wedding, for the best of reasons, Maggie and James decided to plan a large but casual wedding, with all their friends and a few recent acquaintances invited.

'Banish the word "bridesmaid", though, and I'm not wearing a fluffy white dress, either,' Maggie said firmly when discussing details of The Day.

'You could wear rags and tatters and I'd still want you,' James told her.

This sort of remark always made Amy realise how poor a choice of husband she'd made. She probably wouldn't get married again, she decided, and said that one day.

Her aunt fell about laughing. 'Famous last words, my girl.'

Maggie was absolutely loving having her niece around, while Amy felt more at home in the large, shabby house than she had anywhere else in her whole life. The two women were working together to turn the far end of the shortest corridor upstairs into a self-contained flat with an artist's studio in the room that caught the best light, and would bring in tradespeople as needed.

And the small attic staircase at its far end, formerly used only by servants, now led up to a private storage space for some of the pieces of furniture Amy wanted to keep but didn't want to use in the flat.

This transformation had made Maggie take a good look round the big house and wonder whether it might be worth making another flat out of the old servants' quarters in the semi-basement at one side of the house, where the ground sloped away and gave that area its own little garden. That part of the house had been standing empty for years, not even visited for most of the year apart from a former handyman and now James attending to routine maintenance tasks from time to time.

Neither Maggie nor James was into entertaining or house parties, preferring to live casually and spend their spare money on repairs and improvements. As she sometimes said, the family served the house more than it served them.

It was good too to see her niece start on the painting she'd been thinking about for ages, and Maggie was surprised at how good it was looking. Why had Amy not concentrated on her art sooner? The usual reason, presumably, the need to earn a living. But she was good, really good.

On the next plot of land down from Larch House, Lucia still wasn't close to term, though she felt to have been pregnant for ever. She was getting steadily bigger and both she and Corin were longing to hold their baby.

And Corin had just met a man wanting a part-time retirement job who thought Ben's storage facility idea sounded perfect.

Corin also had the contract to renovate and extend the second house in Hawthorn Close, a task he was enthusiastic about.

On the last day of April when Vicki had been on night duty and came home at dawn, she stopped the minute she got out of the car to stare in wonder at the line of trees along her street. They were all lightly frosted with blossom and it was as if the flowers were peeping out at the world, checking whether they'd like to venture out fully.

She hurried inside and woke Murad up. 'Come outside.'

'What's wrong?'

'Nothing's wrong. I just want to show you something.'

On the front doorstep, she flourished her hand at the street. 'Voilà!'

As they stood enjoying the delicate beauty in the soft light of dawn, Rob came out from the next-door house. He heard the sound of their voices so looked along the street towards them.

Then he too saw the beautiful flowers and forgot everything as he too stared along the street. He waved to his neighbours and went back into Number 4, coming back with Ilsa, who had moved in with him.

They stood together, arm in arm, staring in wonder.

'It's going to be glorious,' he said. 'Absolutely glorious.'

'And it isn't even in full bloom yet.'

During the day, word spread and people came to visit the street. And strangely enough, most of them parked in Larch Tree Lane without being told, so that the beauty was left undisturbed by car noises or fumes.

Even Singleton came to see it and decided perhaps the trees had been worth saving for other than financial reasons. He didn't forget, however, to contact his PR agency and instruct them to take photos of it for his next year's general election brochures.

Arthur fell silent when Jane drove him across to the street to enjoy the trees. 'It was worth protecting them, wasn't it?'

'Well worth it.'

She noticed how he perked up after seeing them and vowed to take him there every single day while the glorious display lasted.

Two mornings later, the trees were fully in blossom and people had started to come from all over the district.

As they ate breakfast together, Rob smiled at Ilsa. 'I have an important meeting in town but will you meet me outside the front door at ten o'clock? I need to say something.'

'Can't you just come inside and say it there?'

'Not this time. And I also want you to promise not to go outside into the street till then. You can look out of the window at the flowers but oblige me with this.'

'Oh, very well. Another of your nice little surprises, I

suppose. I usually enjoy them so I'll do what you ask.'

At ten o'clock the front doorbell rang and she went to answer it.

Rob was there, beaming at her. He put one finger on his lips and took her hand, walking down the path to the street.

When they got there, it was like being in fairyland with the canopy of glorious blossoms covering the whole street and their perfume filling the air.

Rob gave her a moment to take it all in, then said, 'Stand there, please.'

She humoured him and took up the position he indicated by the gate.

He placed a gentle kiss on each of her cheeks, then knelt down in front of her. 'Ilsa Norcott, will you please do me the honour of becoming my wife?'

She gasped and stared at him, speechless for a few moments as the words sank in. Then she took his hands and pulled him to his feet and into her arms. 'I can't think of anything I'd like more.'

As they kissed, the people he'd asked to stay back and keep others away till he'd proposed to the woman he loved let out sighs and little cooing sounds, and one older woman unashamedly wept sentimental tears into her handkerchief. The man he'd asked to take some photographs had done that, and now held out his mobile phone, smiling broadly.

Who doesn't like the sight of true love?

After the couple had finished kissing, the onlookers cheered and clapped, and the happy couple curtsied and bowed to them, then went slowly back into the house, stopping outside the front door for another kiss.

Inside, she said in a choked voice, 'I'll never forget that, Rob.'

'I'll never let you forget it.'

And he kissed her again.

The next morning, a message went to every house in the street from Jane saying there would be a street party in the grounds of Number 2 that evening for residents of Hawthorn Close and those outsiders like Corin who'd been involved in saving the trees.

People should bring a garden chair and a plate of something delicious to contribute to the festive supper.

They gathered as instructed and were greeted by Arthur and Mavis in wheelchairs festooned with tinsel. The two of them were presiding over glasses of champagne or fizzy lemonade.

People from the far end of the close were not as well known to one another as those at the Larch Tree Lane end and stood in small clumps at first. However, as the evening progressed, Arthur kept them busy moving on to chat to a new person every ten minutes, and wouldn't take no for an answer.

People who'd never spoken to one another before got to know their neighbours, relaxed and chatted.

Arthur watched them with a benign smile. He'd done this many times before over the years and had known bossing them around a little at the beginning would break the ice nicely.

When it came time for a speech, he took over from Jane and she stepped back with a smile. He told them how wonderful they all were, to have defended their glorious trees and saved their beautiful street, and how happy they would be to know one another better.

No one minded being told they were wonderful and the evening continued with smiling faces everywhere, few people leaving before midnight.

Jane refilled the glasses and chatted till her voice was a little hoarse. She kept an eye on her father and Mavis, but they looked so happy she didn't feel the need to do anything but let them enjoy themselves.

After all, this was Hawthorn Close, a very special street and its people had earned the right to enjoy their beautiful home.

Once again over the blossoming time there was another, smaller miracle to accompany the beauty, a miracle that seemed to happen every year. People visiting the street spoke in hushed voices, cars parked outside the street on Larch Tree Lane, and no one quarrelled or shouted in that beautiful white tunnel of blossoms, not even the naughtiest child or the grumpiest oldie.

Hawthorn Close was repaying the effort people had made to save it and look after it, Arthur said. Once again it was filling their souls with its beauty to help nourish them over the coming year. And this year it seemed particularly beautiful, the best display of blossoms ever.

Anna Jacobs was born in Lancashire at the beginning of the Second World War. She has lived in different parts of England as well as Australia, and has enjoyed setting her modern and historical novels in both countries. She is addicted to telling stories and celebrated the publication of her 100th novel (*A Valley Wedding*) in 2022 and 60 years of marriage to her very best friend and husband in the same year.

annajacobs.com